I0771276

FINAL CURTAIN

FINAL CURTAIN

Tales Inspired by
THE PHANTOM OF THE OPERA

Edited By
STEVE BERMAN

FINAL CURTAIN

ISBN 978-1-59021-686-6

First edition published in 2025 by Lethe Press

Library of Congress Number (LCCN) available on request

This book is a work of fiction. Names, characters, places and incidents are products of the author's imagination. Any resemblance to real people or current events is purely coincidental.

Cover art: Jeremy Parker
Interior design: Inkspiral Design

1. *Introduction* — STEVE BERMAN

5. *Selections from the Memoirs of the Countess of Chagny* — NADIA BULKIN

17. *La Belle de la Mer* — JAMESON CURRIER

33. *The Road of Mirrors* — JAMES BENNETT

65. *The Phantom of the Wax Museum* — ORRIN GREY

85. *Now We Sing the Killing Song* — JOSH ROUNTREE

103. *Two For the Show* — L.A. FIELDS

123. *Trompe L'oiel* — TIM NEWTON ANDERSON

141. *The Music We Became* — ADDISON SMITH

155. *Encore* — STEVE BERMAN

167. *Little Rats* — THERESA DeLUCCI

185. *The Lake* — BECKY THACKER

203. *Exeunt. Flourish.* — PETER DUBÉ

219. *Figaro's Children* — JEAN-MARC LOFFICIER & RANDY LOFFICIER

223. *The Ghost Singer* — CARA DiGIROLAMO

251. *Such Broken Souls* — JOHN LINWOOD GRANT

INTRODUCTION

O NE OF EARLY CINEMA'S MOST infamous moments is the unmasking of Erik, the Phantom of the Opera—his skeletal visage so shocking that audiences reportedly screamed and fainted. Before Jack Pierce, Lon Chaney's makeup skills transformed a man into a fiend, and this was arguably his magnum opus. Though the 1925 silent film is a Universal Studios production, Erik is rarely counted among the horror icons referred to as the "Universal Monsters." Erik and Quasimodo, the other Gallic stepchild of the studio, were denied sequels, and the original films were rarely shown on Saturday afternoons by the many television horror hosts of the late 20th century (Dr. Shock, for this Philly boy). In 1943, the studio released a new adaptation with the talents of Claude Rains, Nelson Eddy, and Susanna Foster. The film was more romantic and comedic, especially the quirky ending between the rivals for singer Christine's affections. New adaptations appeared every twenty years or so throughout the century, with the Phantom haunting London (*Mon Dieu!*) or Manhattan, the play between the figure's cruelty and ardor rising and falling. And then, even stranger heirs were filmed, with a shade of the Phantom haunting a studio backlot, a rock concert hall, and, sadly, a shopping center—the plight of all monsters is eventually to become fixtures of suburbia.

And while most of the Universal Monsters eventually find themselves the victims of paranormal romance, Erik is the original stalker—a tortured gothic beau, remaining mostly unseen until his ardor drives him to kidnap his love and bring her back to the hovel he imagines she'll accept as a fitting stage for wedded bliss. Erik understands that passion drives art, but he fails to see that artists must find their own passion—not that of a mentor or manipulative lover. His control over the young soprano Christine, who, at the heart of the story, pities the Phantom as much as she fears him, is entirely human. It is not the mesmerism of the vampire or the seductive pull of reincarnated love stories.

Gaston Leroux's *Le Fantôme de l'Opéra* debuted as a newspaper serial before its 1910 release in novel form. Inspired by events, some real—a pianist disfigured in a terrible fire who spent the rest of his life hidden away in the Palais Garnier, an actual chandelier accident that killed a member of the audience in 1896, and the flooded foundations of the palatial building—and some apocryphal—a young man who willed his bones to the old opera house and became a prop. Over time, Leroux's tale, rooted in gothic obsession and theatrical grandeur, became a cornerstone of French literature, though more people know the story (or so they believe) based on one of the latter renditions.

I challenged the authors to write stories—strange fiction, if not necessarily horrific—inspired by Gaston Leroux's novel, any of the subsequent films, or even the musical. Their tales need not focus solely on Erik and Christine but could explore the novel's compelling secondary characters: the noble suitor Raoul, the mysterious Persian, or Carlotta, the jealous prima donna. Even the Opéra Garnier itself might take center stage. Some chose instead to write stories thematically tied to the original—a meditation on obsession, on beauty, on art as both salvation and damnation.

And, of course, I would never say no to a clever piece about Lon Chaney in the role of Erik.

This book, planned to coincide with the centennial of the silent film, is an homage to Erik—the first truly human monster of modern horror—and to those still drawn to his tragic song. Step softly into the opera house's shadows. Mind the chandelier overhead. Behold the stage—your seat awaits. The overture begins.

Steve Berman

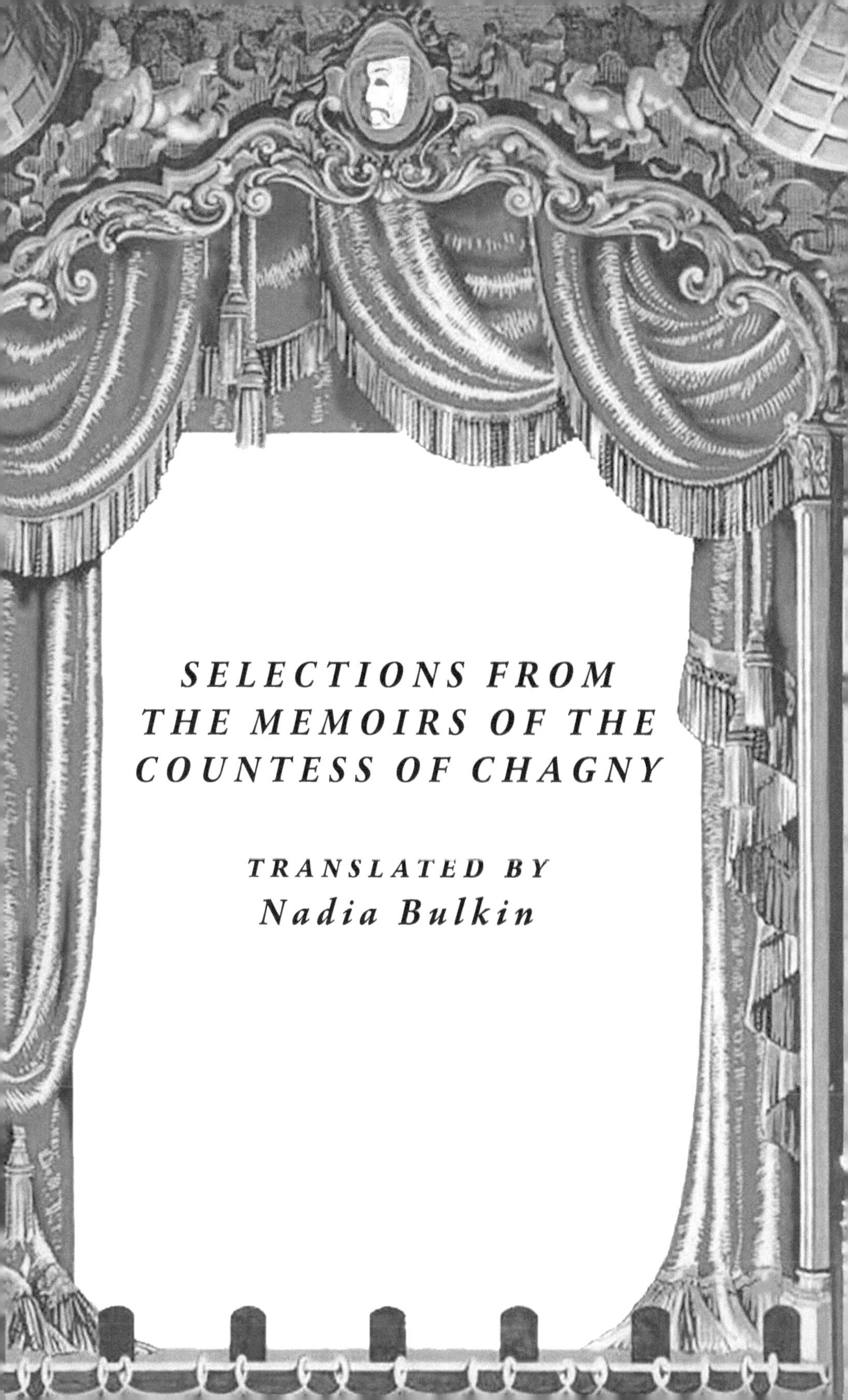

SELECTIONS FROM
THE MEMOIRS OF THE
COUNTESS OF CHAGNY

TRANSLATED BY
Nadia Bulkin

BEFORE I BEGIN THIS SAD retelling of the most puzzling year of my life, I must remind myself of one of the most important lessons my mother imparted to me prior to her passing: to always bear in mind one's true and singular purpose. My true and singular purpose in writing this account is to prove, to myself and all who follow me within these walls, that I am not mad.

I have heard it said, of course, that only the mad protest their sanity, and I have also heard, from my ever-faithful Martine, that the state of my mind is no one else's concern. After all, my husband had no relatives who could hope to strip me of what little he left me on account of my insanity (it would have been comical to see them try, given what happened to their Raoul), and the few women I dared briefly consider my friends in recent years would be just as repelled by the truth as by my apparent madness.

But the state of my mind is my concern. I must know. I must know for the precious peace of my own soul that Raoul did not hate me so much as to choose death over life (his and ours), that my senses did not fail me all those long months of my short marriage, that all my sleeps since have not been tormented for—and by—nothing, and most of all that I did not imagine the presence in my life of that dread PHANTOM!

WHEN I MET RAOUL, I assumed that Christine lived only in his memory. My own father still mourned my dear mother, quietly and on his own, even after he married his second wife Madame Berthe. I was prepared, when I married Raoul, to bide my time as a second wife must – to be patient, to be cheerful, to help ease him from his memories the way I had seen Madame Berthe slowly coax my father from his sadness.

We had met on the shore of the North Sea, on a wet spring afternoon. It had just finished raining—a coincidence that I mistook to be a positive omen—and I had just finished stitching up my father's coat while waiting for the weather to clear. Particularly after the terrible winter we'd had, I was eager to be out of the house as much as possible. I took a stroll to the beach, and there I saw this man. I called out to him—truth be told, I was afraid he was going to accidentally walk into the sea. He was staring at the water as if mesmerized, his hands clutching something that he seemed to want to throw into the waves, but his forward steps were the stumbles of a sleeper. I did not trust them. So, I called out to him, "high tide today!" and judging by how startled he was to see me, I really did think that I had woken him from some dream. A nightmare, I suppose.

His equally innocuous reply revealed himself to be a stranger in our town. His accent suggested he was a stranger in our country too. He explained that he was taking part in the *Ingeborg* expedition and was merely watching the waters, contemplating what might lie ahead. I had always been fascinated by arctic expeditions, much to my father's irritation, and so I eagerly—and rather rudely—began attacking him with questions. At this juncture I did not consider him an eligible man. I assumed he was married, maybe even with children my age, but I did appreciate his willingness to entertain the childish curiosity of a bored doctor's daughter.

Given the brevity of our interaction, it shocked me to learn that he had inquired after me, before the *Ingeborg* set sail for Greenland. This news sent my father into fits oscillating from confusion to joy, as he was very impressed with Raoul's title. Rumors of his interest in me fueled speculation that Raoul might stay in our town after the expedition, and of course there was interest from the mayor and others in making this a reality, in the hopes that he would bring numerous townspeople into his employ and perhaps receive visits from other families of similar high stature. This was all before we understood that the Chagny family's glory days, such as they had ever been, were long behind them, and that Raoul had long since let go of whatever connections he'd had in industry and commerce. When word arrived that the *Ingeborg* was soon to complete its triumphant return, I was ceremoniously rushed to the port in my best gown, as if the town hoped for an impromptu dockside wedding.

For my part, I never expected Raoul to stay. And yet he did, unlike so many others who have passed through this town on the way to more exciting destinations. I suppose that's when I chose to begin caring for him. And the longer he stayed, the more I began to hope that my father and the mayor were right, and he had stayed for me. I would have been willing to go, if he had been willing to take me. I did tell him that I longed to travel. But he seemed to have lost that urge himself. All he ever said was that he loved the way the sea looked on stormy afternoons. This, I believed, was a very chaste nod to our first meeting, as I did not see how any man could actually prefer the color gray. I thought it sweet. Foolishly, I believed myself cared for in return.

It was not until after we were married that I learned the truth about Raoul and the sea and stormy afternoons.

There had been a wife. An opera singer. Very accomplished, as I understand (I have no ear for fine music myself), and now, very much gone. They had married young and had no children, and so she, Christine, seemed like a closed chapter in the book of my new husband's life. I was not so sheltered to imagine that a man of his age and worldly experience would not have had several previous "chapters." As I mentioned, that did not concern me. I only pitied him for having had such a short and sad one, and could only pray that ours would be long and fulfilling instead.

Yet almost as soon as I learned of her existence—of the crisp sweetness of her name—I began to imagine Christine in a way that did our marriage no favors, I must admit. I imagined her unfairly coquettish in her beauty, charming, demanding, dressed in the finest silk and fur and fragrance the houses of Paris had to offer (I still have never been). I imagined her toying with suitors, exchanging affection for gifts, torturing poor Raoul with indecision until finally deciding to give him her hand. I did this to torture myself, to remind myself that I had no right to expect my handsome husband to open up to me when I was merely a consolation prize. It is a sad irony that before I met my husband, I never considered myself plain—I had a good eye for tailoring and Madame Berthe had always praised my posture—but after I learned of this glamorous ghost, my confidence shattered.

Did Raoul speak cruelly to me? No. But he did not have to. I felt the freeze of his disinterest when I fell asleep waiting for him to come in from our bedroom's balcony. When his eyes drifted from mine on our seaside walks and toward the cloudy void swirling over my shoulder instead.

I should have begged him to let me in, I suppose. Even if I could not understand his grief—losing a mother is nothing like losing a wife, I know—I thought I could at least keep him company in his misery. And I did come close several times, in those first few months. But each time I would think, "ah but you are no Christine," and I would halt my advance. At the time I blamed my looks, my personality, even the sound of my own ungraceful voice. But as the years go by, I wonder if maybe a different sort of fear stopped me, overpowered whatever bridal desire or obligation I may have felt. Not the fear of having my own inadequacy confirmed. Rather, the fear of what else might be standing beside him on the balcony. Fear of Christine.

[Editor's note: Per the Countess's timeline, the following incident took place four months after the wedding. The preceding passages detail her attempts at improving her marriage through more conventional means and are deemed irrelevant to this inquiry.]

ONE DAY RAOUL'S VALET PEDER—an earnest and guileless boy, the youngest son of a shoemaker my father knew—came to me and said: "I worry the Count is ill." I inquired as to his symptoms. "He is whispering to himself," Peder said, and before I could remark that whispering was not a symptom of an illness, he explained: "I heard a strange sound from the bedroom, and when I looked in to see if something was the matter, I saw him leaning against the mirror, clutching the edges with both hands, and whispering to his reflection. His face looked like my grandmother's when she was in her fevers—pale like a goat." I conceded that this was a bit odd, but by then, I had revisited my understanding of my husband: *he* was a bit odd.

Still, some part of me must have suspected something more serious was awry, because I asked my father to visit Raoul and make sure he was well. The examination, which Raoul resented as an unnecessary invasion of his privacy, yielded nothing amiss except fatigue. None of Peder's grandmother's fevers. His sight was fine and so was his hearing. I should have been relieved, and yet I felt my stomach turning to stone, wishing that my father had found something I could blame our struggles on. After my father left Raoul miserably asked if I was content, and I wanted to shout at him, *no*—but instead I finally told him what Peder had told me.

He was quiet for several minutes, when I asked him what he'd been doing. At last, he answered, "If you must know, I was praying."

Well, I had nothing to say to that. My father had warned me not to "bother" Raoul with my worries and so I tried to drop it for the sake of peace... but a week later Martine came to me to say that she had seen him pressing his face into the bedroom mirror again, and this time she'd also heard him say a word: "Christine." You can imagine the state this sent me into—he was having more meaningful conversations with his dead wife than his living one!

It was my old self-punishing impulse that sent me climbing into the wardrobe one afternoon when I heard Raoul's footsteps coming down the hall toward the bedroom. He did not speak to her in my presence—again, I would never claim Raoul tried to be hurtful—but I wanted to see the husband he could have been, had Christine not claimed him first.

I couldn't tell you all the things that Raoul said while I crouched in the musty, oaken dark. Some I have forgotten. Some I have chosen to forget. Some I have tossed over so many times in my head that I no longer know which words were his and which were mine. What I do know, what I *still* know, is that someone – a hidden lady with an angelic voice, a hidden lady who was not me – whispered "my dear Raoul" in return.

Peder hid in that same wardrobe for a week at my request and claimed to hear no voice except my husband's. Martine, ever practical, suggested that Raoul had been "playing a trick." I knew Raoul would deny it, so I did not bother asking him, but I did write an anxious letter to his secretary in Dijon—he was the only person I knew who had known Raoul before the *Ingeborg* expedition, having come to our wedding to wish me luck. I still have the letter he sent back to me and will copy his answers below.

> *Regarding the Count's mental state—I do believe that the many months he has spent in the oddness of the sea have taken their toll on him. Mapping the cold unknown can weigh heavy on a man's head, especially when that man has been rattled by losses (his brother, Christine). He is not the hopeful young man I once knew, but I only ask you to be patient with the man he is now.*
>
> *Regarding Christine—yes, I am very sure that she is dead. I watched the Count bury her at sea.*

Unfortunately, by then these answers gave me far less comfort than I had hoped.

I CONFESS I BEGAN TO fear mirrors. I was afraid I might see the hem of a pink silk dress passing behind me, or a sickly face too pretty to be mine peering over my shoulder. I even thought I saw her sometimes, when the light was wrong, when I hadn't eaten for all my worrying. So, I took to tending to my vanity in the dark, and then not at all (it pains me to admit that Raoul did not notice any difference, as he so rarely noticed me toward the end).

My fears were not limited to the large mirror that hung above the dresser in the bedroom; I tucked away my hand mirror as well and hurried past the pretty brass mirror in the sitting room too, though it had been a wedding gift from the mayor. I took to cupping my spoons at the dinner table to protect myself from accidentally spotting Christine, throwing out kettles that I considered too shiny, and when I caught sight of Martine's reflection behind me in a window one day and screamed loud enough to wake the dead, she gently suggested that we remove the mirrors altogether if they bothered me so much. I was grateful for her advice.

You may wonder, upon reading this, why ridding myself of the mirrors would have given me any consolation when in fact all the mirrors did was show me what lurked behind me in my home. One might as well stab out one's eyes on a dark path, so as not to see the wolves. But that is the curious thing—during those two days we spent in a mirror-less house, the air did feel lighter, sweeter, less bound up, less dragged down. I heard Peder and Martine laughing in the kitchen. Even Raoul, I think, seemed to see me for the first time in weeks.

Unfortunately, it was also fleeting. Raoul suggested I stop by my father's house for lunch—he had "some work" to finish, he said—and when I returned, I could sense even before I touched the door knob that the malignance had returned. A wiser woman would have turned around and gone straight back to her father's house, but I was too mesmerized by my disbelief and anger. I stormed inside, barreling through the oppressive cloud of *l'eau de Christine*, flew up the stairs, and threw open the door to the bedroom to confirm what I already knew I'd find.

A mirror! He'd put up a new one!

I looked around for my wretched husband, wanting a vessel for my rage, and saw him standing with his back to me on the balcony, facing the North Sea. This is how I will always remember Raoul, I think: with his back to me, hypnotized by a force unseen.

That is when I finally went down the stairs and back to my father's house. I conceded my defeat. I wrote a letter explaining my decision that I would eventually find, unopened, among Raoul's possessions.

AND STILL I FELT COMPELLED to return alongside my father when we received word that Raoul had collapsed on the beach a few weeks before Christmas. Maybe it was the fact that he'd been feverishly clutching my hand mirror when he was found. Maybe it was something Madame Berthe said to me, that the love of the living must always overcome the love of the dead. "When we allow our kin to be lured into the dark," she said, "everything is for nought."

[Editor's note: Several lines of text that follow have been scratched out, apparently in the same ink they were originally written in. Of what remains visible it appears that the Countess was debating whether her deceased mother had likewise become a phantom, or "lure."]

Raoul seemed very small in the bed—I remember that most of all, how he looked frail enough to throw—and while he had lost a bit of weight since I'd seen him last, it was his presence that seemed most depleted. Or maybe I simply recognized that in his diminished state he could not push me aside, could not stalk off to the balcony, could not shrink from my hand. I still could not say what was physically ailing him, other than a chill and an empty stomach, but his demon was not corporeal, after all. I sat beside him, wiped his face, held his hand, until he opened his eyes.

"Christine," he said—and I barely reacted, this meant so little to me by then— "Christine went into the mirror." What mirror, I asked. "At the opera house. He took her, and she went…." Looking back, I realize he must have been misremembering some stage trick he saw her perform, but at the time I was very confused; I thought he was implying a kidnapping, or an abscondment. "She returned," I said, hoping to reassure. He winced as if my words had hurt him and turned his face away. It wasn't until later, when I was changing the sheets, that he said, "I will follow."

I remember this next moment very well: I recoiled from the bed when I heard this and caught myself in the mirror—that new, damned mirror that Raoul bought to replace the one I had taken down—I gasped, fear closing my throat at the prospect of seeing pale Christine behind me—and I saw nothing. Nothing but the closed bedroom door. Satisfied that we were alone, I pried my gaze from my own eyes and looked to the left of the mirror, to the glass-paned window that overlooked the black, churning sea.

[Editor's note: The Countess had originally written "I was alone," before crossing out the words "I was" and replacing them with "we were."]

And now, at last, I understood. Raoul had not been staring into the mirror in the hopes of catching sight of a dead wife behind him. He had been staring *through* the mirror, *past* the mirror, as if it was a window. All those times he would press his face into the mirror, he was willing it to become liquid—he had been trying to enter the glass!

Enter the glass and go where, you may wonder. I now believe that his madness—her madness, their madness, together! —had already begun to bloom when we first met, on the shore of the North Sea. I believe he really had been intending to walk into the ocean, and I believe he had been holding out a small pocket mirror at the time. Perhaps he thought of it as a kind of talisman. Perhaps he thought the glass would turn the sea into a door. Perhaps I can never hope to make sense of it, because it was only ever some vile secret whispered by the phantom Christine.

And yes, it was vile. I do not believe that fact is in doubt, because everyone knows how my husband's story ended.

[Editor's note: The Count of Chagny was found drowned on the beach of Helleneset later that month. His death was officially ruled an accident.]

My own story did not quite end at the close of that strange year, in the sense that my body has continued to rouse me from bed even on the darkest days, and my voice has continued to speak to those who choose to still speak to me. But I am afflicted, the same way Raoul was afflicted. Who knows, perhaps Christine herself was afflicted too.

I know because I climb aboard steam ships at the port as they prepare for arctic voyages. I nestle myself among the barrels and boxes of supplies and sleep until I am inevitably found. I am close to him there. In dreams I trudge over the bristly grass that I imagine drapes the islands of the far north, and I see him as he once was: open-hearted.

So, you see why I could never remarry, no matter how much my dearly departed father begged and prodded. Some love should be allowed to die.

LA BELLE DE LA MER

Jameson Currier

I AM NO EXPERT ON ghosts and paranormal activity; in fact, I am often skeptical whenever I catch an episode of a team of young and hip ghosthunters and psychics waving laser tools and lighting spirit candles. But I am not oblivious or disbelieving of otherworld phenomena; if I have learned anything from surviving to an older age, it's that sometimes what you think you see and hear is not what was there and said and sometimes it takes more time—maybe years of living and experiences and adventures— to understand what had happened.

When I was twenty-four, I spent a week traveling through Normandy with a guy named Josh. I knew Josh from a short stint in film school—there was a time after I had graduated college in Atlanta and landed in Manhattan that I thought I might become a screenwriter and had enrolled in a class to learn more about plots and structure and pacing and dialogue. I was also hopeful that I might make some friends and find some career referrals— since arriving in New York less than a year before, I had been fumbling through theater auditions, unable to pick up dance routines, and realized my limited acting talents when I felt rock-bottom and ridiculous in a voiceover class. Josh came to the city from a small-town in Pennsylvania; he was a year older but several more experienced and wiser; he'd been a triple-threat in a college production and had now set his sight on becoming a director. Josh was self-absorbed and full of opinions, and, more importantly, he resembled a matinee idol; he had all the charisma that I lacked.

Josh hadn't announced that he was gay, but neither had I, and I would join him and some of our classmates for drinks after class at a bar in the West Village, a noted tavern that catered to actors and writers and artists in a dark, clubby room. Josh would monopolize the conversation, pointing out the facts and twists and turns in movie plots that our instructor had overlooked. The two young women in the class who would often join us had crushes on Josh and would turn boisterous or giggly to keep his attention. I stayed silent until prodded for an opinion and then realize as I tried to speak that I was unintelligible, tongue-tied, and thick-headed from the alcohol. In high school and college, I had been the type of guy other boys never liked—a bookish know-it-all and tattle-tale, and a fool when it came to anything about relationships and sex. I had learned to remain silent and listen and watch to save myself from further ridicule and embarrassment. Conversations were never my strength and experience had demonstrated to me that opinions could be hurtful and backfire.

The class met twice a week and the after-class gatherings would dwindle to me and Josh and one of the young women. I would feel like a third wheel, but those times I would try to leave, Josh would urge me to stick around for one more drink. Josh did not feel that there should be a difference between writing for the stage and writing for film; both should seek to have a faster pace and more fluidity. He liked to talk a lot about the New York theater—what was playing, who was in a cast, what was in rehearsals, what auditions might be coming up. I studied him like a textbook of equations or hieroglyphics. He would often leave arm and arm with the young woman who also conveniently lived uptown near his apartment. I'd watch them walk down the subway steps and wish I possessed some skill or attractiveness to lure someone like Josh to want to spend more time with me. I wanted someone like Josh to guide me through my life, help me make my decisions. I wasn't sure who I was or who I wanted to be. I felt frustrated in and out of class. I didn't feel comfortable in a gay bar; I felt out of place in other gay spaces: dance clubs, bathhouses, and back rooms. I had a job downtown where I proofread legal documents and I was convinced the dry prose had infected my writing style. My writing samples for the screenwriting class were exercises in comic frustration without the wit and characterization I had wanted to depict. And I craved Josh's attention and respect and didn't know how to make myself interesting.

Josh never provided follow-up details about the young women who accompanied him uptown, and I was too much of a gentleman to ask for details. Josh was never open about personal relationships, though once he had confessed to having an "ex," but of which gender remained a mystery. Josh was the sort of guy who flourished through connections; he had hooked up with a catering firm and was often hired as a waiter for upscale parties—I had once seen him dressed up in his tuxedo at a swanky party at the Metropolitan Museum, smiling and carrying a silver tray of appetizers through a gallery; he had arranged invitations for me and another classmate through the caterer.

One night after class, Josh announced he had arranged a summer internship with a film director in Italy. Before the start of his internship, he wanted to fly to Paris and then drive a sportscar to Rome, where the film was being shot. When the young woman who had joined us that evening— Pamela, I believe her name was—left the table for a restroom, Josh asked me if I wanted to join him on his driving route from Paris to Rome. "I bet we would have a lot of fun together," he said. Even though I could not afford this sort of trip, I accepted because I was flattered and in love with Josh— or at least in love with the idea of being in love with someone like Josh, even though I wasn't certain if I was on Josh's sexual radar. I thought this might be my opportunity for Josh to fall in love with me. The luckiest thing about the timing of his invitation—at least on my part—was that I had just gotten a new credit card, and I thought I'd hit it big before any of the bills would become due.

Josh's European Adventure itinerary wasn't direct or simple—in fact, he said he wanted to avoid all the cathedrals and chateaux and monuments and just experience the real France. By the time of our trip, Josh was in a "new wave" phase; he was obsessed with the French film directors who were making movies with new plots and young actors and new cinematography techniques. Because of this, he wanted to visit Normandy and see the locations that these new wave directors had used. I kept my wants close to my chest. I had never been abroad. Seeing Paris with someone I thought special would be enough for me, but when I studied a map of France, I thought it might be wonderful to visit Mont-Saint-Michel, a romantic-looking medieval village and abbey built on a small island off the coast.

We shared a hotel room in Paris for two days that had separate beds. I undressed and dressed in the bathroom, years of self-consciousness were both behind and ahead of me. I scrutinized Josh whenever he wasn't looking. I became obsessed with the way his hair—long and light brown—never obtained the clown-like shapes that framed my head. I'd taken French in high school and college but was pretty much nonconversant in the language, so I thought if I re-learned and repeated phrases, I might be better equipped for conversations. We scurried from the Eiffel Tower to Montmartre to the Louvre to Notre Dame, doing all the things Josh said he didn't want to do because he told me, "How many times will we be able to do something like this?" I had very little opportunity to try out my French phrases because I felt like I was watching Josh have a vacation. Most of our tourist excursions were contained to queues and café tables where Josh flirted with whoever wanted his attention, usually other young tourists who could converse with him in English and make him laugh and smile. I tried to keep my jealousy and envy hidden, but as I've mentioned before, I wasn't a very good actor.

After two days in Paris, we rented a car, not exactly the luxury sports car with a convertible top that Josh had envisioned, but a reliable four-stick Aston Martin, and drove out of Paris headed to Deauville, where Josh wanted to see the beach and the casino. Somehow, we got lost and ended up in Rouen, but didn't find the Normandy coast until somewhere north of this city. For me, it was still a great adventure. The soaring white chalk cliffs of the coastline were extraordinary, the vistas wide, and it was exhilarating to come upon them after twisting maps around in the car and trying to understand road signs. A World War II monument distracted us, and Josh became obsessed with the young ages of the lost soldiers, guys our age decades before. I couldn't imagine fighting in a war. In high school, I begged my mother to convince my father that I did not need to take an ROTC class. I was a boy of books and songs and dreams, not of guns and defenses and conquests.

In the late afternoon, Josh and I reached a small village in a coastal valley where the alabaster limestone cliffs fell away, and we decided to stop for the night. According to Josh's pre-planning, we did no pre-planning at all—our goal was to find places recommended by local tourist bureaus. The tourist office in the village directed us to an auberge located at the footsteps of an abandoned lighthouse, up on a cliffside that overlooked the village.

The name of the inn was La Belle de la Mer. The daughter of the owners checked us in. She was pretty and stylish, thin, blonde-haired, and in her late teens or early twenties. I judged her too sophisticated and pompous for a small village, but I also realized the moment that we entered the lobby of varnished wood furniture, checkered curtains and tablecloths, shelves of knickknacks, and painted ceramic plates hung on the walls, we had entered the real France, or at least Josh's idea of it. I saw a look of possibilities race between Josh and the daughter. The nametag on her blouse read "Sophie."

We asked about a room for the night, about nearby dinner options, and whether there was a bar at the inn without having to drive back to the village. Josh smiled so broadly that his eyes disappeared. Sophie's English was too good, and I wondered if she was a British imposter. She informed us that the inn could fix sandwiches and drinks. "If you'd like, I can give you a tour of the property," she offered. We agreed, left our suitcases in our room, and returned to find her waiting for us in the lobby.

We followed her outside to the windy cliffside and a low row of large, gray stones. "The Romans built a fortress here before moving on to Britain, but these are ruins of a medieval settlement," Sophie said, pointing to the stones. "As you can see, there is a good view of the village from here, and for centuries, this site was important because of its view—you can see approaching and departing ships. We could see ships approaching from Britain—or Spain or Portugal. In medieval times there was a trade route established with Brazil—wood and red dye were important imports—there is still an original structure built in the early 1500s in the village made of Brazilwood. But because the cliff below is steep, there are still coves where a ship could hide. This site has always been associated with tragedy. The Celts were defeated here. The Vikings were defeated. The land changed hands several times during the Hundred Years' War. The lighthouse was destroyed in the Great War and then rebuilt. The surrender in 1940 to the Germans was another catastrophe. The curse of misfortune associated with this land is said to go back to the myth of Salacia."

"Salacia?" Josh and I said simultaneously.

"Goddess of the Sea—La Belle de la Mer? I suppose the bureau did not tell you of the hauntings."

"Hauntings?"

"We have had guests who have... experienced things. That is not unusual at a site like this. We are perched at the apex of many worlds—air, earth, water."

She led us to doorway of lighthouse. "The cast iron structure rises twelve meters, or about three stories. It was rebuilt in 1960. Where we are standing, the ground is stone. Granite. From here you can see the dark granite cliffs to the south. Turn around, and you can see the white limestone cliffs north of the village drop away to the pebble beaches. There are legends of passageways built into the granite cliffside that rose up into a fortress, dungeons, and cells, though none have been found other than natural caves.

Some believe that there is a natural path carved into the cliffs that lead to the beach. Salacia's hideaway."

We followed her and looked at the cliffs and the beach below. She continued, "There was a writer a few years ago who wrote that this location might be the birthplace of modern romance—particularly the ill-fated love triangle. These cliffs, this fortress, the sea—they inspired many stories and many writers. Fairy tales. Stories of knights and chivalry. One scholar posed that this was the location of Camelot, where the ill-fated triangle of Arthur and Guenevere and Lancelot played out, before the stories assembled into *La Morte D'Arthur*."

Sophie folded her arms against her body as if to protect herself and said, "Salacia was the Roman goddess of the sea, but she did not want to marry the god Neptune. So, she sought refuge from him in these cliffs. Her singing could calm or disturb the waters below. Long ago, there was a shipwreck and a man survived and was washed ashore. He climbed the steps of the cliff. He was a deformed sculptor and began working to transform the cliffs into a temple in Salacia's honor for saving his life from the rough seas. He said her singing was pure and enchanting and calmed the waters so he could swim to survival. Some sources say the deformity was a hunchback— hence the inspiration for *The Hunchback of Notre Dame*. Some said he had a club foot or was maimed in the shipwreck. Another source said the sculptor was a feral beast, such as in *La Belle et la Bête*. The journalist Gaston Leroux would have heard this tale while growing up in his grandparents' home in the village, inspiring his version of the tragedy in *Le Fantôme de l'Opéra*.

"Neptune discovered Salacia's hideaway and sent a dolphin to persuade her to return. The dolphin transformed into a handsome soldier and climbed the cliffs to convince Salacia to return to Neptune. She refused and her anxiety caused another storm. The handsome soldier could not leave, so he stayed in the temple at the generosity of the sculptor. The soldier heard Salacia's singing and fell in love with her. They would meet in the caves below. Over time, the soldier knew Salacia must remain hidden because he did not want her to return to Neptune. He wanted her for himself. The soldier grew to distrust the sculptor and knew Salacia must continue to be hidden. His jealousy consumed him. He destroyed the temple and threw the sculptor into the sea. Neptune discovered the soldier's deception and drowned him and tried to force Salacia to leave the cliffs. Some accounts believe that she was successful in keeping Neptune away. Others say that they came to an arrangement and that the sea below reflects her moods and memory—anguish, joy, regret, passion."

After the tour, we returned to the inn and ate at a table in the bar at the back of the lobby. It was a pub-like atmosphere without any extraordinary menu offerings, but it was good to sip a glass of wine and feel inebriated. Josh was more interested in talking with the other guests than he was with me. He'd stop a couple passing by or disappear to order another drink, and I'd discover him chatting with someone else near the door.

Sophie sat with us for a while and I was tempted to ask more about the hauntings at the auberge. Had anyone seen a ghost—who was the ghost, and why was a ghost haunting the inn? She seemed annoyed, and answered, "There have been many deaths here. Soldiers, civilians, lovers." She did not provide any further details about ghosts. Josh drew her into a conversation about French pastries and cheese and chocolate, and I could tell I was being shut out. When I made a motion to leave and return to the room—I was tired—Sophie reached out for my hand and said, in a sympathetic manner, "My mother says the haunting is all nonsense. Those who claim to witness the goddess are haunted before it even happens."

Sophie's gesture did not lighten my mood; in fact, it irritated me. I left the inn alone, feeling dejected, thinking I had made a big mistake in agreeing to this trip. When I wasn't thinking about Josh and why he was so oblivious of me, I was worried about the escalating costs—Josh never seemed to have any cash on hand and I found I was putting more and more charges on my new credit card. I decided that I was done with him, that I would no longer invest myself in a hope for romance or a decent friendship. I would remain polite, finish out the trip, return to New York, and not look back. Back in our room, I felt my unhappiness gathering at my chest and throat and brow. I clenched my teeth to avoid crying, turned off the lights, rolled myself into a tight position, and tried to sleep.

I fell asleep quickly, in fact, into a deep unconsciousness because I was tired and seeking emotional relief. I tumbled into a dream—I was trying to find my way through a dark tunnel, trying to hear my footsteps—when something yanked me out of that darkness and I woke startled in the dim room, my heart beating in my ears. Josh's bed was empty—he had not returned to the room. I sat on the edge of my bed, feeling the heaviness in my eyes, and walked to the door and opened it. I was heavy-headed and disoriented. Outside there was a stillness: no wind, nothing moved. I could not see where we had parked the car or a light on at the inn. Suddenly, I felt yanked again, lifted by a great force of wind that became a high-pitched screeching sound. The scream was long and disorienting. I was shaken but I was aware that I was still standing in the doorway.

The scream was swiftly followed by another pull of air and then a wave of water, a drenching downpour that startled me and I shook my head as if to find a breath of air and realized I was still in bed, trying to lift my head up and awaken from the dream.

I switched on the lamp beside the bed and made myself stay awake. I went to the door and looked outside. This time, I saw the car and the parking lot and the lights on at the inn. I closed the door and went back to the bed and lay down on it, listening for any disturbance. I heard a soft, high-pitched whine that did not go away, a constant ringing in my ears. I turned off the lamp and closed my eyes, but the whining persisted until I fell back asleep.

Hours later, Josh was sleeping when I woke and showered the next morning. I dressed and went to the lobby for coffee and a croissant. I sat at a table for a while, trying to translate a French newspaper headline. Sophie was not to be seen, but her mother appeared to replenish the pastries at the buffet and asked if I slept well. I nodded, and she responded, "*Bonne*. Then *la belle* did not disturb you," but it was only then that I remembered my dream and the high-pitched scream. I had no thought that this might have been a ghost or a haunting or an omen or a forewarning.

I did not tell Josh about the dream or the scream because it dropped from my mind again once we were back in the car and driving. But I stuck to my resolve of remaining unimpressed and as distant as possible. The rest of our trip took us to Cherbourg and Rochefort for more new-wave locations and the "real France." Mid-week, Josh said he thought Mont-Saint-Michel was out of the way—too far to reach and then try to make Rome by Sunday. I didn't display my disappointment or growing depression or even my new belief that I was the source of my own misery, but something someone said to Josh over the next day about the "approach to the cathedral" made Josh change his mind. From afar, Mont-Saint-Michel was breathtaking, a fairy tale rising above the sea, but after we had parked and walked to the entrance, I was surprised and disappointed to find the alleyways of gift shops that lined the ascent to the abbey.

When we reached Rome, I checked my luggage at the train station. We returned the rental car and spent a few hours sight-seeing before I trained back to Paris. I said goodbye to Josh when I realized that the queue to enter the Coliseum was too long for me to wait to make it to my train, and Josh was flirting with two college girls from Canada. As I walked away, he promised to call me when he returned to New York. I didn't expect to see him again.

IT WOULD BE THREE YEARS before Josh reappeared in my life, though it seemed like decades had passed because times changed so dramatically. I was still living in the same Village apartment, but I was now working for an advertising company as a scriptwriter for radio and television commercials, finally chipping away at the bills and loans that had followed me for years. I had started and ended a brief relationship with a married man because I saw no future beyond the sex. Josh mailed me a flyer about a performance that was happening at a nearby gay bar. Josh was now one of the members of an acapella singing group—the group sang arrangements and reinterpretations of Broadway show tunes and new songs about gay relationships. I wasn't surprised that Josh might now be an openly gay performer, but I was curious how he had reached and accepted this awareness. The bar concert was a fundraiser for a new health care service organization. Afterward, I met Josh's boyfriend, Carlos, who was also one of the singers. Josh introduced me as "my first friend in the city," and made me aware that I had misinterpreted the value of our friendship. Carlos was a dark-haired dreamboat—black eyes, black hair, and a thick mustache. They had met at an audition the month Josh had returned from Italy. The three of us had an after-show dinner together at a restaurant. Carlos dominated the conversation. He could articulate all the issues that Josh was often silent or vague about.

There was an amusing tale of his first seduction of Josh. Carlos knew about our screenwriting class and the trip through Normandy and Josh's internship in Rome. "He probably drove you crazy," Carlos reached out to me and patted my hand. "He's got the attention span of a tiny sparrow. He's lucky to have someone like you as a good friend."

I was surprised by Carlos's passion for performing, for politics, and for Josh. Josh was less supportive of the politics—he thought their group should stick to performing recognizable songs, show tunes, and pop standards, not call-to-arm gay anthems. "We're not folk singers," Josh said, to which Carlos responded with a quick reply, "And we're not the Village People."

They lived in separate apartments and were open to other sexual partners, though they seldom acted out on their wandering instincts. Josh preferred Carlos to stay over at his apartment, "He keeps me focused," Josh said. "And I keep him on time." Carlos and Josh were an integral part of a growing and important gay community of out performers and activists. Carlos embraced me as if I were family. I was never a third wheel. I was always included. Their gatherings and rehearsals and performances were full of gossip and jealousy and admiration. We made many memories together: there were trips to Washington and benefits in luxury hotels. There was a road trip to California with the acapella group that surpassed our drive through France. Josh wrote a song that became an often-performed anthem at gay pride events. The group recorded an album that never found a distributor and I made a couple of videos of their songs that can still be viewed online. They kept a rigorous schedule together until they couldn't.

Carlos died first. It was hard to accept and still hard to revisit. I have many memories of those days—of doctors' visits, protests, marches, and of helping before and after performances. Josh became my focus—I often stayed over at his apartment, sleeping on his couch, to help him out in the mornings before I left for my office. I was best when there was a schedule or a list of things I had made that needed to be accomplished. It was harder when it was just the two of us sitting together—Josh was prone to sentimentality and regret. "You know what this all means to me, don't you?" he would say to me as I gathered up a load of laundry that needed washing or had finished scrubbing the toilet after his bout of diarrhea. I would nod and answer, "I'm glad I can help," grateful that he trusted me and we shared these intimate moments.

And I still remember a day when two other friends, Pete and Sean, and I arranged to take Josh to see a Broadway matinee. Even after we had planned it out, it seemed like an impossible feat. We rented a wheelchair and carried it out of Josh's apartment first, down four flights, then bundled Josh into a sweater and coat and carried him down the stairs. We pushed the wheelchair on the sidewalks through Hell's Kitchen and Eighth Avenue to the theater, about fifteen minutes away.

The performance was the musical *The Phantom of the Opera*. It had opened on Broadway but had been a big hit in London before arriving in New York. Carlos and Josh had talked about the show and had wanted to see it together—they had listened to the recording of the London cast album over and over. After Carlos's death, Josh would not abandon his desire to see the show; he was particularly intrigued by how they would handle the chandelier crash. And as the possibility of making the matinee performance came closer, it became a mission to accomplish because I didn't want to accept Josh's disappointment, or my own.

I was nervous and skeptical about the entire outing—I was concerned about Josh's health—we had to unhook his catheter from his IV fluids, and he had not been out of his apartment in close to two weeks. We reached the theater early and Sean had settled Josh in his wheelchair at the end of a row. I sat between him and Pete, but angled myself so I could keep my eye on Josh. There was a nervous excitement in the audience as customers began to take their seats around us. I was trying to hold in my emotions. I thought of this as one of Josh's last outings, one of his last days, and I wanted to hold on to the memory of every moment. This wasn't the first time that I doubted Josh would survive. My unhappiness and despair settled into my body; I felt a pressure tensing around my neck and shoulders. I thought that things could not go on like this, but I did not want to imagine my life without Josh.

That was when I first heard the noise—a high-pitched shriek. My first thought was, *Where had I heard that sound before?* I could see the tops of the heads of the orchestra members settling into their chairs and tuning their instruments in the pit below the edge of the stage. I heard the shriek again— it was a violinist tuning a string.

I had a moment of vertigo, a swirling change of my vision, and I had to lean my head down toward my lap and close my eyes to steady myself. I gasped for breath. I felt a wave of anguish rise from my stomach and settle into my ears. I had heard this sound years before, been through this feeling before, waking alone in our room at the Auberge La Belle de la Mer in Normandy. *Why was this happening now? What did this mean?* As I calmed my breathing, I could isolate all the sounds around me, with the exception of a long, soft whine.

The performance began. I struggled with whether I should remain in my seat or leave. I lost my concentration in the show until the chandelier crashed at the end of the first act, and I noticed that Josh did not react. I seemed to gather strength at intermission and I managed to smile while Pete showed Josh the program. Later in the second act, there was a moment where a singer held that same pitch as the shrieking sound at the crescendo of a phrase in a song. I looked down the aisle at Josh, expecting something to happen. Nothing did. I noticed Josh had fallen asleep. I waited for the note to come again. It didn't. When the performance was over and we stood to gather up our coats and begin to help Josh leave the theater, I realized I was damp with sweat. I felt as if I had survived something. But something was different.

Josh lived another month and then died. I vividly remember the cold March days after his death, cleaning out his apartment, going to the courthouse and the funeral home, and reaching out to the landlord and Josh's family in Pennsylvania. But I am aware that I let go of him at that performance, in that theater, that we had reached the end of something, that I gave up on him before I should have, that I had doubted him when he never doubted me. That was who he was.

More time passed, memories sharpened and softened grief. I would see Josh throughout the city for many years. Someone would have his profile, another his walk, another his height or hair or complexion. I would move through more obstacles, witness other deaths, grieve others, learn to bear it, fall in and out of love two, no, maybe three more times, and accumulate the memories of a life.

Decades later, I would retire and move away from New York City. I would purchase a small house located between farmlands, a village, and a railroad crossing. I remember the evening I was eating dinner and heard a train approaching the crossroads. As it came closer to the house, there was a high-pitched squeal of the train wheels along the tracks as it took a curve around the valley. The pitch was the same shriek I had heard in Normandy and in a theater on Broadway. I was now too old to worry or wonder about it. I thought again about Josh and how I loved and lost him. Some ghosts cannot be seen and never disappear. They live within you, unable to find peace.

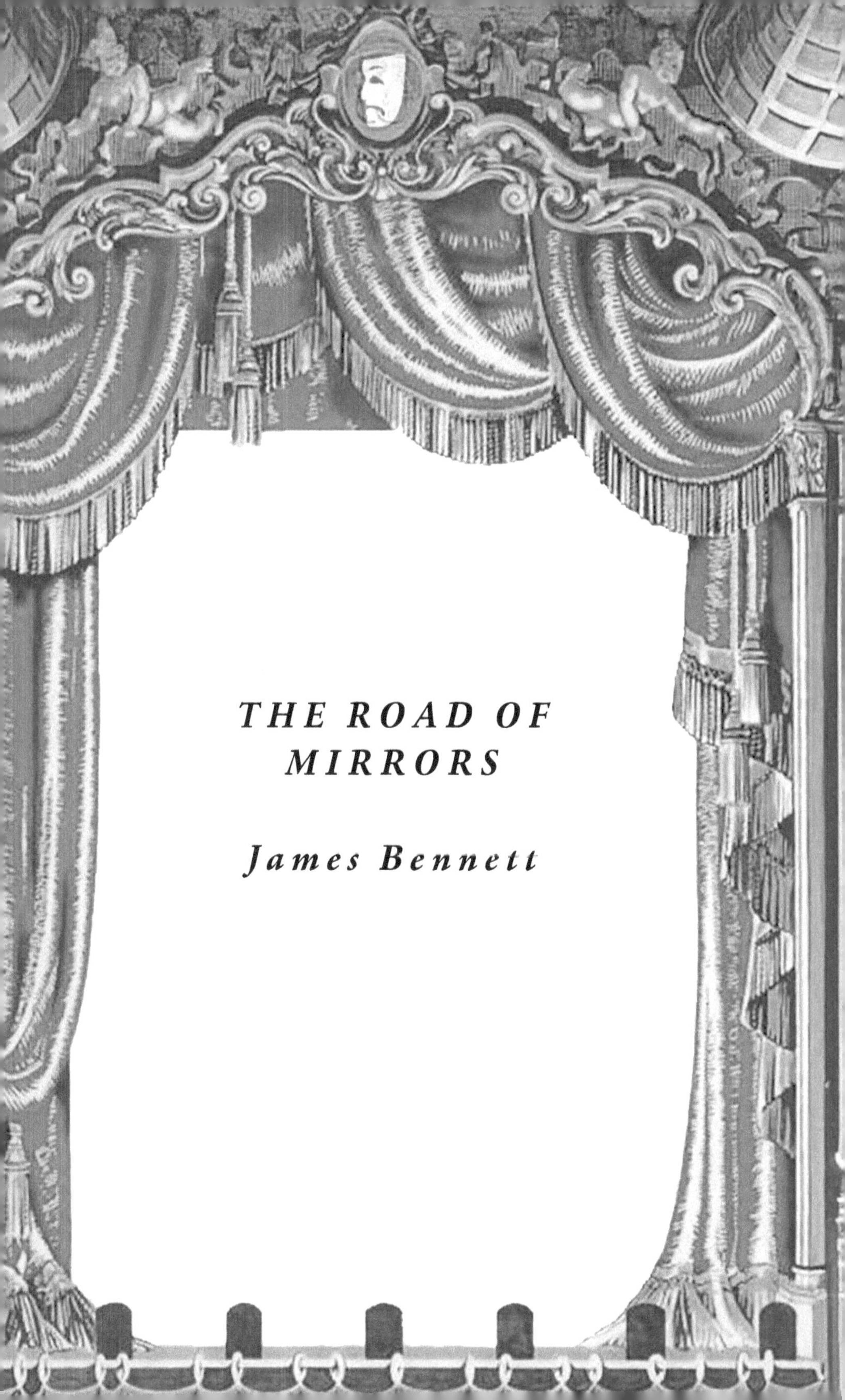

THE ROAD OF MIRRORS

James Bennett

CURTAIN UP ON *LA COUR des Miracles*. Orchestra plays, the soft swell of farewell.

Up until the morning when Claude received the letter, delivered to his lodgings in a crisp white envelope, he had truly believed he was escaping *le Marais* slum into which he'd fallen, an angel granted new wings, plucked from the murky swill of streets between *Rue Rambuteau* and the *Bastille*. He deemed the third arrondissement barely medieval, with slop poured from windows and rats in the *boulangeries* while thieves and whores haunted every corner. *La Belle Époque* was over, shattered by the assassination of a duke and the mobilisation of the Central Powers, the war currently dividing Europe. But life in the city went on regardless; what else was there to do? While thousands perished in the trenches north of Paris, *les gens riches* still went to the theatre, applauded *Faust* and sipped champagne.

The bourgeoisie clung to businesses in the economic chaos. Actors, like Claude, trod the boards for francs where they could and prayed that no zeppelin brought their hovels down upon their heads.

Indeed, it was in the rubble of an antique shop on *Boulevard Voltaire* where Claude found the speculum one bright spring morning, lying unbroken on a heap of furniture that couldn't claim the same. He'd been on his way home from rehearsal at *Le Théâtre Montdory* (some shoddy production of *Cyrano de Bergerac* in which he was playing De Guiche) when a glint of sunlight in the street had drawn his eye to the fateful treasure. He'd crouched there, turning the silver-handled mirror over and over, his heart thudding with a wonderment that had only dimmed when he'd cleaned the glass with his sleeve and been presented with his too-familiar face. Lines of care and greying hair greeted his inspection, reminding him that such awe belonged to a child and not his thirty-seven-year-old self. The mirror – a relic of the Revolution, he thought – seemed too fine to hold such a countenance, one cheek palsied and the lopsided lip, the bulge of his outsized, watery eye.

> *In me,* the inscription on the handle read, *picture your heart's desire*
> *The glass shall make of pain a liar.*

Baroque nonsense, thought Claude at the time. Thanks to a complication of birth, he was never going to be a Valentino. He wouldn't have been a Valentino *without* his disfigurement, he knew, merely another humdrum *homme* in the Court of Miracles, the narrow web of tenements and slums set aside for paupers like him. The future held no leading roles for Claude Sévère and ascending from the maze of the *le Marais* seemed unlikely, for all his aspirations on stage. That afternoon, it hadn't stopped him from removing his scarf—he disliked to expose himself on ordinary days, risking the stares of passersby and the laughter of children—and wrapping the mirror oh-so-carefully, then placing it in his bag.

Had something whispered to him then? In his distorted appearance, the glass was speckled and a little warped with age, had he surrendered the reflected world for an unchartered, inverse one beyond? At the time, he'd simply hastened home to his room on *le Rue du Temple*, there to drink the sourest wine and pore over his find. The mirror, he suspected, would fetch a nice price from some fence or other in the Latin Quarter, perhaps enough to see him through winter. Claude hadn't known then, *couldn't* have known, how meagre those ambitions would later seem.

This morning, the morning of the letter, found Claude much less impoverished than he had been in spring and with a greater degree of vanity. Why, the up-and-coming French director, Jean Allard, protégé of none other than Capellani himself, had invited him to a third audition for a forthcoming production of Leroux's famous novel. And everyone knew that a third audition usually meant an offered role. And in *film* besides. Mirror in hand, he slicked back his locks with lacquer—dark now and without the aid of dye—tightened his cravat and regarded himself in the handheld mirror. Oh, how marvellous his chin and nose, a heady combination of the strong and the delicate. Handsome in a way that none could gainsay. How he trembled to observe himself! Only weeks ago, Allard had been scouring the backstreet theatres for an affordable cast and so Claude had stepped up to the task, buoyed by the good fortune bestowed upon him by the glass. How ironic it had seemed to him then. Before, he would've thought himself the perfect fit for the Phantom, and without the need for makeup! Instead, he found himself eyeing the role of le Vicomte Raoul de Chagny, the noble, heroic lover of the prima donna Christine Daaé.

Oh, Badeaux. If you could see me now.

Come his initial audition in late November, his slight limp and stooped back he could only conceal with the skill of a veteran thespian—but his face, oh, his face! He had the mirror to thank for that. The mirror and something less palatable, which the letter, when it came, served as a grim reminder of. Nevertheless, for an hour or so that morning, Claude had believed himself on a ladder to the stars. The theme was operatic, as grand as any of his dreams, not that he'd be required to sing. A piano in the auditorium and title cards on screen would serve in place of coloratura, for which Claude, admittedly, had little talent.

But you *could sing, Badeaux. How you screamed at our exchange.*

Magic, he didn't think too much about. His current locale, so sardonically named, held nothing miraculous about it, unless one happened to survive it, that was. And Claude intended to do just that. Bastien Badeaux, the young Apollo of *le Marais* with all the jewels of success laid at his feet, was dead. *Surely* dead. The picture houses of France beckoned. Hollywood even. Claude was on his way. Allard had seen something in him, something that might well see him fly from the Court of Miracles for good, borne aloft on his own strange marvel. This wintry morning, Claude Sévère had prepared for his final audition, his *offer*, with speculum in hand. He had every reason to thank his luck and approached the hour with all the anticipation of one who would finally see his ghosts laid to rest, Bastien Badeaux chief amongst them.

The letter, when it came, was like a crack in the glass.

THE MIRROR NEITHER LIES NOR forgets
Come to me, mon voleur, *or the truth shall be known.*

On reading the letter, Claude was trembling for a different reason. There was no smudge of fingerprints on the envelope, crisp and white. No clue to the mystery of who had written it in an elegant yet neutral hand. Who, in this labyrinth of shit and death, had learnt of his humble address? Nor was there an answer to Claude's wheeling fears, the cramp in his chest and the cold sweat on his powdered brow as the message thumped home to him. It was that singular expression, *mon voleur*—my thief—that suggested the letter was more than some unpleasant prank or a case of mistaken identity. Oh, he had taken such pains. There had only been the two of them present in the theatre that night. Who in the Court of Miracles could know of his sorcery?

On the back of the envelope, someone had printed an address. It was an auberge out near Fublaines, a two-hour journey east of the city. Only a fool would travel out there into the waste of No Man's Land and in these violent times. A worse one would miss an audition with an ambitious French film director, but auditions, he supposed, could always be rescheduled. The consequence of such a threat – for that the letter most certainly was – overshadowed both concerns.

C'est impossible. *I watched the curtain fall.*

Cursing, Claude shouldered his bag, the speculum wrapped inside. There was no longer any need to veil his face, but he tipped the brim of his hat nonetheless, ghosts dogging his footsteps down the icy streets as he headed for the train station.

In one of his minor plays, Molière opined that 'La curiosité naît de la jalousie'. Curiosity is born of jealousy. A minor player in life, Claude Sévère gazed out at the snow-patched fields rolling by his cabin window and admitted to himself that he'd certainly greeted Bastien Badeaux with a touch of the green-eyed monster.

One late spring day, the young man had appeared in the gloom of *Le Théâtre Montdory* in the hope of joining the company entrenched there (*Les Petites Reines,* they called themselves, vain to a one), trembling in the stalls with suitcase in hand. It had called for an impromptu audition. Thereafter, the newcomer had succeeded once a particularly inspired turn as Romeo impressed the burly stage manager, Laurent. The costume designer, the elderly *Mlle.* Antionette, which wasn't her real name, had wept authentic-looking tears into the fur of her scruffy Persian cat. The prop master, Lucas, had pursed his lips at Badeaux's *derrière* and therein plunged the blade of resentment through Claude at the sight, which had stayed with him ever since. Tall, dark haired and cleft-chinned, Badeaux presented a heady combination of the strong and the delicate. Handsome in a way that none could gainsay, the youth had won the hearts of the gaggle before the footlights and thus the corps des thespians had their Apollo.

"Bravo! Bravo!" croaked Laurent, in a way that Claude had never heard from him before.

"Oh, *mon cœur*," bleated the powdered Antionette.

Lucas whistled. It was plain what was on *his* mind.

And for the following summer, Claude played villain, foil and fool to Bastien Badeaux. He played Quasimodo to his Gringoire. Danglars to his Edmond Dantès. On some of those evenings, the auditorium was almost full, the hoi polloi of the third arrondissement buzzing like flies over the fresh meat in their midst and all in agreement that the man had talent to burn while the company drooled over its triumph. And their increase in wages.

It was why Claude never thought to sell the mirror.

"Oh, *mon cher enfant*," he would say to Badeaux once the lights went down, the applause the roll of the sea beyond the curtain. "What a gift to us you are. Not since Artemis bestowed a javelin that would never miss has the world received such a godsend."

"*Merci*, maestro."

Badeaux would grin and give a little bow. It was terrible how much he meant it.

Claude was an actor and, he liked to think, not a bad one. Privately, he seethed. In his room on *la Rue du Temple* he drank wine and toyed with his antique mirror, gazing and wishing that the deities he so loved to reference had bestowed on him such natural appeal. Alas, he was ugly, marred from the womb, and he'd long suspected that his place in *Les Petites Reines* was due to a sad combination of friendship and pity. That long, bitter summer saw him put on his most dazzling and most artificial of smiles.

The worst part, he'd thought then, was that Molière was right. Soon enough, Claude had to know all about their happenstance Apollo. He'd ask Badeaux to join him for supper in this or that café and the man would graciously oblige him. Claude would pay for a better quality of wine and thus came to learn how the youth had travelled north from Limoges, escaping a life of farmyard drudgery and wedlock to a woman he had no appetite for, in which Claude had detected a faint, unbidden hope. Thanks to a touch of pneumonia and a subsequent frailty of the lungs, Badeaux had escaped conscription to the Front and meant to earn his living treading the boards, an endeavour that Claude could only tell him he'd succeeded at and more. Again, Badeaux would grin – no arrogance in it – and turn a pretty shade of pink in the candlelight of whichever rickety terrace table they occupied.

"You flatter me, *monsieur*."

As summer rolled towards autumn, Claude reviewed his assessment of the situation. No, the *worst* part, he thought, as leaves swept the Tuileries and the rain painted Notre Dame a deeper shade of grey, was that Bastien Badeaux was kind. Never did he drop his gaze from Claude's bulging eye as they discussed the works of Rimbaud, the activism of Clemenceau and the possible historic peccadillos of Richard Cœur de Lion. Never did his gaze linger on his would-be patron's palsied cheek. Nor did he deign to open doors for his limping mentor as if the veteran artiste lacked the ability to move through Paris under his own steam. Once, Claude had dropped his scarf and the youth had knelt in a puddle, then handed the item to him with no sign of grimace or concern, allowing the older man to swathe himself from scrutiny as they walked arm in arm up the Seine.

Damn him! Had the gods spared Badeaux no largesse?

October had arrived in fallen chestnuts along the Champs-Élysées while Poland declared itself an independent state and Claude Sévère had forgotten all about his magic mirror. The Montdory was set to put on a production of *Dr. Jekyll and Mr. Hyde* for Halloween, with Badeaux and Sévère in the eponymous roles (no prizes for guessing which was which) and the latter might have made his peace with his envy if not for the deeper truth curdling in his breast. Often, it woke him from wine-tinged dreams in the middle of the night, shivering on his damp, ratty blankets until the cold light of dawn threw shadows through the ribs of *la tour Eiffel.*

No. The worst part was that he'd fallen in love.

AND NOW, IT SEEMED, CLAUDE had fallen through a mirror. *Art imitating life?* The riddle nagged at him. *Or life imitating art?* Either way, the letter of this morning, the threat, was the reverse of the future he'd envisioned for himself, the speculum having done its work and the camera waiting to roll on his ascension. Allard's cinematic version of *Le Fantôme de l'Opéra* called to him even as his own led him east across *la campagne*, between low grey hills and skeletal forests, through nowhere huddled towns. Despite the bleak state of the landscape, he deemed himself lucky to have caught a train at all. The ticket inspector informed him, one who believed himself addressing a handsome, scarf less young passenger, that travel past Chateaux-Thierry was impossible due to the battles being fought on the Front. The German lines were retreating, the papers said, pushed back by the tireless efforts of the Allies, but what they'd left behind was horror. A wasteland, according to the inspector, with countless refugees fled and villages left burned or abandoned. If this were indeed the End Times in Paris, the man in the cap grumbled, then it was proceeding under the eye of an absent God, for surely no God could abide such bloodshed.

Claude, better appraised of the doings of gods, and with blood on his own hands, stared out the window in a manner to suggest that the conversation was over. Let war ravage the *Île-de-France*. Could he not have some peace?

In the smoke-stained window, he was barely a ghost. But even this reflection was too much for him. Oh, to grip the handle of his mirror, packed away in his bag, and sense some divine justice in the world! He closed his eyes, half in weariness and half in fearful expectation of what awaited him in an auberge up ahead.

Too much. This is too much.

"Stop making love to your misery," murmured Claude to himself, sleepy with the rattle of the cabin, the endless shutter of the passing scenery. The trees out there. The churches. So much like monochrome figures on a screen. "It eats away at you like a vulture...."

He quoted *Faust*, but his thoughts swirled with the thoroughly modern. With monochrome figures up on a screen. Silent yet immortal. Why now should this spring to mind? *Bah, oui.* It was to *le cinéma Gaumont-Palais* that Claude had invited Badeaux that very first night of November, him waving tickets under his nose in the dressing room once the company had toasted each other with champagne, changed clothes and departed from the final performance of the Stevenson. The film on offer was a British effort called *Masks and Faces*, ironic in hindsight, a melodrama of wicked counts and lovelorn husbands in 18th-century London. At one of their suppers, the youth had confessed he'd never seen a motion picture before, all the rage in Europe and the States. Never dreamed he'd have the opportunity. And so, Claude had snatched his own.

"This is too much, maestro. Too much."

"*Bête*, Bastien. You received a standing ovation tonight."

"*We* did, you mean. You're one half of our success, no?"

Indeed, thought Claude. *A monster to your marvel.*

But the implied kinship between them fluttered through him, nonetheless. When he patted Badeaux's shoulder, the younger man had held it there for a while. Then remarked that his co-star was wearing opera gloves. Why, Claude had dressed for the occasion! This seemed enough to convince the Apollo of the Montdory to accompany him through the twinkling Parisian streets, past *le Palais Garnier* to *la Place de Clichy*. And to the end of the whole desperate affair.

An affair, at least, that was flapping in Claude's heart alone, a trapped dove behind his ribcage.

The auditorium grew dim. The audience shifted and giggled. A pianist plonked through sheet music next to the stage. The projector made silver of the dust in the air and figures in monochrome flickered across the screen. The title cards, most generously, had been rewritten in French.

Later, there was little Claude could say about *Masks and Faces*, his customary critique, often merciless to a fault, rendered mute. Badeaux sat next to him, rapt as a child, gazing in awe at the screen before him. Meanwhile, Claude gazed slyly at Badeaux, the youth's profile etched in an argent glow and turned up as if to greet the angels of heaven. And the dove threatening to break free from his throat.

At some point in the performance, Badeaux leant in closer and whispered at the older man.

"Oh, maestro. It is a miracle."

"*Oui, mon cher.* It is the future."

Though he shook at his boldness, Claude slipped a hand into Badeaux's own, venting a gasp as silent as the players on screen when the youth gave a chuckle and squeezed his fingers in return. It was too much, too much…. While thought of a thousand tomorrows with the fortuitous Apollo filled his mind, a destiny that promised cherishment in place of loneliness, Claude found himself overcome. Encouraged by his first imposition, he forgot himself, leaning closer to slip one gloved hand into the space between Badeaux's parted legs. Surely a man of his talents would make him equally welcome there. Surely the shape of him, his dashing height and frame, would be reflected by his manhood, his passions flaming at his mentor's touch…

"Maestro!"

Instead, Badeaux had wrenched himself in smart retreat, his seat creaking under his weight. An arm came up, shoving Claude—with little grace—away from him. The disruption dislodged the scarf from around his face, his hat knocked askew. As the two men regarded each other in the gilded ambience, wide eyes to bulging one, Claude experienced the dove inside him croak in dismay. *Oui,* even as its feathers went up in smoke, his hope charring to a crisp. And he saw then how his companion appraised him – in anything but the same soft focus. Oh, he must've seemed to Badeaux a wretch, droop lipped and sag cheeked, ghostly in the projector light. Why, he was no more than a Death's Head, some ghoul of *le cinéma Gaumont-Palais* given grim life in the gloom.

Claude shielded his blemished skull even as behind him a dame in a flowerpot hat aired a startled scream. He paid the woman no mind; her fright at his appearance could never compare to the look on Badeaux's face. The younger man's expression sank into outrage as he stood, towering over Claude in the stalls. The piano, the screen, all were drowned out in that moment. An orchestra thumped in his ears, thick with the blood of shame. The veteran called on all the gods from his beloved books, cringing and praying that his seat would swallow him, undo the last terrible minute.

And, with all the glower of Navarre, Badeaux delivered his parting line.

"*Monsieur*, you are mistaken."

Then, like a shadow, he was gone.

Footlights fade. End of scene.

Closer you draw to the glass

Step through, mon voleur, *and face what you have wrought.*

Disembarking at Fublaines, chill on the platform, Claude made his way to the address scrawled on the hateful envelope. He steamed like the train as he walked, rattled by his misgivings. Should he have brought a weapon of some kind? A prop gun from the *Montdory* would've sufficed, for he had only the vaguest clue as to what awaited him. Blackmail, he suspected, some unlikely witness to his crime. Some shadowy figure in the dress circle, perhaps? Antoinette's blasted cat? But a worse inkling bubbled beneath it, and he thought again of his treasured mirror, the trouble he may have stirred up with its usage. Who knew more about the capricious nature of such gifts than him? But he was an actor, damn it, not some streetwise thug. If whoever had sent the letter meant to harm him, then what good would struggle do him? And what reason for the curious game? It was in this fashion, as one heading into mystery, that Claude Sévère went forth, doubting that any mortal method or manoeuvre was going to help him.

And I must know.

He could've told Molière that curiosity gave birth in turn, usually to satisfaction. Oh, but he'd rather not tarry out here. The afternoon was stretching long. Soon, the train would chug back to Paris and hope, the city representing a fairy tale world compared to the rural privation around him. All around, carts lay empty. Crates stood stacked by the walls. The farms hereabouts would no doubt have turned all their goods over to the Allies and the air held dust, snow and traces of an unmistakable military presence, one recently departed. Cordite prickled at his nose. The odd building had been cordoned off, requisitioned for makeshift barracks or control rooms, he guessed. He passed an abandoned armoured truck. While the war had never reached this far south, it made its presence known in every shuttered house, every scurrying passerby, fraught with a certain sadness and dread. The shadow of nearby combat still held all in thrall. As one about his own business and keener on answers than politics, Claude proceeded with determination, his chin stuck out and his collar high.

Who are you? Who are you, my ghost?

If only his newly handsome guise was matched by his gait, his limp remaining along with the other hidden woes of his body. The mirror, he had found, could only do so much. But oh, how the glass had whispered to him, reflecting his pain and promising respite....

The auberge was a mere five minutes' walk into town. There, under the scarred beams of *Le Corbeau Rouge*, he revealed his letter of invitation to the innkeeper and made his enquiry. In turn, he was presented with another letter, as crisp and white as the first. A tall, coated figure in the reception, he opened it, read and gave a shudder. The innkeeper noted it, the large man rubbing his hairy forearms in sympathy.

"It's a cold day for travelling, monsieur," said he through his untrimmed beard. "And I don't mean the weather."

Face what you have wrought, the letter ended. *Sans* signature.

As such, Claude had no time for pleasantries. The place was silent, empty of guests, and nor would he be booking a room.

"Who came here? Who gave you this?"

He learnt that it had been six days ago, according to the innkeeper. A man with his face wrapped in a scarf. Old, perhaps. A little stooped. It was hard to tell. The stranger had handed his message to Manon, the chambermaid, and Manon was presently off duty. Claude absorbed all this, fingers tapping on the wooden counter, wondering whether he was being mocked or not by the news of his phantom's attire.

Into his apparent trepidation, the innkeeper offered, "There was the letter. And the car."

"Car?"

"The very one in which he arrived. He paid handsomely for us to reserve it and told Manon a man with another letter would come." The man spread his hands. "*Fait accompli.*"

To Claude's surprise, the vehicle in question turned out to be a Renault town car, a practical, inexpensive model that had been parked in the adjacent barn. The cab had black and yellow boarding. Brass plates and wooden panels on the snub-nosed bonnet. High spoked wheels. The crank handle stuck out at Claude like a tongue, taunting his confusion. More than that, the florid, confident tone of the letter gnawed at him. The author of the riddle knew he would come. He knew that Claude would curse to himself and climb behind the wheel, appraise the rumpled map placed on the passenger seat. In crimson pen, someone had marked the road to *le Chateaux-Thierry*, twenty odd miles east of here, the line turning north at the hamlet of *Lucy-le-Bocage*, heading, it seemed, into open countryside. Into No Man's Land. Forbidden territory. Peril. Whatever drama was playing out in his extortionist's head, they wanted to meet Claude in the wings.

To go out there. Have I lost my mind?

It was a reasonable question. Of late, he'd often wondered it, puzzling over his magic speculum and his brutal way of maintaining his secret... A madman could certainly have conjured as much, drunk and dreaming in some *le Marais* gutter, let alone one with a flair for theatrics. Like every second-rate script, however, that would be such a cliché. As much as life imitating art, the peculiar resonances that had seeped so insidiously into his own, flickers at the edge of a mirror, masks, ghosts, and vengeance... But whose?

Now he was thinking of Badeaux again, and against his better judgement. Oh, there had been several over the years who might wish Claude Sévère ill. Those he'd scorned and dismissed from auditions. The odd neighbourly dispute in *la Cour des Miracles*. None with a grievance as fierce as the lost Apollo. But that was quite impossible. Wasn't it?

And so was the mirror, a devil whispered in his skull.

The innkeeper spun the crank, the engine rumbling, bringing Claude back to the here and now. With a wink, the hirsute man leant on the edge of the rolled-down driver's window.

"Tell me, *monsieur*, is this to do with the war? Subterfuge and all that?"

Despite himself, Claude barked a laugh.

"*Absurdité*," he said and pressed his foot to the pedal.

REGARDLESS OF HIS EMBARRASSMENT IN the cinema, the matter might have ended in awkward looks and silence if not for Jean Allard. Those early November weeks prior to the director's arrival, events out in the world offered a violent kind of hope. The papers shrieked of King Ludwig's flight from Bavaria, the German troops withdrew their support of the Kaiser and the *HMS Britannia* sunk off the coast of Trafalgar with a loss of fifty lives—though the war, they said, was coming to an end. Not so, however, for Claude Sévère who had found himself locked in his own minor battle. The

Montdory had become a maze of discomfort, for Laurent, buoyed by recent successes, had decided that *Les Petites Reines* were to put on a Christmas performance of *Romeo and Juliet*. How perfectly romantic! Badeaux, as no surprise to anyone, was to play the lead. Céline, the fair but alcoholic prima donna of the little company, was to join him as the object of his affections. Claude, deemed too old for a turn as Tybalt, settled for the role of Lord Capulet instead.

"You shall bring such *venom* to the character," Laurent told him in the closet that passed for a manager's office one afternoon, blind to the resentment brewing in the veteran thespian's breast.

And the spite with which he'd learn his lines, later to spit them at Badeaux on stage.

"And you be not," he whined at Laurent in return. "Hang, beg, starve, die in the streets, for, by my soul, I'll ne'er acknowledge thee, nor what is mine shall never do thee good…."

Oui. It was fitting. The rest of the time, he and the soured apple of his eye had barely exchanged a word beyond the apron. A terse '*bonjour*' at the start of rehearsal. A turned face when Laurent clapped his hands and ordered them to dine, which Claude now found he did alone. While he could hardly refuse the francs that his part would bring him, he was also forced into proximity with the younger man when the whole of him longed to flee from the sting of his rejection, bury his head under his blankets on *le Rue du Temple* and drown himself in wine. Oh, but if he could sprout wings and fly from the Court of Miracles! Yes, wheel like Gabriel above the *Arc de Triomphe* and away over Versailles, over the Loire and out to sea, there to meet a happier fate.

Instead, out of cruel necessity, he was faced every day by Badeaux. Badeaux cupping the fair, and absinthe-reeking, Céline in his hands. Bending to kiss her. Mourning even an evening away from her sight. Handsome, celebrated Bastien Badeaux who in both appearance and manner was nothing like Claude. No, none of it was *real,* yet the pain, the pain could not be denied. It was a knife through Claude's soul and how he forced out his lines between his teeth, so fierce, so believable that *Mlle.* Antionette applauded him as well. If he could only imbibe the poison central to the play and spare himself his misery. In truth, had he loved before now? The vinegar of it, its unfulfillment, proved more bitter than any cheap Bordeaux vintage.

The day before Allard's arrival, Claude had attempted a reconciliation.

"*Mon cher*, forgive me." These lines he had spoken with equal hardship, the dust of the wings where he'd cornered Badeaux sticking in his throat. He could not beg pardon for his face. "I meant no offense. I'm an old fool who drinks too much. I beg you, let me buy you a bouillabaisse, *un salmon en papillote*, anything you like!" He'd clasped his hands before him, an Oliver with a bowl. "*Je suis désolée.*"

With a bow, and his scarf bound tight, Claude then flourished his bouquet, fifteen red roses he'd procured from a stall on *le Rue de Turenne* and all bound in the blackest ribbon of silk. It was the appropriate number, so the florist had told him, with which to make his repentance.

"Sévère…"

Why, they could talk of the poets again. The coming Armistice. The best method of expiring on stage. Claude had practised all of these in his handheld mirror, sat on his bunk and pushing his features into an award-worthy guise of apology while the stray dogs had barked in the alley outside.

Badeaux met this with a gaze down his nose, so aquiline, so adored. There was no kindness in his eyes, however, on this occasion. And he did not take the flowers. Later, they would fall to the boards, there to gather dust and rot along with the last of Claude's hope.

"*Monsieur*, you shall not speak to me," Badeaux told him. "Your friendship has proved as hollow as your words."

With that, the young man swept away from him. Into the Parisian night.

Exit, pursued by tears.

The very next day, Allard had come to the theatre.

HE WAS A NARROW MAN, Jean Allard, a fact that belied the ambition inside him. The director, mentored by Capellani and funded by none other than the *Société Pathé*, had envisioned a grand screen version of Leroux's famous novel, *Le Fantôme de l'Opéra*. A lion of cinema, for so the press had dubbed him, Allard meant to take on Hollywood itself and give France a classic to rival the greats—and before America got its grubby hands on the rights to the script! To this end, he intended to make use of unknowns, albeit theatrical pros to a one, and present a picture on a par with the highest heights of the dramatic arts.

Claude gleaned all this when he arrived for a tops and tails run-through that afternoon, the shards of his heart clanking in his chest, and found Laurent and Allard stood before the small orchestra pit, in truth more of a trench, discussing the matter. Accustomed to passing unseen, the actor slowed in the stalls, allowing the gloom to fold in around him. He would hear more. Framed by the proscenium, it was as if he observed a play himself, one as fateful as anything that Shakespeare had written. As he listened, hat in hands and scarf loosened, he thought himself gazing into a different kind of glass for the future appeared to ripple before him, stark with promised glory and loss.

"And what, may I ask," Laurent was saying, "has brought a personage such as yourself to our humble theatre?"

The burly manager was plainly flabbergasted, leant back with his waistcoat threatening to burst in a shower of brass buttons. And flattered. And prospecting, *oui*, the idea of all the francs that such a venture might bring him aglitter in his eyes. He all but rubbed his hands.

"Why, the reviews, of course." Allard's spectacles winked in the footlights, his beige wallpaper face otherwise inscrutable. "The Hunchback. The Count. Jekyll and Hyde. These were my invitations. All have had the critics of Paris gushing like the *Fontaine des Mers*."

"Oh. Oh. To hear you say it."

"*Bah*," Allard replied. "You should think yourself proud. It seems that this leading man of yours… this Bastien Badeaux? Well, he has proved quite the draw. I had me a mind to extend an invitation of my own. I'd like the *monsieur* to audition next Wednesday. I shall leave you the address."

"But… but Badeaux performs under these eaves, *monsieur*. He is under contract. This coming Christmas, he is set to star in our next production, a Shakespearean outing that's bound to ignite the streets of Paris and -"

"*Bien sûr.*" Allard waved a hand, clearly unfazed. "By all means, continue. We can discuss a release clause should the audition be successful," he said. "I can promise you that compensation for any later performances will be generous. It's so hard to find a worthwhile lead these days. The company has seen so many. Nevertheless, God willing, I will find our Vicomte Raoul de Chagny!"

He laughed, wearily, while Laurent gawped. It was likely that the manager had only heard the financial part of the director's words and had to focus on staying upright, keep himself from tumbling into the pit.

"Well, in that case… if you think it best…" Laurent cleared his throat. "Tell me, what is the address?"

Claude, who had heard the whole speech and absorbed the horrid potential of it, watched Allard reach into the pocket of his bland grey suit and withdraw a calling card, crisp and white. Emotions warred in him, the green-eyed monster tangling with the rose-tinted one, but it was this small gesture that propelled him out of the shadows, hastening down the aisle in a flap of coat and scarf.

"You can't! You can't!" Breathless, he lurched towards the two men, his hands held out in entreaty. "You can't take Badeaux from us. From *me*. I shall not hear of it!"

For here it was, the crux of Claude's dilemma. Bitterness be damned, his passions for the happenstance Apollo lingered yet and the thought of losing him, whether scorned or no, was too much to bear. Curdled with this—a stain that the actor would never admit to—was the starkest envy, that Badeaux alone should fly from the *Montdory,* from the tattered stalls and threadbare curtain, from the Court of Miracles itself. He must intervene.

Overwhelmed by distress, Claude had failed to reckon on his appearance, to which the company themselves were well accustomed. Like a madman, he arrived unmasked and yelling, barrelling through the rows. For his part, Laurent merely started, his covetous hands flown to his cheeks. Allard, so narrow and grey, found his professional reserve undone. Aghast, the man stumbled in retreat, his backside meeting with the edge of a seat and hurling him backwards into the aisle where he sprawled among the husks of chestnuts and stale candy, and God knew what else. Spectacles knocked askew, he must've viewed Claude as a descending demon, some gibbering, distorted spirit from the gloom, aflame with furious eyes.

"Merde!" spluttered Allard as Laurent stepped forth to block the actor's path, his words of reason a shrill babble, his arms a bar against Claude's shoulders.

"Calm yourself, imbecile. Don't you know who this is?"

Claude snarled at the pointless question, his lips peeled back in a rictus of emotion. His fists came up, flailing, and what could have happened next must remain a matter of conjecture, because circumstance stayed his hand.

It was then that Badeaux arrived, a little late for rehearsal and hurrying through the auditorium doors. Tall, handsome in a way that none could refute, the youth skidded to a halt upon sight of the tableau below him, his lips forming a circle of shock. At once, Claude sagged, his rage torn from him. It was all Laurent could do to keep him on his feet as he turned his plaintive gaze from the stunned Apollo to the director on the floor, his drooping lip working to form an apology while his tongue shrivelled up in his mouth.

But Allard had eyes only for Badeaux. Gone was his horror in an instant, replaced by a look that Claude could well recognise, his expression a vice to crush him where he stood. Who could have hoped for a more dramatic scene? It surely surpassed the need for an audition. The hero, so dark and bold, came flying to save a damsel a distress—in this case, Allard.

What light from yonder window breaks?

In that moment, Claude Sévère found himself forgotten, regardless of his grotesque visage. And there weren't enough roses in Paris to undo the twist of fate at hand. As the director climbed to his feet, Claude knew that the battle was lost.

"*Bonjour*, Monsieur Badeaux. Such a pleasure to make your acquaintance."

LIKE THE WARPED SURFACE OF a glass, Claude had exchanged the *Montdory* for the theatre of war. Haunted by the letters and his own reflections, he'd driven through the hamlet of *Lucy-le-Bocage*, the car turning north into wooded countryside. Dusk was settling over the hills, the trees crooked fingers leading him on and the crimson line on his map growing fainter on the seat beside him. He headed now into Belleau Wood, the scene of a summer offensive by the Germans that had resulted in an Allied victory, hard-won, bloody as it was. Like all Parisians, fearful on the borders of the conflict, Claude had read about it in *Le Journal*, though day-to-day survival in *le Marais* tended to eclipse the matter, too much to think about when the procuring of meat, beans and sour wine took up most of his concern. And here the twilight spared him anew, for he could not know how the wheels of the Renault crunched over the shells of used ammunition and the occasional bone. When he glanced out the window, he deemed the thicket no more than that and did not see the strung entrails rotting on the lower branches nor the bodies slumped in dell and creek. The autumn rains had washed away much of the blood, nourishing the forest floor. The December wind had chased off the stench of ash and decay, but left the woodland empty, a snowbound tomb where the locals would not come, fearing ghosts or worse. This was indeed a wasteland and a land of waste, haunted by a lone trespasser whose hands trembled on the steering wheel as he drew near his destination. *Wherever it is. What do you want of me?* Down a road of death, Claude ventured, his headlights flicking on to reveal the spectres of moths and falling leaves, a spotlight on his reverie.

Step through. Step through. The letter whispered in his ears. *Face what you have wrought.*

Alice, with her harebrained pursuit and giant tears, could not have wept as much as Claude on that chilly November night. Vanished was his hope and lost his love, and he'd be lucky if Laurent kept him on at all, even as the poorest understudy. A broken heart was punishment enough, let alone the thought of all in *Les Petites Reines* learning of his strange obsession, his unwanted advances and public outburst, and laughing behind their hands. Badeaux would never look at him again! In that, there lay mercy, for Badeaux would soon be gone, plucked from the murky swill of streets between Rambuteau and the Bastille, drawn up to the stars.

Oh, if only life had held such luck for him. Hadn't he worked hard enough, wrenching out his soul to entertain the rabble of Paris? And in a flash of footlights, they'd forgotten him, beguiled by beauty and youth. How fickle, how cruel they seemed to him then, blind to all of his trials. Where was their compassion as he'd sobbed in his room on *le Rue de Temple*, born twisted and thrust out into the world like a gargoyle, misshapen and accursed? Oh, the fools would never know the depth of his grace. The pain that he had suffered for them. A weaker man would have climbed up into the vaults of the theatre and brought the chandelier down on their heads!

Drunk, shaking, it was these unwelcome thoughts that had turned Claude that night to the mirror. Across the shuttered room, the glass had caught the light from the street outside and glimmered to him in silvery despair. *Whispered.* He would face himself, the ghoul he was, and drive in the last nail of his grief.

Instead, he'd traced the inscription with his fingers and wondered, wondered again at its promise.

In me, picture your heart's desire
The glass shall make of pain a liar.

The first line asked for little from him. What night had passed without his Apollo haunting him, ever bright at the front of his mind? Those dark eyes, his gloss of hair, his chin so strong... It was a familiar phantom and one with whom he always lay, his hands busy under his blanket and his breath coming short, determined to squeeze out the poison inside him. Then he would lie, sweat-covered and shivering in the darkness, left only with the emptiness of dreams. No, it was the second line that held the lure, for pain was the vital part of him, he knew. And while Claude Sévère no more believed in magic than he did in the gods he often referenced, for the blessing of both had been denied him, it stirred him to utter his longing to the glass, his cheeks ugly and wet.

Then he had slept, long and deep, spared by drunken oblivion.

When he had awoken, creaking like a shipwreck, it was with the grimmest determination that he'd again lifted the mirror. He was due for a rehearsal at the theatre. Must he hide in his room forever, lurking in the catacombs of shame? To hell with them all! He was an actor and a good one, and they'd tremble in the face of his pride. His endurance. They'd -

With a cry, he flung the speculum from him, its surface crossed by a crack.

That morning, it had been the face of his dreams that confronted him. Bastien Badeaux had stared back from the glass, his eyes wide in alarm.

Gingerly, gasping, Claude had made sure of it, lifting the mirror to gaze at the miracle, pressing his cheek—so smooth, so perfect—and tugging a forelock so dark. A finger, trembling, had traced the line of his aquiline nose. No, it was no trick of the light. As sure as the sun rising above the smoky rooftops, he had observed Badeaux in the glass. Weeping, gasping, he at last barked a laugh.

"O Romeo, Romeo, wherefore art thou Romeo?"

Here. He is here. I am he.

As Claude wove onward through Belleau Wood, he remembered every line of his wonderment, his transformation, the exchange. In the black glass of the windshield, it was Bastien Badeaux who ventured forth, chasing the mystery. His shadow. To all intents and purposes, the Apollo of the *Montdory* sat behind the wheel.

Claude, wearing Badeaux's face, drove through the night to an appointment with ghosts.

NOT LONG AFTER NIGHT HAD tightened its grip on the forest, Claude bumped and jostled between a pair of ivy-covered gateposts and rolled to a halt before the chateau. In the pool of headlights, he could make out the boundary of an unkempt lawn, broad and gone to seed, the hint of broken statuary in the gloom. Loath to kill the engine, for the moon was yet to rise and the woods deep, he stepped from the vehicle to take in the derelict. It brought to mind the backdrop of an opera, some grand *trompe l'oeil* under low lighting, eerie and unreal. And here he was, an ageing, troubled soul set to sing a private nocturne…

Like many of the country estates around Paris, the building had the typical round tower with a conical roof. Chimneys with decorative caps crowned the steeply pitched gables. Later additions, he thought, somewhere around the seventeenth century. The windows, blank, black squares, betrayed no sign of an inhabitant and he imagined that whoever once lived here would've fled long before the howitzers starting blasting. That's if they had any sense – not that he could judge them, having come out here all alone. Leaf-choked steps led up to a balustraded terrace and, heart aflutter but having come so far, Claude hastened up them to the entrance.

But not before he'd reached into the Renault and recovered the speculum from his bag. It wouldn't serve as well as a gun or a knife, even prop ones, but it was wrought silver, nonetheless. Heavy. Or so he told himself. The truth was he wasn't about to leave the antique out here, part himself from its magic when it was plain to him that he'd strayed into vague and illogical realms, far removed from the humdrum rituals of the city. How commonplace the notion of murder had become; it was a matter of survival in a place that showed no mercy. And miracles, he had learnt, had their price. Oh, he was through the glass now, an Alice himself, and his ghost called him on towards the crux of his crimes. The answer, he sensed, was waiting behind the doors.

Show yourselves, you wavering forms....

On the doorstep, he faltered. Someone had laid a bouquet there, right where the tips of his shoes would scuff it. Claude didn't need a second glance to realise what they were. Fifteen red roses, bound in the blackest ribbon of silk.

But how?

He didn't bend to retrieve them as he entered. No. Let them rot. Why, it was if some force on the small of his back propelled him forward. A force that had caught the elements at work in his life and here sought to reflect them, all muddled and distorted. As if it mirrored the desires beating within, life imitating heart. Had the presence awaiting him reckoned on his darkness, the depth of it? He would show them.

"What's the meaning of this?" he asked of the vestibule, his words chasseing off the cracked tiles and the peeling walls, down the narrow throat of the house. "You summoned me. I came. Whoever you are, you should know I have little money. And less patience. Let's settle this like gentlemen."

Only echoes answered him.

It was then that Claude noticed the radiance coming from a doorway on his right. Silvery, stuttering, it shone through the gaps in the frame, casting shadows where the headlights of his car could not reach, into the heart of the chateau. Stealing a breath, Claude raised the mirror over his head, turned the knob and peered into the grand salon.

Threadbare furniture greeted him. A chaise longue. An *escritoire*. The curtains, velvet and long, had been drawn over the tall windows, better to shade the room. Black and white tiles, art deco in design, stretched out across the floor along with his shadow. Vases with desiccated flowers stood on an elegant plinth. The bust of some unknown philosopher regarded him in blind disdain as he made his way into the chamber, his gaze reserved for the naked walls.

Mon dieu.

Though Claude could discern no obvious light source, no whir of projectors in his ears, images flickered and played on the surfaces around him, looming and silent. There was no trace of acidic odour, which Claude would recognise as nitrate from the picture houses, the vinegar of mechanical decay. The illumination made silver of the dust, lending the impression that Claude had wandered into a blizzard, one as cold and white as the late November night he'd gone to meet Badeaux at the *Montdory*. *Midnight. Stop. You must come. Stop.* The result of the telegram, delivered by a breathless messenger boy to his room on *le Rue du Temple*, had summoned Claude at once.

He hadn't known it at the time, but neither Badeaux nor himself had attended rehearsal that chilly afternoon. In fact, both senior and junior actor had absented themselves for a similar reason, albeit an inverted one. The former had sequestered himself on *le Rue du Temple*, frantic but joyful, and wondering how on earth he was meant to appear at the theatre, confront Badeaux with his own blasted face. The latter… well, the reason became clear when Claude had wrapped his face in a scarf, this time merely to hide his identity, avoid the attention of any passing enthusiast for, much like a lamp in a room full of moths, Badeaux had most certainly begun to attract them, and hastened to meet his former companion, his would-be paramour, the unrequited thorn in his heart.…

Here, in the abandoned chateau, the flickering scenes on the walls had transcended the need for memory.

The breath going out of him, Claude watched himself enter the *Montdory* that night, shaking snow from his shoulders. He unwrapped his scarf, inhaling the staleness of the theatre, the trampled candy, the greasepaint and sweat. On the wall, he watched his pace slow as he approached the stage, the figure waiting there. Tall and taut. His head bowed. Consumed with an angst that rippled off the man like fumes, a point of tension under the proscenium. The footlights were low, the auditorium doused in gloom, and how Claude shuddered when Badeaux at last turned to face him. He saw his unease reflected now, caught in the silvery light. In the mirror of some unseen *lanterna magica*, one that projected the past more easily even than film. The young man's coat, a bulky woollen affair, was not unusual considering the weather. The mask he wore, some black operatic confection, seemed at odds with his usual confidence. What need would a man with his looks have to conceal his appearance? But Claude knew the answer to that. All he could make out of Badeaux was his chin, weak, stubbled and pale, and all too familiar.

Claude started as a title card flicked up on the wall.

"What... what have you done to me?"

In silence, the Claude who stood in the chateau still heard the timbre of rage in Badeaux's voice. And if there had been any doubt about the exchange, Claude himself had arrived to dispel it, sporting the younger man's visage. Then, dread thundering in his veins, Claude had reached out a hesitant hand and, with all the gentleness with which he'd longed to touch the former apple of his eye, he removed the mask from the man before him.

Oh, horror, horror, horror!

Badeaux slumped, falling to his knees on the boards, his hands flying to his face.

Look! the title card read. *You want to see! Feast your eyes on my cursed ugliness!*

In that terrible glimpse, Claude had witnessed the truth of the transformation. It was a sight, he thought, to earn a mother's loathing. Bulging eye, palsied cheek, downturned, drooping lip—all thumped into him harder than any German bullet. The inscription on his mirror, a riddle, an invitation, had somewhat borne out. *Somewhat.* Indeed, he had pictured his heart's desire. And the glass had made of them both a liar. Badeaux, sobbing on the stage before him, wore the face of Claude in turn.

Wordless, Badeaux on the wall demanded that the thief return what he had stolen. How could Claude tell him of the mirror, the dark spell that he had wrought? Such matters were beyond all comprehension and would only conjure further confusion and pain. Wordless, the veteran protested instead, his hands held out, beseeching. Between them, all he desired had come within reach. An audition with a famous film director. A way to fly the Court of Miracles for good. Badeaux, having spurned him, had nothing to offer him now. Perhaps, the title card read, he would consider an attempt to reverse the exchange if the younger man would grant him a single kiss, and more besides, there in the shadows of the stage.

In response, Badeaux had spat at him.

Voleur! Imbécile! Démon!

In the projected images, Claude reeled back, his features souring into pique.

"So be it. You have made your choice."

Now, *now*, Bastien Badeaux would know what it was to be hated, to have children point and laugh in the street, passersby cross the road to avoid him, all the moths flying apart. To toil and toil, tearing out his soul, to an audience who didn't care whether he lived or died. To offer love and find himself rewarded with scorn, with naked disgust in the murk of a cinema one night and all the silence that came after....

A struggle had ensued. One that would've had the audiences of the third arrondissement on their feet and applauding, aghast and awed by the scene. Badeaux, younger, leaner, had proved the stronger despite his disfigurement. The mirror could only do so much, after all. It had taken all of Claude's strength to tighten his grip around the Apollo's throat, squeezing for all he was worth until gristle and bone snapped under his gloves. Then, unlike the god in question—unlike any god—Badeaux had spluttered his last and tumbled to the boards, the life gone out of him.

Claude, shivering, had perched over him like the embodiment of death, a shadow.

For all his fear, the knowledge sank into him, sweet as a stolen kiss. The glass had made good on its promise. There was no one left to expose the lie. Stage darkens. Curtain falls.

THE MIRROR NEITHER LIES NOR forgets. That's what the letter had said. Standing before the flickering past, Claude imagined that the tears on his cheeks must resemble rills of silver. Oh, he was ascendent now. The wretch he had once been had wept for a while onstage, caught between his greatest loss and his greatest triumph. Then, as the film related on the walls, he had rolled Badeaux up in an old rug from the closet and dragged him down the cellar steps, deep under the theatre. Down and down into the sewers where he'd bidden his Apollo a fond *adieu* and left the rats to do their work. No one, he thought, was going to miss Claude Sévère overmuch. Pity had its limits; Laurent could find an understudy in no time. And Bastien Badeaux had an audition to attend the following Wednesday.

But this, the letters, the chateau, his phantom—none of it made any sense. The mirror he'd found… it seemed to him then both an eye and a mouth, watching the warp and weft of his life, theatrics and all, with the most patient of hunger. Then whispering, whispering until the speculum had gaped wide, sucking all of the substance into its throat and him along with it, a medley, a melange of symbols. What it reflected was surely a dream.

Everything had been so perfect. Jean Allard had applauded his turn in his studio and invited him to a second audition. Then a third, the final call of this morning. No one in *Les Petites Reines* had suspected a thing. *Mlle.* Antionette had sat and sighed over their Romeo during rehearsal, on occasion plucking cat hairs from his tunic. Céline, a little blearily, had gazed up at her leading man. Claude, in the guise of Bastien Badeaux, had never been more aware of the prop master's eyes on his *derrière*. All of them had known, as Claude had known, that soon he'd be leaving the *Montdory* forever. And *le Marais*. And them and their pity. An angel granted new wings, plucked from the murky swill of streets between *Rue Rambuteau* and the *Bastille*. Thanks to Gaston Leroux, a mirror and sheer desperation, Claude was on a ladder to the stars.

What had brought him to this place if not his own guilt? Haunted, mad, he had gazed into the face of a god and made his bargain, a Faust dealing with shadows. In turn, the mirror had made use of his own, wearing the reflection of his poor, discarded shell to lure him deeper into the web. *Oui,* he thought, *a shape that was nothing more than air in a coat and a scarf, drifting to an auberge in Fublaines....* And there to leave further crumbs and a carriage in which to proceed to its lair, this nowhere house of ghosts. Travelling through the surface of envy and desire, he had ridden into a land of death. Yes, he grasped it now, even if it lay beyond all comprehension. His summoning was the price of the magic. The glass would have its way. And like any audience in Paris, laughing, weeping at the players up on the stage, the gods must also have their entertainment.

Clutched at his side, the glass whispered to him.

Come to me, mon voleur, *and the truth shall be known.*

In his skull, remade, reshaped, the speculum glimmered and sang.

Step through and face what you have wrought.

Beguiled by silver, Claude Sévère held his antique mirror and moved towards the walls. All around, the scene of his crime flickered and shone, captured forever. Immortal. Weeping, smiling, Claude knew that the film would never end, as constant, as enduring as any ghost. At the same time, he knew that he would never leave this place. All was but a symbol; chateau, tree and rose. And Claude, granted his wish, had become an innate part of it. The spirit of the glass hungered for his soul.

Into impossible light, he went.

Into silence unending.

The End.

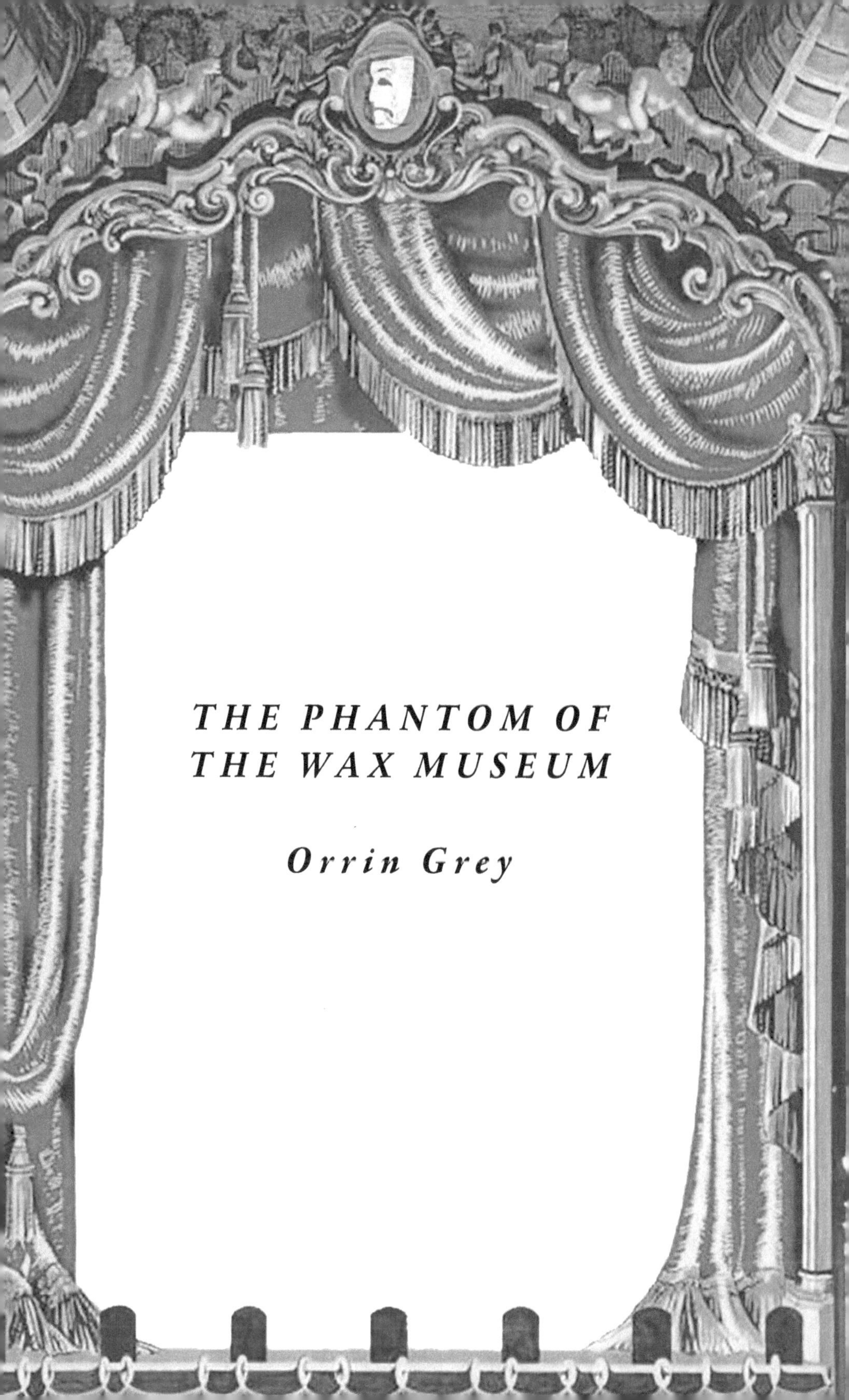

THE PHANTOM OF THE WAX MUSEUM

Orrin Grey

LON CHANEY DIED ON AUGUST 26, 1930, and was buried two days later in an unmarked private crypt in Forest Lawn, per his wishes. When Universal rolled out the James Cagney-led biography years later, it opened with the claim that "the entire motion picture industry suspended work to pay tribute to the memory of one of its great actors," but I was there, covering Chaney's funeral, and I'm here to tell you that it was only for a couple of minutes – still a pretty impressive feat.

August 28 was a scorcher in Glendale, and I can only imagine that the various famous pallbearers were sweating through their black suits as they loaded Chaney's silver-bronze casket into the family vault. Hundreds of mourners gathered in the ninety-degree heat, from idols of the screen and a

Marine honor guard to fans and nobodies come to pay their respects, and all of us watched as the man who had so completely disappeared into his roles disappeared from our lives forever – or so we thought.

THE FOLLOWING FEBRUARY, I WAS standing in the midst of a different kind of overheated crowd, breathing and shifting like cows in the slaughterhouse as we waited in a darkened chamber of the Montmartre Wax Museum on Coronado Avenue. After a period of public input – the Montmartre had put out an ad in our paper, asking people to write in and tell them what role of Chaney's they would most like to see commemorated – a new exhibit honoring Chaney's legacy was set to be unveiled.

The Montmartre was the new big thing, having pulled in a famous French sculptor named Xavier LeGrande who had made his name in Paris before being lured – as had so many others before him – to the land of Hollywood. A notorious recluse, all I had ever seen of LeGrande was a picture in the paper showing a white-haired guy with a stern face and a prominent nose.

The version of Chaney that the museum had gone with was supposed to be a surprise, but the secret was given away by the fact that Mary Philbin was present in the crowd that night, the newly retired young ingenue in pride of place near the front of the huddled mass of icons and journalists. It proved to be one of her last public appearances and, so far as I know, she spent the rest of her life as a recluse herself in that little house on Fairfax that she bought for her parents after becoming a star.

Standing in front of the curtained display was Dr. Werner Kebbler – an actual medical doctor who had left Germany and sunk his considerable funds into real estate speculation in California. The wax museum was only one of his many holdings, which also included a silent film theater across the street that was showing a special screening of Chaney's *Phantom of the*

Opera that same night, in case we needed more clues as to what we were about to see in the Montmartre's newest exhibit.

Even as I was dutifully scribbling down the key points of Dr. Kebbler's speech in shorthand on my notepad, my eyes were scanning the crowd, taking in who was there, and who wasn't. Which is why they settled on a young woman, not much older than I was, standing in the shadows and obviously waiting to draw back the curtains.

Her name, I later confirmed, was Mellie Garcia, 29, originally from Salt Lake. I knew the name already as one of the assistant sculptors who aided LeGrande in his work, but this was the first opportunity I had to put a face to it.

Plain by Hollywood standards, she wore tortoiseshell glasses and had somewhat frizzy brown hair and a prominent beauty mark above her lip. Later, I would have cause to wonder what drew my eye to her in that moment. She *was* my type – surrounded by platinum Hollywood starlets with porcelain complexions, I found myself drawn always to the mousier girls instead – but I don't know that I was necessarily attracted to her. Call it a reporter's intuition, if you like, but I think it was just that I had been to so many curtain calls, grand openings, and ribbon cuttings that my eyes were eager for anything out of the ordinary.

They were about to get just that.

What was it the intertitles said after Chaney's legendary Phantom makeup was first revealed? "Feast your eyes – glut your soul on my accursed ugliness!" I had seen *The Phantom of the Opera* with a date when I was nineteen. Back then, I was still living in Ohio and still trying to date boys to make my parents happy. Nobody fainted or threw up in my theater during the famous unmasking scene, but there was a beat of awestruck quiet that followed it – a collective reaction that even stopped my date from trying to run his hand up my thigh.

As the curtain drew back in the Montmartre that night, a similar bit of alchemy took place. "A shudder passed through the crowd," I wrote in the piece that ran the following day, "like a breeze rippling grass, followed by a moment of breathless, funereal silence."

The tableau was arranged such that the audience was where the camera would have been. The wax statue of Philbin, as willowy and pale and bright as a flame in the dark, was to the rear, while the organ itself made a sort of half-wall between us and the figures. Behind it sat Chaney's Phantom, his death's head exposed in a batlike scream, the horror not directed at Philbin's Christine nor even at the audience but ultimately inward, our own terror at the fragility and inconstancy of our treasonous flesh.

I'm not exactly a Bible-thumper myself, but my folks were Lutheran and I remembered my mother reading to me from what she called the "Good Book." A passage in Isaiah about how "all flesh is grass, and all its beauty is like the flower of the field. The grass withers, the flower fades."

My beat was events and premiers and galas, not the movies themselves. That job belonged to the men who made the rounds glad-handing the celebrities and writing reviews that would make or break the careers of would-be stars. My job was just to say who was there, what they were wearing, and the like, so no one ever asked me my opinions about what a movie *meant*, but here's my two cents: Chaney's Phantom was a reminder that we are all born with death already inside us. That was what frightened us, not the shock of his hideousness.

The necessity of color had done little to change the appearance of his infamous visage. The flesh was gray, a pallor that called to mind caves and the dark, deep catacombs in which the Phantom made his home. The lips peeled back, the teeth ragged and ruined, the ears stapled, the nose – how did Buquet describe it in the movie? – "there is no nose!"

It was all captured marvelously, freezing in time what had been, on the screen, a sudden shock, yet losing none of its power. The models of Philbin and Chaney looked like they could have stepped down from the display at any moment, and I saw Philbin's own face in the crowd, flushed with the uncanny recognition of her doppelganger.

As the onlookers stirred back to life and flashbulbs began to explode while Kebbler and Philbin and the other guests were bombarded with questions, I pulled my eyes from Chaney's frozen shriek to scan the shadows for Mellie Garcia, but she had already vanished back into whatever hidden alcove she had emerged from to begin with.

BACK AT THE OFFICE, I was stopped outside my editor's door by raised voices from within. "I don't know where you got that Chaney story, Ernie," an unfamiliar voice was saying, "but if you run with it, by God, you'll find it hard to do business. The last thing that poor man's family needs right now is this kind of nonsense."

My editor's voice was considerably more conciliatory – not a tone he tended to strike when talking to *me*. "I have no idea what you're talking about, Mark," he said, "but you know as well as I do that my paper doesn't print any story that isn't backed by solid facts."

"Don't you 'Mark' me," the other voice replied. "It's 'Detective Pearson' until I'm sure you didn't have anything to do with this."

The door opened and a big, broad-shouldered, squarehead guy who looked every bit the part of a cop came pushing out, pretty much crashing right into me with a brusque, "Pardon me, miss."

I learned what the scene was all about the same way everyone else did, on the front page of the *Los Angeles Evening Bulletin*, although, true to Ernie's word, it wasn't anywhere in the pages of *our* paper. The *Bulletin* was one of those less reputable rags that specialize in celebrity gossip, but "HOLLYWOOD BODY SNATCHERS" was a particularly bombastic headline, even for them.

"Mourners were shocked to find the tomb of one of the screen's greatest legends ransacked," read the piece, which was given no byline. "The marble seal containing the remains of the great Lon Chaney was cracked open under the cover of night, his casket removed from its resting place and left in disarray – the body missing!"

"So, is it true?" I asked Clete, who was behind the circulation desk when I arrived – the place in the office where gossip was most likely to circulate *from*.

"The Chaney thing?" he replied, as if there was any other big news. "I guess the boss sent Miller down there, but the police had sealed the mausoleum up tighter'n a drum. They wouldn't let him see the crypt for himself, but when he tried to push 'em for confirmation, they said it was just a precaution against gawkers because of the story in the *Bulletin*. So, who knows?"

I tried to catch Miller, but he wasn't at his desk. "Probably down at the station trying to get some answers," Ganz, the reporter at the next desk over, told me.

THE FOLLOWING DAY WAS VALENTINE'S Day and, wouldn't you know it, I was covering the LA premiere of what would become Universal's new big thing, a movie version of *Dracula*, with Bela Lugosi reprising his role from the stage, the theater lobby all draped with fake cobwebs and rubber bats on strings. Good thing I already didn't have a date. My love life had been the pits ever since Dana moved back home to Denver. Dating is always hard, and my schedule as a reporter didn't make it any easier.

It was my first time seeing Lugosi, and his sinister yet strangely mellifluous voice was something else. "There are far worse things awaiting man," he intoned, as the lights fell over the box where the protagonists had gathered to listen to the symphony, "than death."

I'm not one who can necessarily spot these things, but I'm told that scenes from *Dracula* were shot in the massive Paris Opera House set constructed on Stage 28 for *Phantom of the Opera*. And while I was watching Lugosi and writing about the stars who came out for the premier, the *real* story was taking shape on that same soundstage.

Of course, Universal had a hit on their hands with *Dracula*, but no one knew that yet, and they were hedging their bets. Ever since *Phantom*, they had been tinkering with a sequel. They'd even gotten Gaston Leroux himself to write a treatment for it before he passed away in 1927, which had been the complication that led to the sound re-release in '29 instead.

With Chaney's death thrusting one of his most famous characters back into the forefront of the public imagination, however, they had fast-tracked the follow-up, now titled *The Return of the Phantom*, back into production, to be directed by Marcus Barry.

Of course, one of the big coup de grace moments in *The Phantom of the Opera* was the giant chandelier falling on the crowd. So, naturally, Universal had to do it bigger and better for the sequel, never mind that the sequel's budget was less than half what the original's had been. Purse strings were a little tighter all over in '31.

All this I got from Tracy, who covered the production beat for the paper. Apparently, someone had tampered with the apparatus that was supposed to control the scene of the falling chandelier, and it plunged down on the crew, who were working on the set between takes. It killed two grips and injured several others, shutting down production for a few days while, among other things, the chandelier prop had to be rebuilt.

"They probably would have chalked it up to a bad accident," Tracy told me, "but for what another crewmember found." The apparatus that controlled the chandelier was located at the top of the enormous set, and an electrician working up there said that he had seen a figure in red, but had assumed it was just someone in the cast until after the catastrophe. It was only then that he found the message, scrawled in red paint in the rafters: "There is only one Lon Chaney."

IT DIDN'T TAKE LONG FOR the *Bulletin* to seize on what it called "THE CHANEY CURSE," with another anonymous article filled with the kinds of swooning half-truths and implications that would have made Universal's marketing people proud had they been ballyhoo for a movie instead of a scandal.

"It seems that someone — or some*thing* — doesn't want Chaney's legacy sullied with a sequel," the *Bulletin* mused, dubbing the possibly speculative figure glimpsed on Stage 28 "the Red Death" and drawing parallels to a case in London a few years earlier when a man had killed a housemaid in Hyde Park and told police that Chaney's beaver hat vampire from *London After Midnight* made him do it.

I wasn't on the Red Death beat, though. I was on the wax museum exhibit opening beat and, despite what the pictures will tell you, those are very much not the same beat. Nevertheless, I worked in the same offices as the reporters who *were*, which meant that I heard things. "The cops think it's a deranged fan thing," Tracy told me.

"Do they think it's the same person who broke into the Chaney vault?" I asked Miller when I found him back at his desk.

"I can't even get a straight answer on whether anybody *did* break into the vault," he replied. "They're keeping it locked up tighter'n Fort Knox."

"No leaks?"

He shook his head. "Contradictory ones. Some say yeah, some say no. Some say the studio is covering it up, some say the whole thing is a studio publicity stunt."

I, meanwhile, had used the news to convince my editor to let me take another swing at the wax museum.

"Why the hell do you want to go back there?" he asked me as I took a seat on the corner of his desk, as was my wont. "Don't I keep you busy enough?"

"With all this Chaney stuff swirling around, I think there's a bigger story on the Phantom exhibit. I did some legwork, and they bought some of the original props from the movie — ones that weren't used in the exhibit I saw. I think they might have something in the works, and it would give us an excuse to fill some column inches with Chaney's name without stooping to grave robbing."

Ernie frowned at me, but I knew he was going to say yes before he pushed me off his desk and told me to get going.

IT WAS RAINY ON THE evening that I headed back out to the Montmartre, planning to arrive just before closing time, in the hopes that I could get an interview with LeGrande or one of his assistants. "We're closing up," the hat-check girl told me as I ducked in out of the rain, shedding droplets on their red carpeting.

I flashed her my press badge and said that I was there to talk with the sculptors. My paper already had a good relationship with the Montmarte and I could have – probably *should* have – called ahead, but some hunch had told me not to.

"I'll see if Dr. Kebbler is available," the poor hat-check girl said doubtfully, locking up the door with me still inside and heading deeper into the museum to find her boss.

A wax museum is a weird, eerie place to stand by yourself on a rainy night. The only figure visible from the lobby was one of Valentino as the Sheik, which was up a short set of four steps. From my previous visit, I knew that you could take either a right or a left at the Valentino statue and make a circuit that would lead you through the museum and back to where you had started.

Previously, the Valentino statue hadn't struck me much. I knew that he was a heartthrob and I could agree that he was handsome enough, but he had been a bit before my time and I hadn't ever really watched many of his movies. The figure had seemed innocuous enough on my first visit. Now, it seemed haughty and terrible, its eyes at once staring and shadowed as it held up one hand in an imperious gesture. I was reminded of Lugosi, who I had seen so hypnotically just a few nights before.

My reverie was interrupted by the arrival of Dr. Kebbler, with the hat-check girl in tow. Immediately, I noticed that something seemed off about him, but I couldn't put my finger on it as the girl left and he locked the door behind her. "What can I do for you?" he asked me. His voice was different, raspier than I remembered, and I wondered if he had a cold.

"I'm working on a follow-up story to the new Chaney exhibition," I said. "I was hoping to speak with Mr. LeGrande or one of his assistants to get a little more insight into the process. The public has a real interest, especially with Chaney's name back in the headlines."

Kebbler made a sound, like something catching in the back of his throat. "The public," he scoffed. "What do they know of a great man like Lon Chaney? While they have him, they crucify and exploit him. When he is gone, they spit upon his legacy."

"Sounds like you're a fan," I said, with what I hoped was a light chuckle.

"There is only one Lon Chaney," Kebbler said and then, as soon as the words had left his mouth, his dark eyes darted to the side, scanning my face to see if I had reacted, if I knew that he had said too much. "But we are now beside the point," he hurried on. "While we appreciate the enthusiasm of your paper, I am afraid that Monsieur LeGrande is a private man who refuses interviews. 'My work shall speak for itself,' is his constant refrain. And he keeps his assistants too busy to take time out to speak with the press."

"Could I perhaps see the workshops, at least?" I asked, though I had little illusion that he would acquiesce.

"Perhaps another time," Kebbler replied. "The sculptors have all departed for the day, and Monsieur LeGrande would be wroth with me if I showed someone around his laboratory when he was not present."

"I would like that very much," I said. "Should I call tomorrow and arrange it?"

"Please do so during business hours," Kebbler said. "And I make you no promises. It will have to be cleared by Monsieur LeGrande. He has the final say on such matters."

As he ushered me out the door, I reached out to shake his hand, and he drew back at the last moment, almost involuntarily, as though afraid of the touch. "Do not stay out in the rain, fraulein," he said. "You will catch your death."

The door locked behind him and I watched him retreat into the darkness before turning to walk away myself. Finally, what I had noticed at first clicked into place: When he had presented the Chaney exhibition, Kebbler had walked with a limp in his left leg – one that was perceptibly absent now.

I MAY ONLY HAVE BEEN assigned to the society beat, but I still liked to think that I had a reporter's instincts, and they were certainly aroused. So, rather than walking back to where I had parked my roommate's car, I slipped around the corner of the Montmartre to the alley, where I found a basement window that radiated heat and light through its frosted glass.

The window was locked from the inside, but I had a penknife in my handbag and I was able to use it to slide the latch open. From what little I knew about the inner workings of wax museums, I imagined that the room beyond would be one of the workshops I had just been asking about, filled with half-finished figures and bubbling vats of molten wax. Instead, I was hit with a wall of damp heat, but could see little, as the interior of the window proved to be hung with gauzy curtains or veils, letting light sift through but precluding vision.

Pushing these aside as best I was able, I stuck my legs through the window and prepared to slip into the room below, hoping that it wasn't too far to fall. I imagined broken legs or twisted ankles as I dropped, but instead felt something constricting suddenly and tightly around my neck, filling my vision with stars and my ears with the sound of ringing bells.

After that, everything went dark.

As I CAME TO, THE first thing I was aware of was the cord twined bruisingly tight around my throat. Instinctively, my hands flew to it to try to force my fingers beneath, but they were bound together inside a black bag tied at the wrists, rendering them functionally useless.

The gesture upset my perch atop a wooden stool, which rocked precariously as I moved, causing the cord to dig even harder into my windpipe. "I wouldn't," a woman's voice said from somewhere in the darkness.

It was only then that I finally took in my surroundings. The stool on which I balanced was center stage in a recreation of the Phantom's lair – now I knew where those other props that the museum had acquired had gone.

A wheelchair in one curtained alcove held a hunched figure white with stalactites of hardened wax. Even under the tallow, I could recognize the facial features of Xavier LeGrande. In another alcove, Dr. Kebbler leaned against the wall, harder to make out under his own coating of wax.

Pride of place, however, belonged to the coffin bed in which Chaney's Phantom had claimed to sleep. In the movie, we never saw him use it, but he was there now, dressed in a reproduction of his Red Death outfit. Though months in the grave had rendered his features eerily similar to the Phantom's death's head, I recognized Lon Chaney's desiccated corpse.

"They tried to take him from me," the voice said from the shadows, and as it did, a figure stepped forward. It was still dressed as Kebbler, just as it had been when it spoke to me in the lobby, but now it was shedding its disguise, bit by bit.

"LeGrande was first. He wanted to do the Phantom sculpture himself. 'It will be my crowning achievement,' he said. But I've been the one doing his work ever since he came to America. Maybe he was great once; I've seen photographs. Now, though? He's a dope addict, and his hands shake. I couldn't let him mar Chaney's likeness. So I strangled him, like the Phantom would have."

First to come off was the jacket and top hat that Kebbler had been wearing. Then, it was time for the makeup, beginning with the hands, which had looked old and weathered, now gradually scrubbed clean of their wrinkles and liver spots.

"Then Kebbler found out. Of course he did. How could he not? I thought he would discover LeGrande's absence first, but no — the old sculptor was so unreliable, Kebbler was used to leaning on us, on me. It was the body that he found. Not LeGrande's, but the one I had taken, to serve as my model, as my muse. To keep it safe from those who would let it decay, forgotten. He had to die, too. It was only once he was gone that I realized… if he disappeared, then sooner or later they would take *this place* from me, and I had worked too hard to build it. So, I did what He would have done, and I *became* Kebbler, whenever the need arose. "

The figure had finished scrubbing the makeup from its face now, and it reached up to peel off the wig of Keebler's gray hair.

"The chandelier was a mistake. I know that. Too much attention. But they were going to make people forget Him, don't you see that? I couldn't let someone else be the Phantom. It was sacrilege."

"They won't shut down production over one little accident," I said, the words croaking out of my mouth, my throat raw from the bruising pressure of the strangling cord.

"Oh, I know that," Mellie Garcia said, now stepping into the full light for the first time. "I'll have to do more to stop them. But first, I'll have to take care of you."

"So, why not let me strangle to death already?" I asked. I don't know why I thought that antagonizing her was a good idea.

"I need to know," she said, her demeanor changing, her voice faster, harsher. "How did you find me? What brought you here? What was it that gave me away? My next role will have to be better. I'll learn, like He did, and I'll do better next time."

My nose for a story was what had brought me back to the Montmartre, and then the absence of Dr. Kebbler's limp had tipped me off, but that wasn't going to do me any good in this situation. "I'll show you," I said, "but you'll have to let me down from here."

She looked at me with sharp, cunning eyes. The glasses, I realized now, had been another disguise. She didn't need them. The beauty mark was gone, as well. I really *was* attracted to this girl; this dangerous, half-crazy snake. Too bad she was going to kill me.

"If you think you can get away, you're wrong," she said.

"No," I said. "I think you're right. There is only one Lon Chaney. They can't ever be allowed to forget that. I'm a reporter. I know how they think. I'll show you how I found you out; how you can make them remember."

For a long time, she stared at me, my heart hammering in my chest as I tried to keep my eyes, the set of my face, the sweat that rolled its way down along the edge of my ear from giving me away. Then, she walked over to the wall and pulled a lever, and suddenly the cord around my neck was slack and I was falling, my hands still uselessly bound, and cracking knees and elbows against the hard floor.

"Now show me," she said. "But don't try anything."

She was holding a device similar to those I had seen used to subdue wild dogs. A long stick with a loop of wire at the end, a weapon ready to close around my neck if I made a wrong move.

"It's in my purse," I said, and she gestured with the hoop toward a curtained alcove. As we walked, me ahead and her behind, telling me which way to turn when the time to turn came, I realized that we were still beneath the wax museum, and with each step away from the Phantom's lair, the heat grew.

"I left it where it fell when you came in," she said. "But the window is shut now and there's no one on these streets at this hour, so don't try to scream."

My make-believe image of the workshop had been pretty close to accurate, its shelves lined with grotesque, half-completed heads, a bubbling vat of cooking wax in the center of the room. Worktables lined the wall nearest the street, atop which small burners were lit, keeping specific pans of wax at particular temperatures.

My purse still lay beneath the window, below the hanging veils which had concealed the noose that caught me. "I'll need my hands free," I said, holding up the black bag that bound them.

Mellie Garcia shook her head. "I'll get it," she said, picking up the purse. "You just tell me when."

Cautiously, she set the stick with the hooped wire on the floor, leaning it against the wall so that it was within easy reach as she began to rifle through my purse, taking out first a compact, then a notepad, then the penknife. That was when I rammed her, putting my shoulder down and driving it as hard as I could into her sternum. I followed that up by stomping on the bridge of her foot, then throwing my elbow into her nose.

She stumbled backward, blood spilling from her face, her feet going out from under her as she struck her head against the worktable. The whole thing went over then, spilling wax which ignited as it struck the open flames. In what seemed the blink of an eye, the draping veils had caught as well, and the whole wall was a curtain of fire.

I was already backing away as Mellie Garcia rose shakily to her feet, but I knew that I wouldn't be able to escape in time. I didn't know the layout of the wax museum, while she knew it like the back of her hand. It would only be a matter of time before that wire was around my neck.

"The fire!" I said, trying to throw panic into my voice, which wasn't too hard, given the circumstances. "He'll burn up in the fire if we don't save him!"

Mellie's eyes cleared in a moment, the pupils dilating with panic terror as she ran *past* me, back the way we had come.

Much of what happened then, in the smoke and chaos that followed, has been lost to me. I couldn't tell you now the route that I took to get out of that place, how many false starts and dead ends I turned down. I can only tell you that the fire spread faster than I would have thought possible; that my exodus was like a stereoscope of Hell itself, wax figures writhing and deforming beneath the flames.

Did I really pass through the chamber where Mellie had first held me captive and see her there, embracing the corpse of Lon Chaney because she was too overcome to move it? Did I see a figure, dressed in red, vanishing down a distant passage? I have never been certain.

What I know is that, eventually, I found myself back at the front door and, from there, out into the rainy night, where I collapsed on the sidewalk until firefighters came and put a blanket around me and loaded me into the back of an ambulance.

ERNIE AND CLETE AND TRACY and my roommate and even Detective Pearson all came and visited me in the hospital over the next few days, where they told me about what had happened. The fire had spread much too fast, and the Montmartre was lost, though the fire department was able to save the neighboring buildings. They recovered three sets of human remains from the burned wreckage, which dental records matched to Werner Kebbler, Xavier LeGrande, and Mellie Garcia – no fourth body was ever found.

When I got out of the hospital, with a clean white bandage around my throat, I had my roommate drive me out to Glendale, where I laid white lilies in front of Chaney's crypt. By then, the stories about graverobbing had died down, and I saw for myself that the unmarked marble face of the crypt was unbroken, unmarred – as Detective Pearson assured me it always had been. Did it look newer than the ones around it? Well it would, wouldn't it? Chaney had only been dead for a few months.

So what, then, did I see down there, beneath the wax museum? Ernie and Detective Pearson both said that it must have been a model of Chaney's body. That Mellie Garcia had snapped, and that she had created the wax effigy after reading the bogus story about the tomb robbery. I tried to convince myself that they were right, but I've never been quite so sure.

Though my paper covered the story, painting me as the "brave reporter who single-handedly stopped the Red Death," I didn't write about it myself. Ernie offered to graduate me up to the crime beat, but I told him I'd had enough of it, and I was happy to keep covering less exciting stories.

Just two years later, Warner released a movie starring Fay Wray and Lionell Atwill, about a crazy sculptor who kills people to make his statues. Supposedly, they based it on an unpublished short story by this guy named Belden, so neither me nor my paper saw a dime. But the main character was a cute, blonde reporter who looked a lot like yours truly. A coincidence? Maybe so. But in this town, you'll never make me believe it.

NOW WE SING THE KILLING SONG

Josh Rountree

Of course, you have secrets; you always wear a mask.

But we have secrets too.

We know your true face, *Angel of Music*.

LISTEN WELL AND YOU'LL HEAR a heartbeat. A rhythm that commands the slow progress of an underground river; the river of the dead or the river of the *not entirely dead*, there's little difference in this place. Voices cry and wail. They sing. But there is no voice like *hers*. You might have been forever lost to us, had she not placed that ring on your dead blue finger. But you loved her, and that silver band shimmers like moonlight across the surface of the afterlife. Hear the heart of the river grow stronger as you splash about. Don't resist. This is your nature. Follow the music. Climb the slow violin whine, upward from the depths. Open your eyes to brittle sunlight, and heave air into your new lungs.

We have given you everything but a face.

That's what the mask is for.

Feel the tooled leather boots on your feet, and the long cowhide coat that hangs from your broad shoulders. Notice the weight of the pistol at your hip. The weapon of choice in this new land. The quickest, surest way to deliver death to those deserving. Stumble into town beneath a hellish sun, flesh burned red, and sour with sweat. An unwelcomed stranger. Feel the ache in your bones and the stiff motion of your limbs as you learn to inhabit this new shape. Steady your legs as the blood flows back into your being and open your ears to the songs of this place.

Spit out the taste of your old life.

Become our servant anew in this awful world.

Hear a voice singing. Not *her* voice. She's an ocean away. A memory from another life. This voice is untamed, yet no less beautiful. Violence lurks in every shadow of this continent; it echoes in the ears of every living being, and it lies at the tip of the singer's tongue. She is not aware. Would never choose it. But the song you bring her can ruin souls. You may not want to teach her, *Angel of Music*, but you know you're unable to resist. You love too easily, and your love for them weakens you. Allows us to draw you back from the dead again and again.

You'll teach her the same song as all the others.

You'll teach her the *killing song*.

THE WHISKEY HALL BELONGS TO a man name Bull Ransom, and it's not the sort of place you usually haunt. Hastily hammered lumber forms a building two stories tall, and its murky-eyed windows watch your approach. A lone horse stands lashed to the hitching post outside, suffering in the heat, while a couple of tired old dogs cling to the shadows beneath a leaning second-floor balcony. Other neglected buildings crowd around, bound by unpaved streets, bereft of life, like haunted houses in the making. The song summons you up the steps of *Ransom Hall* and onto the groaning porch. The singing captivates you to the point where you don't think to wonder where you are. And does it matter? You are west of the Mississippi and east of the Pacific, we can tell you that. You are in the beating bloody heart of the West and there is no escaping such a place.

Through the door and into the gloom.

A splintered bar runs the length of one wall, backed by a tarnished mirror that reflects nothing but darkness. Tables and chairs form haphazard patterns across the sawdust floor, and a performance stage dominates the far wall, bordered with heavy blood-red curtains, lit from above with a brass candelabra, its light swaying in drunken patterns as the candles gutter and spit. A piano waits in the wings for fingers to give it voice.

The singer is a sharp-edged beauty in a thin blue dress with yellow hair piled high on her head. She sits on the edge of the stage with her legs dangling, like performing from the stage itself is too lofty an aspiration. The song is not an old one. The song is *American*. But she builds the simple melody and words into a rising temple of sound. Her raw talent is striking. Tentative, now, but growing. She throws you a curious glance as you climb onto the stage and take a seat at the piano, but she does not grow silent. When you begin to play, she raises her voice to match, and this new song comes alive under your fingertips. The piano is half out of tune, but no matter. The music between the two of you is still lovely. And when the song dies, and you approach to sit beside her on the edge of the stage, you are delighted to see how she beams at you. How the candlelight lives in her eyes.

Already you are beaten.

"You play beautifully," she says.

"I was a music teacher back east. Before the war."

The lie becomes truth as soon as you speak it. You have no history beyond what you create for yourself. When you motion to your mask, both of you imagine a bloody battlefield, artillery explosions taking the flesh from your face, leaving nothing but a leering monster that must be hidden away from the world. Might be you had loved ones waiting for you somewhere, but you'd never be able to face them again. Better to wander in this new land, a stranger, than to see the pity blossom in their eyes. None of this really happened, and yet it's entirely *real*. Already you have wandered for years, and this land has burned the devil into your soul. You flinch when she puts a palm on your mask, but you let it stay.

The look she gives you is not pity.

More like *wonder*.

Are you the *Angel of Music* her grandmother used to talk about? The one with the magical gift to elevate a person's natural talent to something extraordinary? Of course you are, and we make certain she understands this deep in her bones. Simply being in your presence, she can feel a more beautiful voice rising in her throat, and though she has known you only a moment, she takes hold of your arm for fear you might vanish and leave her searching once again for such a miracle.

Now *she's* beaten too.

"How often do you perform here?" you ask.

"Oh, I never do."

"But just now?"

"I love to sing. Nothing more. Lady Ransom sings every evening, though, if you're looking for entertainment."

"Don't you wish to perform?"

"Certainly."

"Does Lady Ransom have a better voice than yours?"

The woman only smiles, and her expression reveals her every thought on the matter.

The two of you draw closer, clasping hands now. So engaged with one another that both of you are surprised to find the bartender standing before you, having emerged from the shadows with a heavy iron rod in his hands, and a sour expression on his drawn face. Your eyes found only *her* when you entered the saloon, but now you realize there are other women here, leaning over the second-floor balcony in various states of undress, laughing and smoking and examining your sudden romance. Dirty men seated around a table by the front window pay you little mind; they trade curses and whiskey shots in the still early morning, and like as not have been seated there since deep in the night. The bartender clears his throat. Scratches his scrawny beard with an overgrown fingernail. Offers an unconvincing smile when he speaks.

"Time with the ladies is not free, sir."

The bartender's mouth is edged with white foam, giving him a rabid sort of look.

"We're only talking," you say.

"Talking ain't free. Nothing you want to do with her is free. You may rent a room and the lady's time if you wish."

"I haven't any money," you say.

"Then you have no business in this place."

The singer still holds you tightly, and concern colors her face.

"I only wished to hear her sing," you say. "If I return with money, might she be allowed to perform for us tonight?"

"Open your eyes, sir. She's too beautiful to waste on that sort of work. She earns her keep in other ways."

"Even so, why not let her sing?"

"I asked you nicely to leave, sir."

Your hand rests uncomfortably on the pistol at your hip; you've never fired such a powerful weapon. "I'll go. But I'll return tonight to hear her sing."

"You will go, but you will not return."

"Let her perform, or things will go hard for you. I cannot say it more plainly."

"You threaten me with violence?"

"If need be."

The bartender grins broadly, reveals a mouth full of surprisingly white teeth. "Your threat falls on idle ears, sir. Violence is my constant companion."

The bartender's iron rod strikes like a snake, connects with the bridge of your nose. The brown leather mask absorbs some of the impact, but it's enough to send you toppling from the edge of the stage, and when he swings again, the rod connects with the back of your skull; that leaves you dazed on the ground, befouled with blood. The singer's lovely voice is all shrieks now, the natural song of this place. The bartender shoves her away and grips your coat collar, drags you bodily across splinted wood, out the door, and deposits you in the middle of the street.

Two richly dressed people gawk at your inglorious arrival, the two of them having just disembarked from a regal coach pulled by stomping black horses. You roll aside to escape the falling hooves, rise to your knees with your head swimming and blood warming your clothes. The gawkers are not impressed with you. The man is maned with bright white hair and is of ample girth, the woman slim and quietly pretty, but with an expression that reveals a disdain for every living thing in sight. As they approach the saloon, the bartender steps aside, doffs his hat. You don't require our supernatural intervention to know these are the Ransoms.

"Trouble Chester?" asks Bull Ransom.

"Little enough," said the bartender.

"Did he abuse one of the girls?"

"No, but he thought Annabeth might be available for a free tumble. I set him straight on the matter."

Annabeth. Even her name makes lovely music.

"Job done, then," says Bull Ransom.

"And gladly done, sir."

The three of them disappear inside, leave you bleeding in the street. So, you do what's natural to your kind. You seek out the dark places. Wedge free a board from the porch and crawl into the vile, cramped space between the earth and the floorboards. You seethe. You wait. You *listen*.

Haunt them. Seek out the cramped spaces behind the walls, and beneath the floorboards. Places only accessible to tragic creatures like yourself. Understand you have no choice in what's to come. Feel the killing song inside you. Soon it will live in her too. And she'll pass that gift along with tooth and blade. That song a feral intoxication in her blood.

Resist, like you always do.

It won't make a difference.

Feel the love that draws you through claustrophobic passageways, choked with spiderwebs and rat skeletons that snap beneath your boots. Sideways, upward. Coughing out dust and death. Unable to stop your heart from chasing her; happy endings are hopeless, but you seek them out, always. Find the peephole. Gaze into Annabeth's chamber where she conducts the business for which Ransom has hired her. Naked in her bed, atop a groaning man. One of the ranch hands who ride into town on paydays and burn all their money in one night. This one still has his boots on, but his trousers are down far enough for Annabeth to writhe on top of him. Listen as she sings a different sort of melody than before. Wail like a ghost in the walls as your love for her comes under assault.

Wait until they have finished. Until the man is gone and Annabeth lies shaking in the darkness. Open the secret door we have provided, the one backed with the long dressing mirror, and creep into her room, into her bed, into her arms. Inhale her. Feel the pulsing rhythm of her heart. Time your own heart to hers. Place your lips against her ear and whisper the song. Hum the melody. Allow her to absorb the song into her blood and her bones. Listen as she sings your song back to you. Lose yourself in the night when she places her lips against yours and whispers, *we shall sing our songs together for the rest of our lives*.

Pretend this unnatural love is real.

Believe you are more than servants of the inevitable.

We will allow you this night of dreams.

You SPEND YOUR DAYS IN the walls, and your nights singing the killing song to Annabeth. You burrow your way to other rooms, peering up through gaps in floorboards, gazing down through ceiling cracks. You learn the nature and the routines of this place. Twelve women in Bull Ransom's employ, some wholehearted participants, others driven by simple desperation. A stooped piano player named Jake, who leers at them all with red, weepy eyes. The lovely Elizabeth Ransom, star of the stage every evening. And, of course, Chester the bartender, who enjoys the unlimited services of the ladies as part of his employment compensation. You haunt them all. Visit them in the darkness like the phantom you are and turn their dreams to ashes with your whispers. Annabeth and her song invade their sleep, and they wake unrested, wondering why she is all they can think of.

Still, she is not allowed to perform.

Eventually Chester visits Annabeth's chamber, and murder comes of age in your heart. Chester uses her roughly, all the while shouting that if it's singing she enjoys, he will sing her a song of pain. Annabeth sings the killing song through bloody teeth, and the burnt scent of dark magic suffuses the air. Perhaps she will kill him right here. But no. We find she is not yet ready. Has not yet taken the song *entirely* into her soul. Your job is not finished. When Chester leaves, you sit beside Annabeth on the sagging bed, towel the blood from her battered face with water from the basin.

You offer to take her away from this place.

This is not a promise you can keep. You know we'd never allow it. But no matter, she is not ready to leave.

"I'd go with you forever, gladly," she says. "But I must perform here first."

"You can perform *anywhere*."

She shakes her head. Crippled by sadness. What began as the tiniest of dreams in her heart has grown into a desperate desire. One she can never escape. We have done this to her. *You* have done this to her. There is an inescapable end to this story, an ancient pattern that cannot be denied. You always try. You always fail. As your blood grows hot and violence expands in your chest, we must remind you that you're a creature of evil. You don't deserve even this semblance of love.

"You will perform here," you say. "I swear it."

"Make it so."

"And then you'll leave with me? You'll be mine?"

She nods. "I'm already yours."

From your pants pocket you produce a simple gold ring and place it on her finger.

Always, you have been a fool.

No matter how much you wish it, there is no *real* love for you in her heart.

There is only obsession.

When Annabeth finally sleeps, you watch the gentle rise and fall of her chest for half an eternity, then you venture boldly downstairs, not bothering to travel through the saloon's hidden pathways. Sunrise approaches, and only Chester remains as he slops dirty water across the bar top, working to clear away the nightly sludge. He has no sense of you, *phantom*. You are silent as smoke. Dressed in deep morning shadows. Chester might have died at his post, but bodily urges draw him out the side door, where he pisses against the side of the building and whistles bits and pieces of Annabeth's song. Few things have ever offended you more. On quiet feet you approach. Lift your pistol from the holster and place it against the back of his head.

You pull the trigger.

Chester's face escapes his skull, takes flight.

The town is no stranger to gunfire. No one will investigate until morning. When they do, word will spread of the faceless man hanging by his neck from an elm tree, pants around his ankles and belly sliced open, his entrails spilled to the ground.

A couple of hungry dogs, lapping at the mess.

And written in blood, on the side of the saloon:

BY COMMAND PERFORMANCE
THE LOVELY ANNABETH
A DIVINE VOICE YOU WILL FOREVER REMEMBER

Sometimes we forget how willful you are.

Hide away in your crawlspace and we will show you the price of such rash action. Murder is not your business. Such violence is reserved for your students. Hear the wilting tones of Elizabeth Ransom from the main stage, while Annabeth sings only for cowboys in her room upstairs. Wait breathlessly every night until the hour comes for you to join her, warm and alive as you have ever been. Lie with her in the heat of her bed. You are no better than the rest of them, seeking her out to soothe pains they cannot themselves name. Your lessons are carnal. Your love for her is cursed. And yet you can't resist the jealously that burns inside you.

The bartender was hers to kill.

Did you think you could take her place?

We know your secret heart. We know how you maneuver against us.

You have changed some of the words, coloring them with love instead of death. But you've tried that before. It never works. Don't you remember? The *words* don't matter. Only the *music*. And do not speak to us of fair Christine, your last student. Perhaps you think your love for her helped avert her fate. She embraced the song like all the others before her. You think she truly loved you? Fool. She was *terrified*. Enchanted by the killing song. Placing that ring on your dead finger was her way of thanking you for your dark gift. It took a while longer for the song to mature inside her but mature it did.

Nothing remained for Christine in Paris; her association with you was a scandal. But England was not so far away, and even now she stalks the midnight streets of London, delivering death with a gleaming silver blade.

Wonder at this, *Angel of Music*. Are you an angel for true? Or are you a devil.

Even we cannot say for sure, but there's little enough difference between the two to matter.

WHEN YOU MURDER THE PIANO player in his bed you leave a handwritten note on his chest that reads:

OH ANNABETH
SHE OF THE CELESTIAL VOICE
LET MY ANGEL SING

But Bull Ransom does not believe in you, phantom. He does not entirely believe in young Annabeth as a murderer either, but he's worried enough to lock her in her room until he can divine the true nature of your bloody crimes. She lies in her bed, besieged by the suffocating heat of midday, spinning the gold ring around her finger again and again, as if you are the only thing she can think of. Perhaps this is true, but what exactly does she think of you?

You appear from your hidden mirrored doorway, moving quietly through Annabeth's room like the ghost you are. A creature of death and terror and desire. Mask firmly affixed to shield her from the truth of you. She's in tears when she welcomes you to her bed, and you kiss them away once again with your whispering song. Even now, as she draws you close to the heat of her, you are working our will for us, twisting her into the creature she'll soon become.

The killing song is ancient. Irresistible.

Just like you, *Angel of Music*.

You are more than our instrument in the world; you're a fairy tale passed down through generations. A legendary creature who whispers to babes in their cribs and leans over young students as they pick at piano keys with tentative fingers. You haunt the minds of the old and infirm as they recall all the dreams that died in their youth, giving them misguided hope they might still claim some measure of talent. You deliver them all our gift of genius. And they pay us back with beautiful madness. When they draw bows across strings, when they place their lips against the clarinet reed, when they open their mouths wide to sing, the sound they create is like nothing of this earth. Glorious and true, something more than human. And when the killing urge blossoms inside their heart, the skills we've gifted them for murder are no less otherworldly.

Enjoy these moments with your beloved.

She will know your true face soon enough.

And she'll discover her own face too.

BALANCE ON THE OVERHEAD BEAMS while Elizabeth Ransom delivers her workmanlike aria from the stage below. Few in the saloon pay attention, content to drink whiskey and gamble away their money. They laugh and carouse with the half-dressed women, every one of them with bold makeup and high-tossed hair. Even Bull Ransom himself, seated at the table closest to center stage, is otherwise engaged with his hand of cards, throwing down two pair with a yelp of triumph.

Elizabeth continues her performance, undaunted.

Cling to the elevated shadows, sharp knife in hand. Wait for the would-be starlet to settle herself directly below the blazing chandelier.

Some patterns can be steered in new directions, while others are inescapable.

Elizabeth has done nothing to offend you, but she is a sturdy dam, holding at bay the river of violence that sweet Annabeth must unleash, and though you would not choose such madness for your beloved, things are far beyond your control now. You are dying from love. Like always. We count on your weakness every time. Draw the blade across the rope that suspends the swaying chandelier. Wipe the sweat from your brow and mouth our wicked song as you wield the knife. Every word tastes like death and rot. Every word emboldens you. Sing our violence into the world, and the world will repay you in kind.

Watch the chandelier sway and the shadows shudder.

Feel the rope unravel and come apart.

Listed to the screams as the chandelier plummets, knocks fair Elizabeth bodily to the ground. Her voluminous dress is claimed by candle fire. By the time Bull Ransom and the others clamber over the footlights and join her onstage, Elizabeth is a conflagration in full. Inhale the smoke that rises to meet you. Embrace the madness of the moment and unleash a harrowing cry that draws all eyes heavenward. Know the terror they feel. The sudden *understanding*. And retreat to your hidden labyrinth while onlookers summon the bucket brigade to save the saloon, if not the life of young Elizabeth Ransom.

She was not yours to kill either, but we'll allow that sometimes drastic measures are required. And after all, you cannot help yourself. Love drives us all mad.

Oh, what a perfect villain you are.

They will hunt you, but they won't find you.

And now they *all* believe in ghosts.

THE NEXT NIGHT, ANNABETH IS allowed to sing.

You watch from beneath the stage, peering through cracks in the boards, so close you can hear them bend and whine when she steps into the spotlight. Would that you had a better vantage to view her triumph, but there was no hiding behind the curtains this night; they surely would have found you there. So, you press your face against the underside of the stage as Annabeth summons her voice and, at last, gives life to the killing song with wholehearted fury. Her audience is comprised of Bull Ransom and those few men he could convince to return to his demon haunted saloon. When word of your deeds spread through town, few enough had the courage to return. By allowing Annabeth to perform, they think to draw you out. To snare the phantom. But they misunderstand.

The phantom is not the one they should fear.

Annabeth raises her voice in song, and all are ensnared by the music she makes. She is a terrible beauty, a siren none can resist. You've fostered true genius in this one. Everyone abandons their chairs; they draw close to the stage, and crowd before it like worshipers of an unholy god. Annabeth commands them with her voice, while they watch in awe, eyes teary and minds adrift. You mouth the words along with her as you push up a trap door and climb onto the stage. Unafraid of the spotlight. Adrift in the magic she creates. Luxuriating in this music of the night. Standing behind Annabeth affords you a view of the whole saloon, and there is no creature unaffected by the power of the killing song.

Annabeth motions with one delicate hand and Bull Ransom shoves his way onto the stage, lays himself down before her, a willing sacrifice.

Annabeth straddles him like a lover, removes a long knife from her boot. Never stops singing. Wields the knife in both hands and plunges it over and over into Ransom's chest. Her music transforms into screams, her face becomes a mask of ecstasy. Never has murder been so beautiful. Never has such bloody congress between two souls been so sublime. Annabeth wails as she draws her blade across Ransom's offered throat in one violent pass. She punishes his body with hatred and steel. With tooth and fingernail. Blood boils from Ransom's wounds, and Annabeth buries herself in the death of him. He shudders and gasps, spills his life out like a red river that waterfalls over the edge of the stage and washes clean the feet of every worshiper.

Annabeth continues her assault, letting the blade chew away everything that made Ransom a man.

Everything that made him human.

When she stands, chest heaving, she's a red ruin, grinning through bloody teeth.

Behold this perfect machine you've created. This engine of death.

You hold out your hand and she accepts it. With her other hand, she removes your mask and tosses it to the floor. Her fingers explore the ruin that is your face, tracing every protruding bone, caressing the scabrous meat that stretches to cover your leering skull. Her eyes peer through your sunken sockets, and into your soul. For the first time, you believe, one of your students truly *knows* you. And she understands. She brings you close and, for the first time, kisses you *deeply*. The blood in her mouth tastes like the afterlife. Like fallen souls and human pain. Her hands cup your face now, and she peels away all your rotted flesh, until only skull remains. Until there are no more secrets between the two of you. Her kiss never falters, and you imagine an eternity together.

You're utterly enraptured.

A corpse in love.

With the song grown quiet, the spell begins to lift. Howls of terror fill the gloom. Screams of outrage. Several men climb onto the stage, thinking to capture your beloved. But you halt their advance with a few well-placed bullets and the rest of them dive into the shadows to avoid more of the same. You pull Annabeth through the trapdoor, down into your domain. Lead her through labyrinthine passages until you emerge from beneath the front porch, laughing and singing together beneath a sliver of moonlight, sharp as Annabeth's blade.

You flee the town on stolen horses, and neither of you will ever return.

SLEEP NEAR THE BANKS OF a churning river, with you love in your arms. Hear the beat of her heart as it follows the rhythm of the killing song. That song belonged to you once, but it's her song now. No matter. Recall her promise, *we shall sing our songs together for the rest of our lives and* have faith in the love you share. Feel the touch of her hand as it moves along the raspy surface of your skull. You are miles from town, and the wilderness sings a different version of the song. A truly *honest* tune. Feel Annabeth's willing lips against your teeth, and her skin, bloody and red, colliding with your own. Together in a tangle. Feel another kiss, this one sharp against your gut, a knife asking questions of your soul. Gasp at the disemboweling twist of her blade and welcome the flow of hot blood as it pours forth like floodwaters, washing away everything you believed and everything you hoped. Embrace the bite of the blade as it carves a furrow through your chest and hollows out the space your heart used to be. Let her take it, still beating. Cup it in her hand.

This is love; you understand that now.

Feel the gold ring as she slides it onto your finger.

Follow her progress as she kisses you one last time, and rides away into the rising sun. Wait for the river to overflow its banks, to ferry your corpse home once again. Don't resist. Let the music of the river carry you to your reward. Let the ring on your finger be a beacon that lights your way through death.

You've done well, *Angel of Music.*

Rest for a time.

We'll call for you again, soon enough.

TWO FOR THE SHOW
L.A. Fields

T HE DAY Simon Spoke met his boyfriend, he knew they were fated. Call it a symptom of mental illness, but pattern recognition was a true asset, and it alerted Simon to the presence of his beloved when he heard the guy's name: Will Told. They were the past tense of the childhood games Simon Says and William Tell, matchy-matchy.

They bumped into each other when Will transferred to Simon's art college to study the theater craft, particularly stage makeup. Will was born with a port-wine stain birthmark that mottled half of his face and had learned to hide it with layers of concealer. When Simon saw Will step out of the shower on the night of their first sleepover, the splash of red over half his pale blond face reminded Simon of the *Phantom of the Opera*.

Will felt an affinity for the character, the mysterious phantom who lived beneath the Paris opera house and murderously meddled in the affairs of the singers, particularly the beautiful Christine Daae. Simon, a film student, knew that the demasking scene in the silent 1925 film was one of the most enduring shocks in cinema history. Throughout their courtship, Simon and Will watched each new movie adaptation to critique and examine how the Phantom's deformity was interpreted, hidden, and then revealed.

The Phantom of the Opera became such a founding part of their relationship that when they got their first apartment together, they chose a basement one to live underground as the Phantom did. When they adopted a kitty cat, they found a most regal and fluffy Persian-looking girl, named her Christine, and doted upon her for the rest of her natural life. When Andrew Lloyd Webber's *The Phantom of the Opera* premiered on Broadway in 1988, they scraped together the money to get tickets. They clutched each other's arms in wild excitement whenever the Phantom's sting blasted through the organ pipes and shook the very air of the theater.

They recommitted to careers in the theater and, throughout the 90s, paid their dues and honed their trades. For Simon, that meant developing his study of film story structure into an ability to write his own scripts for stage and screen. For Will, that meant mastering practical effects like the ratio of corn syrup to cornstarch for fake blood or using household items like Cheerios to create upsetting clusters of open wounds through makeup. His grotesqueries were commissioned for music videos and off-Broadway productions, but they both agreed their ultimate goal, like many before them, was to get on Broadway.

Simon believed they were destined to fulfill their ambitions. They embraced the madness of New York, aka The City That Never Sleeps. They threw themselves with abandon into every project, imagining that this could be the one they were interviewed about later, their big break into an industry as glamorous as it was grueling. They studied as if they were still in school, and they discussed what they learned together, each teaching the other in beautiful reciprocity and nourishment.

HOWEVER, THE JOB HUNT WAS abysmal for them both. Day after day, week after month after year, they took gigs and contracts and seasonal work and somehow never broke into a full-time position. At long last, Simon got an interview with a woman described as "warm and caring" with a charitable heart who liked to collect strays. He was so sure his luck had finally arrived that he bought a bottle of champagne and stashed it in his sock drawer, hoping to whip it out in celebration with Will when the good news came.

The position was perfect for him, and his interview was flawless, or so he thought. They needed a general manager? Simon had done everything from construction to lights, to comforting wounded actors, to breaking up fights between vendors. They needed someone who practically lived in and for the theater? Simon's apartment was within sprinting distance of the venue, and he had done nothing else with his personal development except pursue a role like this for the past decade. He arrived to the interview early, had florid answers for every question, and just beamed with enthusiasm, verve, and zest.

And apparently, his exuberance was the problem. The woman who interviewed him, Sharla Parr, who was billed as so kind and generous, apparently did not appreciate the brightness of Simon's light. She called him at home. His heart leaped to see her name on the caller ID. Will knelt before him in a prayer pose, hoping for good news. He saw Simon's face fall as reality walloped him.

"We're moving forward with different candidates, but I just wanted to offer you feedback that could help you," Sharla said. "You have a lot of great experience, and I can tell you have a heart for your work, but one of the challenges during the interview is that you talked quite a bit. You talked so much that it was hard for me to get in a question. Does that resonate with you?"

It did not; it was, in fact, quite discordant with Simon, but out loud, he said, "I suppose I can be chatty."

"It's good to know your audience. You know, early on in my career, I had to think about what were my best skills and highlight those without being overwhelmed. If the person I'm with wants more from me, they can ask, what do you think of that?"

Simon was not at the beginning of his career; he was already a decade deep and getting nothing but the runaround. The hand holding the phone felt numb. Will was holding and kissing his other hand to comfort him.

"I guess it depends on the interviewer. Usually, people like to see high energy." It would be more accurate to say people liked to exploit individuals who were in the industry with starry-eyed naivety, willing to work late, work overtime, and run themselves ragged just for the honor of serving the theater.

Sharla laughed, and the sound slithered deep into Simon's ear like a slug. "Sometimes it really is about fitting into the style and vibe of the team. You see, I work with some people who are a little more quiet, and it might be more helpful to find someone with a listening ear? Does that make sense?"

Simon sighed. "So you're saying it's just a matter of the vibes being off?"

"Yeah, nothing personal, we are just going with candidates who can communicate a little more succinctly," Sharla said.

"Okay."

A beat, and then, "Okay, well, I hope that helps you at least understand the decision. I hope you don't leave thinking, 'Sharla is telling me there's something wrong with me,' because that certainly is not the case. I know that looking for a job a lot of times is not fun, but you'll find the place for your skills soon enough with the right attitude.

Right. Well, you have a good night then, Sharla," Simon said, his voice dead in his mouth.

"You as well. Okay, bye-bye." The line clicked off, and Simon lowered the phone back into its cradle and himself ever so gently onto the bed.

Will sprung to his side and started kissing his face.

"How dare she, I'm so sorry," Will told him. The kisses moved to his ear. "Let me just cleanse this ear of her putrid voice."

A dazed Simon repeated their worn-out mantras of gumption and drive.

"Every rejection brings us closer to acceptance. Struggle feeds creativity. This moment won't even be a footnote in our biography."

"That's right," Will said. "Someday, she'll see your name in lights, and you won't even remember hers."

"I'm not sure about that, stupid Shart-la," Simon said, bitterness foul on his tongue. He leaned over to get the champagne out from under his socks. Getting drunk would be his consolation prize that night.

PERHAPS THAT BOTTLE OF BUBBLY would have been enough to soothe a bruised ego. In the normal course of events, perhaps the memory of Sharla's simpering and arrogant pity would have had time to fade away like all the other rejections that had come before. But it just so happened that Sharla's call was the first wound onto which salt would pour and pour, and it wasn't just bad luck for Simon; the unfairness also came for Will.

Sharla's call came on a Friday. On Saturday, they worked a bruising catering job to make rent, running around rich people with trays of food worth more than dental work. On Sunday, they recovered together, taking turns to make breakfast and then dinner, wallowing in bed and rubbing each other's aching feet. On Monday, the torrent of shit resumed.

First, Simon was pickpocketed on the subway. It wasn't a disaster because they didn't have any money, and his ID was in a lanyard in his bag anyway. All they got was his library card, a director's phone number from two years ago, a couple of punch cards and coupons, plus the wallet itself, which had been a gift from Will in their early days of courtship. This was what stung the most.

"I'll pickpocket you a better one," Will promised, and they kissed and kissed and repeated endlessly how lucky he was that he didn't have to replace his ID and how the wallet was going to wear out and need replacing anyway, so it was fine, really. It was a ding but not a disaster.

ON TUESDAY THEIR NEXT CATER waiter job fell through, meaning they'd have to find another gig before the end of the month to stay housed. On Wednesday, Simon got an email from his agent about a script they were shopping around—it had been rejected for reasons that didn't make sense until Simon checked the reply history and found out that his agent Barney had made "edits" that were actually errors all the way through. On Thursday, he called to chew the man out over this, and in a huff at being confronted over his unprofessional behavior, the agent terminated their contract.

"The egos on these people," Simon said, seething as he hung up the phone. He was breathing through his nose like a furious bull, the room felt like it was closing in on him. His skin felt both hot and cold, like the sensation of sticking one's hands into scalding water to wash dishes to make rent in the most expensive city in the country.

"Barney wasn't helping you anyway," Will said, rushing up to hold Simon's face and cool the heat of his anger with those long, thin fingers, pianist hands like the Phantom. "Five years with that guy, and he's never sold anything? We'll find you a better agent, or I'll be your agent and submit you to things. Why should anyone else get a cut of our fortune?"

"You're right," Simon said, clinging to Will the same way Will held onto him. "We have each other, that's worth more than they'll ever achieve."

BUT THE NEXT FRIDAY CAME around, and Will had a golden opportunity snatched from him, too, for the most unacceptable reason.

"What do you mean they don't like my face?" Will was on the phone with the secretary of some big-time photographer who only went by a single name, Kristeh, and refused gender labels. "I'm not trying to be one of the models, I just do makeup."

Simon watched his lover's hope deflate and decided he was done being angry; he was ready to take action.

Simon got up, squeezed Will's shoulder in solidarity, and went to the phone table to hit the speaker button so they could both hear the carnage coming through the call. He picked up a pencil and one of the scrap papers they used to take down messages. While he listened to the bullshit reasonings for crushing his beloved's dreams, Simon jotted a few notes.

"Kristeh needs the vibes of their whole team to be in sync," the secretary explained. "And since Kristeh works in aesthetics, they need to see and surround themselves with the proper environment and energy."

"When you say 'energy,' you mean discrimination, you realize?" Will asked. "The same as if you were rejecting me for having a hair lip or being in a wheelchair."

"I'm sorry you feel the need to make yourself into a victim," the secretary said. "That kind of attitude doesn't work for Kristeh either, so this simply isn't the job for you."

"I could sue," Will said, though they all knew he wouldn't.

"You do you! The position has been filled with a more appropriate fit." An icy click, and then dead air. Simon hung up the call from the phone's base. Will let the portable slide down his body and onto the floor.

Simon finished his writing and handed Will the paper. On it were three names and a plan of action:

Sharla

Barney

Kristeh

— Let's take revenge …?

Will tilted his head to one side as he read it, then the other side as he considered it, and when he looked next to Simon, he nodded. They were always on the same page, matchy-matchy.

THE BOYS DECIDED TO USE their significant theatrical skills to wage a campaign of terror. If only they had been allowed to apply their pageantry to gainful employment, but since they'd been sabotaged or cast aside for a decade, it was time to become disruptors instead. They booked as many weekend catering gigs as possible to cover rent and supplies, and their dawn-to-dusk efforts were dedicated to study and strategy for the rest of the month.

They began with their patron saint, the Phantom, a man of many faces and many masks throughout the century since he was first invented in a book in 1909. In the first American edition of the book, he was in a skull-like, *Masque of the Red Death* sort of style. By the 1920s, his costume was more court jester, and his mask was like a bandit, just covering his eyes and forehead. When the movies found him in 1924, Lon Chaney had a mask with empathetic eyebrows that went from cheek to hairline and with a veil for the mouth. The grotesque face beneath was more along the lines of a sleepless burn victim — dark eye circles, no eyebrows, uniform scar-like skin. Its revelation was one of the most enduring images in the history of cinema, but mostly because cinema had only been around for about 30 years. Still, shock value, unlike stock value, stayed strong.

The masks got uglier as the decades wore on, as more directors and costume artists tried to make their mark on the brand's legacy. It wasn't until the 1980s musical that the white half-mask arrived and became iconic. Beneath every mask were deformities that ranged from a nasty sunburn to chemical peels to acid attack survivor to burn victim. The most gnarly mask was Robert Englund's 1989 *Phantom*, in which the mask itself was stitched together skin like Leatherface. The face beneath was also the most upsetting, mostly because it made the nose look like bloody hamburger meat.

"Remember the stage performance we saw, they made the face look like bone was showing through," Will reminded them as they took their notes and brainstormed.

"And his hair looked peeled back like he'd been partially scalped," Simon said, wincing a bit before noting that scalping was quite disturbing and could be useful to them. Not to do, of course; they were actors, not doers. But they wanted their enemies to believe the threat they posed was real.

They interviewed other uncanny monsters in their quest to make the most frightening mask. Their eyes were drawn first to overly large mouths, especially ones with shreddy little teeth. Next, they felt chills when a creature's eyes were either too open (lids cut off) or not there (gouged out). They started trash hunting for items to make their horror with: lamp shades for a light, stable frame; old rainboots for their thick, rubbery material; any wig or wig-like approximation such as fringe, tassels, and doll hair.

They were ready to rock and roll in less than three weeks with their new nightmare friend. They named him Whir for the whirling sound of the sewing machine used in his creation. That soft, whispering sound not unlike a bird's coo or a cat's chirrup was so unnerving compared to the overwhelming grinning stare of the mask that they decided it had to be the noise he would make. Simon recorded an audio file of the sewing machine's occasionally squeaky purr and looped it so it could be played for hours.

THEY AGREED THEIR FIRST VICTIM should be their oldest foe, Ms. Sharla, with her condescending rejection. Because she knew Simon's face, he would be the one inside the mask, and Will would be there for distraction if needed. The plan was to attend a show, hide while the crowds cleared out, and pop up in her office or any other opportune spot if she was isolated enough to catch unawares. Simon was prepared to stay the night in the theater to get her the next morning if she left early. It would be just like a manager such as her to let the crew handle the closing work on their own, but somehow, she still believed she was essential to running the place.

Luck was on their side. No one came looking for them when Simon and Will hid after the show. When Will saw an opportunity to lock the security guard in the bathroom, he took it and whistled an all-clear. When Sharla came to investigate the banging of the security guard trying to get out of his captivity, Simon positioned himself at the other end of a long hallway in which there was no escape. Once Sharla was halfway down, he lowered his mask, donned a robe to hide his street clothes, and turned on the creepy whirring noise as loud as his little MP3 player could go.

"What is this racket?" Sharla was wondering. "Nestor, is that you? How'd you get stuck in the bathroom? What idiot locked the door?"

Between Nestor's muffled answers, the sound of the whir entered into Sharla's perception. When she turned to see where that noise was coming from, she saw Simon in full terrifying glory.

"What...?" was all Sharla could manage before she started backing away.

Simon sprinted right towards her. As he ran, a savage glee filled him, a runner's high of invincibility, power, and devious delight. He said nothing, he thought nothing. He simply moved like an animal of prey, faster than his pathetic target, who quickly tripped and smashed her face against the flat, dirty carpet of the theater's hallway.

Simon flew past her and, once around the corner, covered his mask with the robe and exited the building. He took a deep breath so as not to be panting as he made his way two blocks west, to a park bench that was their pre-agreed rendezvous point. Will met him there 20 minutes later with wonderful news.

"She's got a big carpet burn all down her face," he said, having observed from afar as Sharla got herself together, freed the security guard, and then had a little cry about why people were so mean and sick.

"One side of her face?" Simon asked, a maniacal laugh bubbling up in his throat like a clear spring of refreshing water. "The Phantom blesses us and all that we do."

"Makeup won't be able to cover it for weeks," Will assured him. "It's going to scab over; it might even make her eye look a little uneven as the skin tightens. So sad for her."

"Karma calls for blood, just a little," Simon said.

"Just a little skin off the top," Will agreed. "A debt due on karma's payment plan."

Simon kissed his beloved with exuberance, feeling like Bonnie and Clyde, like Leopold and Loeb. They hurried home to enjoy an exhilarating and jubilant fuck in front of the Whir mask's alarming stare.

NEXT ON THEIR DOCKET WAS Barney. Unfortunately for him, the stakes of their little game escalated quickly. The boys infiltrated his office at dawn, and hid behind the waiting room couch until he arrived. They watched Barney unlock the door to his inner sanctum, and then visit the bathroom. This was their window to sow chaos.

This time, neither wore the mask; they had it head-on-pike style on a broom handle. Simon's idea was to distract the man with the mask while they perpetrated other forms of low-level mayhem: unseen fishing line tied between furniture to trip him up, other petty disrespects like dumping out his files so they'd be a terrible mess, and snipping the cord to his computer mouse so he couldn't operate before getting a new one. Small slights to piss the man off the way he frustrated Simon with his "notes" that actually just broke everything in his otherwise functional script.

Barney did not get to experience all they had planned for him. Upon seeing their scary mask, he clutched his chest and fell back on his own fainting couch with a heart attack.

Simon and Will, not prepared to be murderers quite yet, used the desk phone to dial 911 and left it off the hook while they made their hasty escape.

"They'll trace the call, right?" Simon asked as they sauntered down Broadway in the rising dawn.

"I assume so," Will said. "Would it bother you if they didn't, and he died?"

Simon explored the depth and breadth of his mercy before answering. It didn't take long. "No, I don't think it would. A heart attack isn't our fault;

that's years of buildup, and we were just one of many potential triggers. They might say that, but for us being there causing a ruckus, the heart attack wouldn't happen, but…."

"But without him messing up your script, we wouldn't have been there at all," Will concluded.

"We also didn't fill-pack the man with a lifetime of rich food and liquor," Simon said, absolving himself of even more responsibility. "We didn't cage him in his sedentary lifestyle."

"The man treated himself like *foie gras*," Will agreed, throwing up his hands. "His demise was inevitable."

The talk of food made them hungry. They walked until they found a street vendor selling tender morsels of meat on sticks, and shared one back and forth as they made their way home. Fine young cannibals, were they not? Savages of arts and letters.

Tʜᴇʏ ꜰɪɴᴀʟʟʏ ʀᴀɴ ɪɴᴛᴏ ᴛʀᴏᴜʙʟᴇ when it came time to mark Kristeh off their list. Kristeh had more money than the others, more security, and fewer normal human habits. Kristeh did not grocery shop for themself. Kristeh did not hold reliable office hours. Kristeh was sometimes in Paris or Berlin for a shoot, sometimes on an island to recover from the existential burden of being Kristeh.

But Kristeh did have two little dogs, and the little dogs had a full-time minder. That minder had a very regular schedule, and it was inevitable that Kristeh would interact with this person again, so they waited. It took a month.

In that month, the boys learned that Sharla had gone back to church, believing the thing that attacked her had been a demon. Barney survived his attack but backed off on his workload, planning to retire. Simon picked up another side job as a dog walker so he could get closer to Kristeh's pup minder without causing suspicion. It was possible because Kristeh's dogs were grubby little chihuahua mixes, unattractive and without breed value. They were another piece of Kristeh's performance of self: the act of taking two trash mutts and treating them to a luxurious life as if they were rare, attractive, desirable. The woman who cared for them found them pathetic.

"It doesn't seem right to invest so much in these little rat dogs, but you know how rich people are with their pets," the dog minder told Simon, who played on the lady's class hatred by inviting it to dance with his own. The tactic worked like a charm, and suddenly, Simon was being paid comfortably under the table to walk the little dogs of his enemy.

"I think part of our plan with Kristeh should be that we keep the dogs," Will said after the yippie little things took an instant liking to him and curled up on his lap in their weird fetal way. "Clearly, they are love-starved, and it would add to the mind-fuck if Kristeh's dogs go missing alongside whatever else we do to them."

"Can we afford dogs? Do we have time to love them?" Simon asked. If his man wanted dogs, Simon also wanted dogs if it pleased his Will, but he had some concerns. "These dogs wheeze, they get eye problems, they eat random objects that have to be surgically removed."

"Right, but look at them," Will said, and they both cast their eyes down at the cold little creatures, sleeping in a yin-yang position with one another in the warm comfort of Will's lap.

"Alright, we'll do it, we'll make it work. What shall we name them?" Kristeh called the dogs Tissue and Hamper, which Simon found loveless and unacceptable.

"Erik and Raoul, of course," Will said. Just as their first pet had been the cat, Christine, these two would be named after her suitors.

"Of course," Simon agreed. "Matchy-matchy."

Stealing the dogs could have been enough revenge on Kristeh. They heard through the theatrical grapevine that the loss was putting Kristeh on the verge of a mental breakdown. Already barely tethered to reality, Kristeh's superstitious nature was grasping for meaning in the nonsensical dog-napping of two unsellable animals. Simon and Will were committed to using their skills to push Kristeh over the edge for closure.

The opportunity arrived neatly when Kristeh rented Sharla's theater for a performance space. Simon and Will quickly purchased tickets under fake names and attended disguised behind false glasses, fake noses, and new haircuts. The show included an interpretative dance done by two models wearing dog ears. They hopped, they yipped, they twirled around together, and then they fell. Over their collapsed bodies, Kristeh recited a poem of mourning in a language that didn't exist at a frequency that was not pleasant.

The plan was to follow Kristeh home and get just far enough inside the grounds to drive them out. The dogs had chips in their collars that would pass them through the security entrance of the building and grant elevator entry to Kristeh's floor. Getting any further would require feats of burglary they were not prepared to exhibit. They were planning to mount their scary mask somewhere for Kristeh to find with the doggie collars hanging from its mouth.

But easier opportunities to terrorize Kristeh presented themselves at the theater, which no longer had a lock on the bathroom door, thanks to their previous shenanigans. When Kristeh climbed out onto the fire escape to have a pensive smoke after the show, Simon was in the wings donning the Whir mask, while Will rigged a fly system so the dog collars could be flown at Kristeh from afar.

When Kristeh climbed back into the building, cigarette still dangling from their lip, a masked Simon approached in a jerking tarantella-style spider dance. Kristeh let out a hideously impressive scream and ran smack into the dangling dog collars. Kristeh grabbed at them as if they were the last shreds of sanity available but couldn't disconnect them from the fishing wire.

This caused a jam for all of them. Will was behind the scenes, trying to release the dog collars so Kristeh could flee with them. Meanwhile, Kristeh was becoming increasingly tangled in their panic and madness. Simon was out of dance moves and considered fleeing down the fire escape to meet Will at their previous rendezvous point. None of them noticed Kristeh's dropped cigarette had started a fire until it was too late to douse it.

Simon could not see the flames through the smoke that was suddenly everywhere, enveloping him, concentrating in the upper floors of an old building in a crowded city. He was unaware that his mask had caught fire before he passed out.

Simon awoke in a hospital bed. Will was by his side. Police were at the door.

Will quickly hugged him and said, "You remember nothing after the show."

When questioned, Simon told the police he remembered nothing after the show. "There was a dance and poem of sorts, and then … I'm blanking. What happened?"

There had been a fire. Most of the patrons had already left the building. Kristeh said they were attacked by haters, Sharla said the building had demons. Kristeh didn't recognize Will under his makeup, but surely the name would ring a bell as the investigation continued. Sharla remembered Simon, but he had not been barred from seeing shows at the theater just because he didn't get the job. She would have barred him now, except the theater was burnt beyond repair. The police suspected Sharla might have made up the demon story to set the fire herself for the insurance money. Simon did nothing to dissuade them from their suspicions.

When the officers were gone, Will filled in the details.

"I saw the mask in flames and thought I had lost you," Will said, holding Simon's hand. "I shoved Kristeh down to the first floor, where they got tangled up in wiring. They're fine, physically. Mentally scrambled, but physically fine."

"Sounds like you saved their life," Simon said. "Not that you can go asking for credit since we kind of caused the peril in the first place, didn't we?"

"That we did," Will said. "I ran to you to get the mask off and dragged us both to safety. The mask went up in flames, all they found was the wire frame. We almost got away scot-free."

"What did they find?" Simon asked.

"Oh, the authorities have nothing on us, we just have to stay quiet. But I'm afraid you're marked for life."

Will placed a large handheld mirror on Simon's chest. Simon raised it to see his reflection.

Half of his face was covered in salve, encased in saran wrap. His eyebrow, his ear, and a fair portion of his hair were gone, flayed off by the flames. But Simon still had both eyes, still had his fingers and toes, still had half his good looks. His burn was on the opposite side of Will's birthmark, and their faces made a perfect reflection even after Simon lowered the mirror. They were like Thalia and Melpomene, the comedy and tragedy masks of the theater.

"I'm so sorry I didn't get to you faster," Will said.

"I think you got to me just in time, darling," Simon said, setting aside the mirror and holding his arms open for a hug. "Matchy-matchy."

Will smiled and hugged him, kissing Simon's unburnt cheek. "Matchy-matchy, my love."

"I think New York might be too hot to hold us anymore," Simon said, adjusting himself so Will could cuddle with him in the hospital bed. "We should move on, maybe. Us and the dogs."

"I was thinking the same thing. How does Los Angeles sound?"

"The City of Angels," Simon said, nodding. "Hollywood, here we come."

TROMPE L'OIEL

Tim Newton Anderson

T HE PALAIS GARNIER WAS MY world from a young age. I had been
taken there at four when my mother died, and my father Joseph,
who was a carpenter there, had no one to look after me. We would
walk down the steep streets from our flat in Montmartre, stopping only
for a baguette from one of the Butte's many bakeries, weaving through
Haussmann's roadworks, toward the universe of the opera house. There,
I would be left in the dressing room of the ballet corps while my father
worked. However, as I grew older, I left that haven and wandered the
endless corridors to explore the wonders around every corner.

There I encountered Erik. They said he was Christine's Angel—but
he was truly mine.

After I had finished my studies at the Ecole des Beaux-Arts, I started
working as a scene painter at my childhood wonderland, only to find it had
become a nightmare of drudgery. Corners filled with beauty were now full
of dust and the broken dreams of a thousand singers and dancers who had

sought fame and found only disappointment. The vistas of beauty glimpsed from plush seats are hasty daubs on vast canvases—distinguished by size, not style. Most of the friendly faces from my youth were no longer present, and even my secret friend was no longer to be heard or glimpsed in his box. I write this account, to be tucked into one of the cobwebbed corners of this palace of broken dreams, for any who, like myself, wander its silent halls in search of hidden glories.

THE MANAGEMENT OF THE PALAIS Garnier has foolishly decided to stage an opera based on the tragic events of 1881. Although it is a mere 15 years since they occurred, they have already entered the domain of distant myth, but I remember them clearly. What I recall with greatest sorrow is the moment my secret friend—my Angel—became not only invisible to the world but forever lost to me. Left alone as I was by my father and ignored by everyone else as too young and insignificant to register in their search for fame or fortune, the so-called Phantom was my only friend. I never saw his face--that visage which those who glimpsed him said struck terror in their hearts, but his wonderful voice would guide me as I wandered like one of Baudelaire's flaneurs through the endless corridors and levels of this fantastic building.

While the management believes their creation will render the Phantom larger than life, I know it will merely make him louder, just as the world outside is noisier but not as rich as the universe inside these walls, so any petty melodrama can only touch tangentially on the magic essence of my friend. Just as the scenery I have been asked to paint is a thin canvas representation of the riches of the Palais Garnier, so will the performance be a two-dimensional mirror of the infinite expanse of his soul.

I said as much when Director Eugène Bertrand visited the stage as I was working with my assistant Robert on the backdrop for the scene in the dressing rooms of my magical kingdom.

"It is a story, Theophile," he said. His bushy moustache danced above his full lips like a caterpillar doing the can-can. "Your job is to render the backcloth with as much accuracy as you can muster and leave the artistic decisions to me."

I thought his grip on art was as weak as his chin. He behaved and looked like the second-rate comedian he used to be before fate, and connections helped him rise to his current position. The rumours which constantly swirled around backstage had it that he knew things about people in power, and in return for silence, they had helped him ascend the ladder.

"Speaking of art," he said. "I am afraid you have been letting your bohemian friends influence your work again. The section you are working on... too many flourishes. Look at how simply and effectively young Robert renders the scene. All that is required is that the audience have the illusion of reality while you seem determined to create a masterpiece. Too slow. Too much detail. No one will ever look at your work with any critical eye, so why bother?"

I bit my lip in frustration.

"Do you ask the same question of the composers who write the operas?" I asked. "Or suggest to the orchestra or performers they miss some notes because the audience will not notice?"

"It is the music and performance they come here for," he said, "not the backdrop. How many would realise that much of the scenery has been repurposed from previous productions? The answer is none. Take a leaf from your assistant's work, and you will continue to do well. If not...."

I knew that he would follow through on the implied threat. Unlike some of his predecessors who had pandered to the whims of the lead performers, he ruthlessly disposed of anyone brave enough to suggest that art was not secondary to profit. A star name may encourage a few more sales at the box office, but what attracted most people to the Opera was a few hours escapes from their humdrum lives, and the illusion that watching art made them, in some way, participants in that display of talent. They were the phantoms: two thousand featureless faces with scarcely a whole soul between them. My angel had a greater soul than all of them combined could aspire to.

I first heard his beautiful voice after only a few visits to the opera house with my father. I had been left, as usual, with the corps de ballet to watch over me, but they were so absorbed with their appearances and giggly gossip that after half an hour, I became bored and slipped away to explore. It is a mystery more profound to me than the story of the Phantom, and only Erik, as he soon revealed his name, and I could find the endless spaces behind the curtain more fascinating than the spectacles that took place on the stage. The wrapped and stored detritus of a thousand shows were locked carelessly in a dozen rooms—costumes, props, sections of stage sets, and most wondrously of all, the vast folded canvasses of backdrops that, when unrolled, revealed whole worlds of space and time which, I longed to explore. Oh, how I wanted to walk into those far-off places. Ancient Egypt, the mountains of Scotland, the legendary landscapes of ancient Greece and Germany. Viewing those vast panoramas, narrated by Erik's soft, soothing voice emanating from the walls of the storage space, made me determined to become a painter in my own right and create my own worlds of wonder, and Erik encouraged that dream.

The most magical space of all was the vast lake that lay at the very foundations of the building. When I asked my father about it, he gave the mundane explanation that it was just a large tank created to assist in the building's stability, but for me, it was an enchanted grotto that was home to the Phantom's lair. He would sometimes play sepulchral music on his violin that filled the space with strange echoes and eerie overtones formed by reflection on the waters of this mysterious cavern as traffic rumbled overhead, stirring eddies and ripples across its black surface. Someone, perhaps even Erik himself, had placed lanterns above the dark expanse of water, and they made the oscillations into jewelled ribbons of light. How could painted myths and papier-mâché shores onstage compare to such majesty—unless I painted them myself?

I managed to persuade my father to obtain some of the paints and canvasses that were left over from the scene decorators' work, and I set up my first studio in an unused store room that Erik guided me to. Here, hesitantly at first and then with growing confidence and ability, I transferred the pictures in my mind onto the misshapen scraps I had been granted. The early attempts were discarded with the other rubbish from my daytime home, but I soon created worlds where I could take some childish pride.

Painting became my escape from the world in which I was imprisoned. The lack of affection from my father was not the worst aspect of that existence. His drinking, which had been slight when my mother was alive, became excessive after her death, and every small transgression earned me a slap. As his consumption increased, the attacks became more violent until even the self-absorbed artists at the Opera noticed the bruises on my face and arms. When he was demoted from carpenter to ordinary stagehand because of his drunken behaviour, his assaults on my person became more and more violent until I was released from his torments by my avenging Angel. One morning, my father was found hanged backstage, which was at first assumed to be suicide, until it was discovered that the noose that had choked the life from his body had vanished. The management might have pitied my orphaned state and found me a good family—but instead, I was sent to an orphanage, cut off from the only comfort I had known. In the orphanage, I learned quickly to defend myself from the fists of the other boys and, at times, became so violent I was referred to Monsieur Charcot at the Hospital Pitié-Salpêtrière. He had the audacity to suggest Erik's voice had stirred my outbursts. However, his colleagues suggested it was merely the violence I had experienced and the traumatic scenes at the Palais Garnier that were responsible.

There was one who, like Dickens' hero, had great expectations for me. There was a fund to pay for my apprenticeship on the understanding that if I mastered my craft, I might return to the Paris Opera as an employee.

Although much of my training at the atelier consisted of emulating the creations of the past, my fellow students introduced me to the bold experiments of the avant-garde artists who had made Paris their home.

There was more life and glory in a back street cabaret in Montmartre than in the expensively created productions staged by my employers.

When I returned, however, my angel had flown, sending me into a spiral of depression. I was told the story of the events of 1881 in fragments and fevered fantasies, but I knew the truth. Such a giant spirit could not be contained in the bourgeois boulevards of broken dreams the corridors of the Palais Garnier had now become. Hundreds of souls surrounded me—yet I was utterly alone.

I PERSUADED ROBERT TO COME to the Chat Noir for a drink that evening. I told him he would encounter the creators of the very cream of the new art being produced in Paris, and I would introduce him to them. Although I knew them all, I could hardly count them as friends. Some had studied with me at the atelier, and their skill had often been compared poorly to my own. However, their crowd believed that starving in an unheated studio and begging for a few sous to buy a drink made them my superiors. I, they believed, sullied myself with commercial work—while they wore their poverty like a halo.

"Théophile, come and sit with us," said one of my former classmates. I could see the bottle of red wine he and his friends had been sharing had only a few drops in it.

"Is that Gaston Bussière?" asked Robert. "I heard he's been commissioned to illustrate a work by Balzac."

Bussière was sitting with the self-styled mage Joséphin Péladan, whom he was doubtless trying to persuade to include his paintings in an exhibition.

"Who is your colleague?" Bussière asked as we joined them.

"This is my assistant, Robert," I said. I ordered a bottle of vin rouge and two more glasses, but Bussière insisted he and Péladan were moving on to absinthe. I added three glasses of the green fairy to the order, deeming Robert too young for the bitter potion.

"You're also engaged in splashing paint on those vast monstrosities, then?" said Bussière.

"It is an honest profession," said Robert. I felt a twinge of pride, even though my heart agreed with the other painter.

"Joséphin here has written operas—perhaps you could paint for him as well," Bussière said. "But you'd need to learn his occult symbolism. He doesn't simply ape reality; he seeks to inspire the marvellous. Théophile, meanwhile, offers only the sterility of the mundane. You once had promise. Why abandon it for glorified house painting?"

What did either of them know of the marvellous? For all of Péladan's posing, I doubted he had ever experienced anything more transcendental than an exceptional croissant. I had walked in miracle—led by Erik. Every object we saw as he led me through the Palais Garnier had glowed with meaning and beauty. And now he was gone, they were simply the discarded detritus of the everyday world. Every fibre of my being longed to return to a time when a pipe was not a pipe, but a portal to the infinite.

As the evening progressed, more of Bussière's friends joined us, and somehow, Péladan and I seemed to dig into our pockets to place more drinks on the table while their purses remained safely in their jackets. I raged inside, my face locked in a mask of false camaraderie. I was too artistic for the Opera but not artistic enough for these poseurs.

The cabaret had only just begun when I stood and took my leave, suggesting Robert do the same.

"The night is yet young," said Bussière. "You may have an old soul, but this boy ought to stay—with us whose spirits remain youthful."

I did not care enough to persuade Robert that he would need a clear head in the morning. He would learn, or he wouldn't. I wrapped a scarf around my neck as a barrier to the December chills and left, stumbling back to my attic studio.

At times, when I have drunk too much—or when the red mist of anger descends—I enter a strange state. I find myself far from the scene of my last memory, with no recollection of the events between. The doctors at the hospital could not ascertain the cause of these blank periods but merely prescribed some medicine to help retain a calm composure. I had long since finished what had been prescribed and refused to get more—fearing it might dim the visions I needed to paint.

As I entered my home, the moonlight illuminated the canvases stacked by the wall. I had sold a few of my early works to galleries but was dissatisfied with my later paintings. Something always seemed missing from them, something I could see at the periphery of my vision but never bring into focus. Perhaps I was doomed to spend my life executing huge yet hollow canvases for the Opera.

Whether the absinthe or thoughts of my childhood inspired my dreams, they were full of the face of the Phantom. I walked the endless corridors of the Palais Garnier, finding strange turnings and hidden rooms. And always before me was my friend, half a dozen steps in front, as if I were Alice following the white rabbit. Like Alice, I seemed to grow and shrink because of a strange logic I had failed to grasp.

And then, as dawn's light through my window drew me up towards consciousness, he turned. And I saw his face.

It was not the ruined mask the survivors of 1881 described—but the radiant face of an angel. The angel who would deliver me from the tedium of my days and lead me to the paradise I had glimpsed as a child. And in that instant, I knew what had been missing from my paintings. Erik.

And then I awoke—and felt a rock of regret sink into my heart.

THE DAY AFTER I WROTE the preceding words, something amazing happened. I heard my friend again.

I was still working on the backdrop for the scene in the dressing rooms of the opera. Although the director had made it clear he wanted a simple representation of the real room, I could not help but add some touches of my own. Instead of the usual classical trompe l'oeil painting showing the depth of the room behind the performers, I experimented with the new style of Monet and his fellow artists, using dabs of colour to create the impression of depth and vibrancy. It would bring the scene to life far more vividly for the audience. I also added some touches that reminded me of my friend—a shadow on the back wall, a mask on a painted table, a dress tie on a hook. I had heard the rehearsals of the overblown music created for the opera, and to my ears, it did not represent the Phantom I knew and loved. That arch theme, in particular, is far too melodramatic for Erik, whose music is haunting and melancholy. Bertrand had hinted that following my artistic inclinations could result in losing my job. Let him fire me, then. I would follow Erik wherever he led.

It was that music I heard played on a solitary violin, low and spectral as if the building was fingering the notes and the air was the bow. I left my brush resting on a tin of paint, the red juice dripping to the floor, leaving Robert behind without a word, and followed the sound in search of its source. As I pushed past the ballerinas and singers bustling towards the stage, seemingly oblivious to the siren melody, the sound seemed to retreat farther and farther in front of me as if it was guiding me to its lair. I wondered whether last night's dream and adding the touches to the backdrop that reminded me of my friend had somehow conjured him back into existence, and he was, in turn, leading me towards some enchanted arbour amid the slain forest of floorboards and doors.

The pursuit first led me to the roof of the Palais Garnier, where I had a clear view of the city's rooftops stretching away on all sides and up to the Butte of Montmartre, where the endless construction of Sacre Coeur was still underway, as workers toiled in the roads around me building boulevards. The city was being renewed, but I cared only for the renewal of art that was taking place inside its studios and ateliers. I had barely time to scan the rooftops for my friend before that ethereal music summoned me back— down, down, down through the building to the lower levels and the capstan room where former sailors toiled to draw the giant sets and backdrops onto the stage. The matelots nodded to me as I entered, seemingly oblivious to the strains of Erik's violin, which, in truth, could scarcely be heard above the creak of ropes and grunts of their operators. Its notes formed a counterpoint to their work, and I half expected them to weave it into a work song.

Despite the aural interference, I followed the music across the room, weaving past the slowly turning mechanisms to a seemingly blank wall to one side of the space. It emanated from within the wall, and I spotted a recessed catch that opened into a tiny closet upon turning. Stepping inside and closing the door, I was enveloped in darkness and had to feel around at the entrance to find another catch that I hoped would allow me to exit. The music seemed to swirl around me, and my dark, adapted eyes could almost see its patterns dancing in the air like coloured ribbons. Despite the strangeness of the situation, I felt a sense of great peace enter my soul. I was once again in the presence of my friend, even if, as ever, he was invisible to me. He may have inspired terror in others, but he represented a time of joy and discovery to me. I felt no fear. The anger and frustration that had plagued my soul at the pedestrian work I was forced to perform evaporated, and the melancholy music melted my bitterness, replacing it with solemn joy—like an epiphany in the pews of Notre-Dame.

Then the music stopped, and I experienced a moment of panic as I stood alone in the small dark room before I heard his voice.

"Théophile," it said, in those low tones I had longed for years to hear again. "You must join me."

I SPENT THE REST OF the day obsessively searching for Erik. I instructed my apprentice to finish the dressing room backdrop and left him to complete it. Only a few patches of the vast canvas remained, and I trusted he could finish without my supervision. Although he lacked my artistic imagination, his work was more than adequate for the demands of the management, even with a hangover from last night's overindulgence. I informed Bertrand that I needed to survey the scenes to fix them in my memory and spent the next hours wandering the building as I had in childhood, seeking hidden rooms, listening for footsteps.

It was to no avail. There were a few scattered remnants of his existence left after his disappearance all those years ago, but no sign of the man himself. A white glove, a curled violin string, a cigarette stub—souvenirs of a vanished ghost. It was as if he now truly was a phantom who had evaporated into the stifling air of the Palais Garnier.

My search led me again to the lake in the bottommost basement. Someone had lit the lamps, and their soft glow reflected off the water's surface. At one end of the water, he had constructed a modest dwelling: a bed, a chaise, a table, a cupboard stocked with absinthe, two glasses, and spare violin strings. Dust lay on every surface, and the floor was unmarked with footprints save my own. I took a bottle and gazed into the glass before unstoppering it and tasting the bitter wormwood and anise inside. The absinthe's fire ran down my throat and warmed my stomach. Then I saw something white on the table. It was another cigarette stub, and when I carefully raised it to my face to see more clearly, I could still smell the smoke—warm, recent. He had been here. Yet the floor was undisturbed. How had he come and gone without leaving a trace?

That evening I went to the theatre by myself. I would have invited Robert, but he had disappeared when I returned after my reverie. The canvas we had been working on was rolled up at the side of the stage, and a fresh one had been hoisted in its place. The play was by a new writer. Alfred Jarry. My so-called colleagues in the art world had been raving about it at Le Chat Noir. A vile puppet-like creature strode the stage, killing and stealing and eating in a hideous parody of the bourgeois creatures who made up the audience around me. I admired the sparse set and simple music, which could teach my masters at the Opera something about restraint, but I was disturbed by the central character, Ubu, even as I applauded its creator. Here was a real monster, created by his appetites, unlike Erik, who was made monstrous by his history and the aspersions of lesser men.

The Ubus of the world—and the baying Yahoos who worship them—need monsters to feel safe in their mediocrity. They belonged in the wings, while true talent—Erik and I—strode center stage. By exiting when he did, my angel became immortal. Poor as the opera was, it had sealed him into legend. My only regret was that I had been left behind among the shadow creatures. They would never understand him—only fear him. Just as they would never understand me. Perhaps only after my death would they find the paintings in my flat—and realise what they had lost.

I SPENT PART OF THE following morning retracing my search, hoping to find my friend, but to no avail. There was also no sign of Robert, and everyone assumed he had taken up Péladan's offer. Then, as I returned to the stage, a shudder shook my body as I saw a shape on the floor. The shadow of an outstretched arm and instrument lay across the boards at my feet, as if the figure casting them remained, invisible. There was no sign of the spectral shadow on the new canvas as it was raised towards the ceiling, but I swear I heard his violin melody again beneath the noise of the mechanism. Then it too vanished.

I started to shake, not because I had been reminded of Erik, but because I remembered the other person he had killed for me.

It had been a year ago to this day. Although the Director and I disagree about art, our arguments are tempered by a false professionalism. He is a fool and a Yahoo, but at least he is successful. Not so was the former Assistant Director Gerard Borel, who had a personal dislike for me that bordered on the pathological. He would go out of his way to insult everything and insist that several canvases be re-painted. The crisis came when he grabbed a pot of red paint and threw it across a scene I was particularly proud of. My blood pulsed at my temples, and I could feel my face become as red as the liquid that stained the canvas. I must then have had one of my episodes. The next thing I remember: Les Deux Magots, Left Bank, a black coffee, a carafe of red wine. Although I had become reconciled to the loss of my angel, I could almost hear his voice inside my head, giving me counsel.

It was night by the time I had returned to the Palais Garnier, and the cold air had cleared my head. I climbed up to the stage to see if I could repair the canvas without having to start again, feeling surprised and annoyed when I saw it had been taken down and rolled up.

I got down on my hands and knees and started to unroll the large backdrop we had finished to check it. It was hard work as it was cumbersome, but once I started moving the material, it continued under its own power. As it made the last turn, I saw a shape at its core. A body. Borel's. Numb with shock, I moved closer, the corpse lit by the flicker of a gas mantle. The bruises on his neck, which indicated strangulation, were not the most shocking aspect. Half his face had been stripped of its skin, exposing the red muscle and bone beneath. His appearance had been transformed into an obscene parody of Erik's tragic features.

I knew that I would be blamed if the body was found, as everyone in the company must have heard our explosive arguments. I found a knife in my pocket (when did I acquire that, I wondered?) and sliced off a section of the backdrop to rewrap the corpse. Painting scenery gives one good upper body strength, so I could lift Borel's body on my shoulders and slip out of the subterranean door by the basement lake. It led to the catacombs that crisscross under Paris, and I found a small alcove where I hoped it would be undiscovered. As I made my way back to the surface, I could still hear Erik's voice in my mind, comforting and calming me.

I CANNOT EXPLAIN THE EMPTINESS I felt unless you have experienced and lost something or someone marvellous. The empty space left by my angel seemed more solid and real than all the mundane shapes surrounding me. I meditated on the paradox that that which is deliberately left out of a painting--or the spaces between the notes in a score—can be more numinous than the things that are present. Erik's absence was more powerful than any presence, as the masterpieces I had yet to create vastly overshadowed the paintings I had been able to realise.

The new backdrop represented the lake beneath the Palais Garnier—not the mundane water tank, but a magnificent grotto with a shore decorated with a hundred candles surrounding a magnificent pipe organ, rather than the reed organ my Angel played so sweetly. However, the Phantom's theme was to be played on such an organ for melodramatic effect, so it had to be represented in our creation.

If I were to realise this fantasy, then I determined that I would do it in such a way that it would truly honour my friend. There is a technique Monet and his group have perfected of using small daubs of contrasting colour to make the main ones more vibrant. I would use this to make the grotto truly enchanting. I told the lighting crew to suggest a way of having candles behind the set, flicking illumination through small holes I pierced in the canvas in their painted counterparts to create a magical effect. I also mixed crushed glass into the paint so the front lighting would make the painted velvet drapes and gilding shine and shimmer. My backdrop should even take away the audience's attention from the humdrum drama in front of them. Their applause would be for me, not the mediocrities who trod the boards and sang the composer's dirges. This would be a far more fitting tribute to my friend.

The scene was painted so that a boat could travel towards it across the stage, carrying the Phantom and Christine. Christine, another person befriended and encouraged to greatness by Erik who also disappeared after the events of 1881. In this tawdry tribute she is supposed to be rescued by her lover, as if anyone could abandon my angel. If his whispered invitation was to be believed—if I had not simply imagined it—I could share in the life Christine could not.

I employed every trick I had learned in creating what I was sure would be my masterpiece. Every brush stroke was painted with love, and each added to the others to bring the scene to a life more real than the one I was living.

Yet strange things kept happening on the canvas in my peripheral vision. I would catch a glimpse again of that hand holding an instrument, peeping out from behind a curtain, or casting a reflection on the water. A reflection with no original, like a face in a mirror, that no one is watching. And I heard that music again, not from the space around me, but from within the canvas itself. It summoned me. I had to fight the pull, keep my brush steady, daub after daub rather than run off to seek its source. Once, I even saw a glimpse of Erik himself out of the corner of my eye, moving behind the pipe organ as if continuing that childhood game of hide and go-seek. My heart leaped as I saw him, as it had when I caught glimpses of him in the dressing room scene until Robert had clumsily spilled paint and spoiled it. A future glimpsed, never grasped—forever on the edge of sight and sound, forever receding. The ache in my heart grew with each glimpse until I could no longer bear it. I hurled my brush to the floor and fled the Palais Garnier.

I strode madly around the streets, bumping into passersby and scarcely seeing what was around me. This world was flat, insubstantial. People: cardboard cutouts. Buildings: lifeless backdrops, less vivid than my painted dreams. Sky: dull and lifeless. Pavement: papier mâché. The sounds: a thin echo of the orchestra. The Opera had always been the truer world. Today, Paris was a pale sketch—tawdrier, thinner than any backstage fantasy. And those fleeting glimpses of Erik only deepened the void.

The Palais Garnier was dark and empty when I returned that evening. The previous production had reached the end of its run, and everything was being readied for the new show's start in a few days' time. Only the doorman was still at his post in case any of the staff had left something behind they needed to retrieve. I had left my heart there. He hardly glanced up from his cubbyhole as I grunted a greeting and entered.

There were still a few of the gas mantles lit inside, although I had not noticed them from the street. They were enough to light my way backstage and walk to the front of the apron to view my masterpiece, which was drying on its wooden crossbeam like washing on a line. There were no candles behind it—yet someone had left a light. It shone through the tiny holes, just as I had dreamed. It only vaguely resembled the real lake, but that was to the good. It was so much bigger and better than reality. The crushed glass in the waves caught the light perfectly, glinting just as I had envisioned. It was perfection. My best work is a fitting tribute to the man who inspired me in my childhood, who filled my mind with vivid dreams, which I now realise on canvas. I now dared to recheck the dressing room scene and see if it could be rescued from Robert's clumsiness. I started to unroll it, and at its heart, I found the body of my assistant. Like Borel, he bore the marks of strangulation, and like him, half his face had been sliced away. The gory fragment lay beside his head like a mask.

As I stood in horror, the argument came rushing back. I found myself searching for my angel. I remember shouting, screaming even, at him to stop. But he ignored me, each brushstroke defacing my creation. Then he spilled the paint, and I remembered no more.

It was then that I saw my angel, no longer at the edge of my vision but right in the centre of the canvas. He sat at the pipe organ, but with his back to the instrument, facing me. The white, bone-like mask gleamed—brighter than any stage light could allow. His mouth curled into a smile. One arm lifted—beckoning.

"Come to me, Theophile," he said in that voice I had heard whisper through walls as I explored my childhood kingdom. "Come to me."

Surely, this was madness. The stress and disappointment of my work and the death of Robert had surely disordered my brain. Yet nothing had ever seemed so real. I had to honour his wishes. I picked up the ruined fragment of Robert's face and, with his blood, glued it to my own in homage to my hero.

I paused only to write this chronicle. I will hide it somewhere in the opera house—a place of gifts and grief alike. Once it is hidden, I know what I must do. I will climb into the boat and punt it forward with the pole. It will take me out of this world and into my painting. I have created a place more real than my mundane surroundings, where my friend and I can live forever. No one will miss me. No one ever understood me. Only Erik. We will haunt this place, phantoms together, for all eternity.

THE MUSIC WE BECAME

Addison Smith

WE THOUGHT THE MUSIC CAME from the cavern—that strange space that opened into our lives and devoured our futures. It didn't. I suppose you know that by now since you're a part of it. What's that meme? "The real music was the friends we made along the way?" Yeah, that tracks. Let me explain.

THE HOLE WAS WET AT the edges. I thought it was just water, but it dripped from the dirt in strange and viscous clumps, like a white sac of frogspawn congcalcd around the dirt.

"I don't want to be here," I said. My hand grasped my headphone wire, tugging at the headset around my neck and reminding me that it was there if I needed it—if I couldn't cope with the world.

You heard me but didn't answer. You stood at the edge of the sinkhole behind the downtown theater, slip-grasp close to falling in. You knelt and touched the strange wetness, lifting it to your nose to smell its biological essence. I tugged at my headphone wire. "What is it?"

"I don't know," you said, wiping the offending goo on your flannel. It wasn't natural, I knew. There was nothing natural about a sinkhole opening in our favorite spot—the backlot behind the theater where the abandoned dumpster stood with our names knife-scratched into the rust, giving evidence of our existence. This was our place. This was where we sat, backs against the wall, to listen to the performances inside the theater. This was where we hid from angry parents and ate shoplifted beef jerky as the sun beat down on us during the high summer. It was where you held me and told me the world was safe. It was our place.

And there was a hole in it.

The sinkhole appeared overnight, and you called me breathless with excitement. You said it was a sign, and I had no idea what you meant, but you were excited, so I came with you. I've always loved how excited you get and how passionate you are about life.

"We've had a lot of rain," you said. "Maybe the dirt washed out beneath it. Whatever happened, it's ours now."

I thumbed the in-line buttons, ready to drown out the world. I wanted to hide away in a place of basslines and synthesizers and vocal accompaniment. I didn't. Dust and wet clumps of dirt fell into the chasm, and we listened to its sound hitting the water below. The dirt landed with note-perfect splashes, rippling the water and introducing new biology into an environment that had surely been sequestered for thousands of years. As the players performed *The Phantom of the Opera* within the theater, we heard their performance in the cavern below, echoing and self-harmonizing on dark cave walls and mildew condensation. I heard the music of the night as tiny rivers wandered through to create little streams within the vast and empty lake. The pool below was a beauty I had never heard, each note carrying emotion and a life worth of meaning to my ears.

Intrusive thoughts waged within me as I imagined stepping forward, falling into the hole, and becoming a part of the music, my body integral to the acoustics of the cavern.

"It's beautiful," you said, and I agreed. We stood at the side of the hole, hands clasped, sweating between us as the water flowed far below. I felt safe with my hand in yours, like every other time since you found me friendless and alone in the school cafeteria. Ever since that first confident smile and invitation. Since you entered my life and became the music that anchored my mind. We stayed most of the night, and when the time came to leave, my feet didn't want to move.

"Come on," you said. "We'll come back tomorrow."

I smiled, and you took my hand.

THE HOLE WAS BARRICADED THE next time we saw it. Orange safety cones surrounded it, with bright caution tape draped between them. Workers stood around the hole in reflective orange vests, discussing safety concerns in adult tones. They didn't see us waiting for them to leave, hidden behind the adjoining fence. They didn't see us sneak in as they left the hole at the end of their shift. A wooden pallet laid over the hole, a poor protection from our curiosity. Still, my anxiety spiked at the thought of getting caught. You passed the ladder over the fence, and I pulled it over, rungs catching on twisted wire. When you climbed over it yourself, we stood and regarded the safety cones.

"You think they went in?" you asked, and I shrugged, fiddling with my headphone wire. The thought made my gut wrench. The theater was a staple of the town, so people had been there. As much as I wanted the world to be ours, we were not alone. I wanted it to be our secret, locked away in a place that was only for us. You didn't hesitate at the barrier, slipping beneath the caution tape and pushing the pallet aside with your foot. I looked around, expecting someone to come in through the gate or step out of the theater's back door and ask what we were doing. Nobody came.

The ladder was heavy, and we'd had to trade it back and forth as we carried it from your parent's garage and through the two blocks that separated us from the theater. Nobody stopped us. We were just a couple of kids, and nobody paid us any mind. We joked and laughed the whole way, and you asked me what I wanted out of life. I told you I just wanted to be happy, whatever that looked like, and again, I saw a future with you. You made me happy.

The ladder dropped heavily into the hole, coming to rest with only a single rung above ground. You stepped over the rung and down, gesturing for me to follow. You grinned like an idiot, and I loved you for the adventure. When you made it to the bottom, you called to me, muffled by my silent headphones. I pressed play to give myself courage and stepped over the rung.

My hand slipped frog-back slick on the metal ladder, and I concentrated on the music in my head. The song was a remix of a remix, originating with "The Point of No Return." The vocals were sped up, the instruments replaced with electronic gabber that cut and hashed in frenetic breakbeat chaos. The pool lay below, illuminated by the swinging flashlight on my belt, but I couldn't focus on that—only on the music, and the next step.

You stood in the pool below, already waiting in water-soaked shoes, but all I knew was the music. It guided me down, calming my mind as I squeezed my eyes tight and rested my hands on each rung in turn. My feet settled into ice-cold water that washed over the tops of my shoes and soaked my socks. I gritted my teeth and let go of the ladder.

The water was shallow, and the cavern was beautiful, illuminated only by our flashlights and the hole in the sky above. It wasn't far to the surface; a dozen feet of dank air separated us from the backlot. I turned my flashlight to look at you, and your lips were moving. I pulled my headphones from my ears and let them hang around my neck. I let them play at my sides for a moment, savoring the musical clarity. Finally, I pressed the in-line pause button.

"It's beautiful," you said, and I tried to see what you saw. The cavern was large and water-worn, with rounded lumps of rock all around us and bulbous stalagmites rising and falling where water dripped over centuries. You stared all around with wonder in your eyes, and I saw the beauty myself. You paused, staring around with a slack-jawed smile. When you took my hand, it was wet and clammy, saved by your warmth. "Say your name," you said.

I stared, but didn't question. I turned and addressed the cavern, my point of no return. "Kate," I said, my voice subdued. It came back to me as an echo, twisted and modified by the acoustics of the cavern. It was almost too timid to hear, but it pulled at my senses with wonder. "I am Katherine," I shouted.

I was embraced by a wall of sound, comforting and beautiful, and entirely myself. The music of the cavern washed around me and made me a part of its song. My name was the vocal track, and the cave was the distortion, the reverb, and the filter by which I was changed and created anew. It echoed all around me, the music of the night and the music of myself. I laughed, and it was joy and wonder. For the first time, I imagined what it would be like to become a song myself, to bring clarity to those who hear me.

You laughed at my expression and stared into my eyes. You leaned toward me, and lighter than air, you kissed my lips. I didn't have time to return the kiss, or to process it, or to tell you how it felt. In a moment, it was gone, but it would never be forgotten. You brushed your hair with your hand and grinned, looking back to the cavern.

"It's amazing," you said, and the word couldn't do it justice. You were amazing. You called your name into the cavern, and I waited to hear it return, to hear the song it made of you. Only silence returned to me as if you had not spoken at all. Water dripped, and you stared around as if you could hear something I couldn't. It was your song, I knew. Your song was meant for you alone. When you turned back to me, I saw the change in your eyes and knew you felt the same truth that was within me. You wanted to be a song. And this place could make it happen.

You lost weight. I saw it in your face as we sat at the bottom of the cavern, listening to our voices and letting the music accompany our conversations. You were already thin, but over our days in the hole, you gained a gauntness about your face that worried me. I asked if you had been eating, and you assured me you were, though I had tasted the lie in the air. I had taken to hiding my dinner and feeding it down the disposal. I didn't need food as long as I had the music. I didn't want it.

We piled stones in the water so we could stay dry, but still we let our feet slip into the pool, taking comfort in its presence. My shoes fit loose upon my feet, so I took them off and dipped my bare feet beneath the surface. Even as I went without food, I couldn't deny the water. I drank it thirstily, cupping it in my hands and sipping it, cool and refreshing to my body.

"What if we stayed here?" you asked. I looked up from the pool, barely able to break my gaze. You stood in the water, stripped to your boxers, your pants lying on the rocks.

"What do you mean?" We couldn't stay, but you'd grown whimsical over the recent days. I wanted to hear what you had to say, even if it was impossible.

"We could stay," you said, turning to me. "It could be our cavern. Cover up the hole and live down here. We could have the music to ourselves. We could become the music."

The way you said "become the music" pulled at me, but it was a distortion of reality. You said it as if it was possible and not a dream-sick metaphor. As if we could discard our bodies and truly become the music of the cavern.

"There's no food," I said, knowing the argument was weak. "And no light. And what about our families?" Those concerns seemed real, but so did the idea of staying. My headphones hung still at my neck, but I hadn't needed to use them since our first exploration. I had the music I needed, and my mind no longer thrashed and revolted.

"We have the water," you said, "and we don't need food anymore. Our families would be fine. Just think about it, OK? Imagine becoming the music of the cave. Imagine living forever."

I picked up a stone, small and rounded without any edge, and ran my fingers over its surface. You were right, I knew. Somehow, I knew it was possible. And I wanted it more than I wanted anything in the world.

OUR CLOTHES NO LONGER FIT our lanky bodies, and our parents sent us to the hospital. They were certain we were on some strange and horrible drugs. "That kid's a bad influence," my mother said, but pursued it no further. The doctors said we were fine. Mine referred me to a nutritionist, and yours referred you to therapy. It didn't matter. When those appointments arrived, we would already have slipped through the cracks.

The cavern was stealing our meat, and we returned to it willingly. Every day, our bodies thinned, and our minds expanded. My ribs showed through my sallow skin. I couldn't bring myself to eat. I wanted to lose weight, to shed my body to the water and become ever smaller until I disappeared. I shouted my name into the cavern and gave myself to it completely so that I could be returned in song. Tiny creatures emerged from the depths of the cavern, no longer afraid of our intrusion. They swam to our island, frogs and fish and strange salamanders with translucent skin. We spent so much time there that we became a part of the cave as surely as they were.

The first time we saw a creature disappear entirely, we cheered for its ascension. A bullfrog stood upon our pile of rocks and croaked loudly into the dark. The frog was already thin, barely able to walk with toothpick-thin legs. As the song returned to it, the frog listened. Its body thinned and faded, and soon, there was no frog to be seen.

You treated it as a religious experience like we had seen the power of God.

"Where do you think it goes?" I asked. I imagined the frog all around us, a small part of the cave's symphony.

"I've been thinking about that," you said. "I figure it must be the water. There's no inlet in here, no outlet. The water doesn't move, it just sits here. I think the water is made of all the things that have become a part of the song."

I stared at the water and pulled my feet further upon the rocks, imagining water made of skin and meat and organs. But the water was clear, pristine even. "Is that what we want?"

You turned to stare, bewilderment upon your face as if the answer were so obvious there could be no other truth. I saw the sinking of your eyes into your skull and the dark skin around your cheekbones. Already, so much of you was in the water. Something inside me changed, and I no longer wanted the water. I wanted you, just like I always had. I wanted you to be safe.

At that moment, the music lost its appeal and the spell it had over my will. I didn't care about the music anymore.

A smell reached my nose, and I suppressed a gag. The scent of rot and decay suffocated me, and I clung to the ladder, covering my nose. "What is that?" I said through my shirt.

"What is what?" you asked, and I stared. You stood gaunt in the light of the hole above, not covering your nose or wrinkling your face. You couldn't smell it at all. Like the songs of our souls, it was a smell not meant for you.

I stared into the water, and it was foul and wretched. Instead of the clear depths, a layer of film covered the surface, like fat rising to the top, a layer of filth and decay from our bodies and the remains of those who came before—bullfrog skin, human tissue, and fat, all dissolved by song.

I gagged and retched as the smell dripped down the back of my throat and infected my lungs with its foulness.

"We have to go," I said, putting my foot on the ladder's first rung. "Please, we have to leave."

You called your name into the dark, sacrificing more of yourself to the cavern, and I turned to stare. As your song washed back upon you, you caught my eyes, a grin on your face. "You can go," you said, and the words cut deep into my flesh, incising more of my body and giving it to the cave. "This is all I need."

Tears formed in my eyes from the smell and the betrayal and the loss.

"I'll come back for you," I said, not knowing if I meant it, not knowing if I could ever return.

You turned away and stared into the cavern. I stared back as I ascended, hoping you would still be there when I returned.

I TUGGED AT MY HEADPHONE cord as my body shook and my stomach groaned. Knowing you were beneath me, I stood behind the theater, slowly dissolving into nothing. The music buoyed me, but it couldn't make me go back into that hole or see what I knew was beneath. I flipped through the tracks, stimming on the in-line controls, catching snippets of techno aria and bassline vibrato. The show was still playing at the theater to my back, and I catered my playlist to the experience. Again, "The Point of No Return" played its remixed tune in my ears, and I cried, thumbing the button over and over and over.

You were in the hole, but you weren't gone. You were right there, twenty feet away, letting the cavern destroy you. And I was too broken to save you, too unworthy of fighting for.

And I grew less by the day.

I saw the pool below, dissolving flesh into its waters in exchange for its beautiful song. Even now, I want to hear my song, the transformation of myself, knowing what it costs to be in its presence. With the music pounding in my ears, I could resist the cave's song and think clearly for the first time in days. You didn't have that luxury so firmly in its grasp.

But I could help you. I had everything I needed. I had my phone and a hyper-pop playlist of opera remixes. I had a small but loud Bluetooth speaker clipped to my jacket with a carabiner. I could save you.

Staring down at the hole, I pulled my headphones from my neck and let them fall to the ground. In an instant I heard the music of the cavern, not some theater performance, but something foul and rotten. I connected the speaker and let it play.

I stepped onto the first rung, focusing only on the speaker's tinny music and plastic-rattling bass. With the music in my head, I took the ladder two steps at a time, descending into the hole as my atrophied muscles protested the climb.

My feet splashed in viscous water and as I broke the surface the smell erupted upward. I gagged into the open air, inhaling more of the rotting flesh smell. I covered my nose and mouth and shone my flashlight all around. You weren't on the island.

My operatic musical intrusion reverberated through the cavern, and the water rippled with displeasure, fat and flesh foaming on its surface. I turned sharply about, shining my light all around and trying to find you. When I did, I nearly wished I hadn't.

You lay in the pool, body surrounded by the dissolved flesh that caked over your skin, stuck to you like seafoam. I sloshed through the thick water and reached into it to take your hand. Your skin sloughed off your wrist, a thick slurry in my hand. I wretched and vomited into the pool and called your name. I couldn't hear the music, but it returned your name to you, taking ever more of your body with it.

Your lips moved, and my heart clenched as I realized you were speaking my name. The music of my name came to me, trying to break through the techno trance that blasted from my tiny speaker. I focused only on my own music, the beautiful creation of real people, not some eldritch abomination. With the music, I could do anything.

I ached to hear my song and to let it take another piece of me for its collection—a fair trade for its beauty. "Get up!" I yelled, breaking the flow of the music all around. I dipped my arms into the fat-layered water, reaching them under your body, which squished and dissolved in my hands. I lifted and strained to pick you up, even as slight as you were.

My foot slipped on the bed of the pool, and I fell thrashing into the rot. It filled my mouth with decaying flesh, and I spit and cried and fought for the surface. Bile rose in my throat, but it was nothing to the taste of the cavern's flesh. When I regained my feet, tears streamed down my eyes. I heaved upward and lifted you in front of me. Half of your flesh remained in the water, and still, you smiled, mouthing my name.

And there was no opera to drown you out. My speaker lay dead and drowned at my side, still clipped to my jacket and perfectly silent.

The cavern called to me, speaking my name in a beautiful chorus that suffused my body and my mind. Your lips scarcely remained, but still, you spoke my name, and still, the cavern threw it back at me. I tried to resist, but my body lowered to the water. I lay by your side as the music ate me away, and I knew I had nothing left to give. And so, I gave you up.

I shouted your name as I held your hand, and the vile fluid filled my ears. The cave sang back to you, its attention diverted. I gripped your hand and shouted until there was nothing left. Your lips dissolved, and you could no longer frame my name. Your hand squished into nothing in my grasp. I shouted, and I cried.

I STAND AT THE MOUTH of the hole. My speaker is dead, but the cave's music stopped when you stopped speaking my name. Without any words to return to me, I could slip from its grasp and back up the ladder. I'm covering the hole, but there's something I have to do first.

I kneel beside the cavern's entrance and listen to my headphones. My phone still works somehow, and I have all the music to drown out the cave. All of the songs, except for one. With a whisper, I speak your name into the hole and press record on my phone. It records everything that is left of you. I let it go for several minutes, making sure I captured every scrap of your being.

Someday, I'll listen to it when the hole is covered and filled, and the cavern has no power over me. For now, nobody will know your song. Nobody will know you the way I did.

The way the cavern knew us both.

ENCORE

Steve Berman

T HE Sword of Damocles had fallen—or rather, the Chandelier of Lacarrière, Delatour et Cie. Six tons of bronze and crystal. The crimson upholstery of the parterre could never soak up that much blood and remain true to its color. Mme. Biabcarolli remembered the screams of the audience but not the deafening crash of the chandelier. She fled the stage—staggering out through one of the many back doors of the Palais Garnier, swept along in a torrent of costumers, wig attendants, and supernumeraries. She, herself, could not scream because her throat remained disagreeable—whatever the Opera ghost had done to her throat spray had left her mute but for an unpleasant croak.

Three days and three nights passed, as the physicians recommended by M. Debienne treated her injury with pastilles and compresses. Her dreams were not haunted by the Opera ghost and his threats, nor by the great chandelier's fall, but by her being unable to sing again.

Mme Biabcarolli threw a modest soiree in her apartments to celebrate her hopefully complete recovery.

While her guests claimed to attend out of a surfeit of concern for her, the conversations she began or overheard all revolved around the Opera ghost and his protégé. The older women were particularly venomous, whispering among themselves—while their husbands, or those suspiciously sudden nephews, drank Mme Biancarolli's champagne—that waif Christine Daaé ought to be held responsible for the tragedy. After all, hadn't someone perished in the fall?

None could quite recall the name of the deceased, but didn't Pr de Fontenelle look noble with that bandage around his head?

But that, my dear, one woman muttered, *happened at his home, in the library—a sudden fall.*

He does seem fragile. When will his wife return from Capri?

Legouvé claimed that, from his perch in the paradis, he had seen the Opera ghost sabotaging the very chains of the chandelier. But he was a poor poet and an out-of-season lover, hoping to secure a benefactor from among the night's guests. Naturally, M. Firmin Richard, one of the Opera House's new management, paid him no attention.

"It is a terrible year for opera in France. First the fire in Nice, and now this. Perhaps it is time for you to tour—or accept an engagement at La Scala. Milan would welcome one of its beloved daughters," said M. Alexandre Luigini. The conductor had been kind to her when she first arrived in Paris nearly a decade ago, and he could not entirely conceal the concern on his face. "Once the authorities have found this madman," he said, softer now, "the stage will be yours again."

Carlina Biabcarolli was born in Lomazzo, while Carlotta began in Milan. She trained under M. Lorenzani, who poured the frustrations of caring for a sick husband into every lesson—pinching Carlina black and blue along her arms and chest. And Carlotta could not help but remember the Devil. What would be awaiting her now? A family she had little spoken to?

"But I don't dare stray—"

A hush fell over the salon. Guests parted as if moving down the aisle that cuts through the nave, pairing off into new couples—a man in the winter of his life finding himself standing beside the much younger daughter of a banker who insists she is a musical wunderkind, awkward nieces paired with the powdered dandies their aunts brought for show; cousins separated by church and state who had not met eyes in over fifteen years.

A handsome man in an expensive tuxedo escorted a lovely young woman. He helped her slip a shawl from her pale shoulders with great care—a shawl, practically a relic, one that might have drawn remarks for its tastelessness in any other moment. But there were no whispers. Breaths were held as the Vte de Chagny took her gloved hand and led her deeper into the room. Christine Daaé had arrived.

Of course, she had not been invited.

The other guests stared at her with the fervor of Galileo observing a new heavenly body—a beauty that dazzled and burned—as she came close enough to M. Debienne to curtsey to the vicomte. Mlle Daaé dipped her head in return: a gesture of respect, or perhaps the acknowledgment of an opponent before a duel.

"It is good to see you have recovered from that awfulness," Mlle Daaé said, taking Carlotta's hand in her own before Carlotta was even aware of it. "No need to speak; you should rest your voice."

And with that word—*that spell, for what else could it be but sorcery?*—the silence broke. The guests resumed their vapid praises and polite protests while keeping Mlle Daaé in the corner of their gaze.

Carlotta did not linger after the young woman's slap. Without an excuse, she slipped free of the circle of guests and found herself retreating to the solace of her music room.

Her hand touched the brass doorknob but remained still as she heard music through the old wood. A piano performing the third act of *Robert the devil*. She groaned. Yet one more unexpected, unwarranted, unbidden guest.

With the curtains drawn, the interior was dark and without song. Carlotta turned the switch for the gas lamps, and the flames revealed the Devil on the bench, his soot-covered fingers traveling the keys. His suit was once elegant, but now its seams have fallen like its owner. Worst, his head was that of an immense black cock. The glossy curve of the beak caught the light, and the comb a sway of ebony.

"You look surprised, Carlotta," he murmured, his voice a baritone any man would envy.

Seventeen years since their first meeting and the last.

"I did not think the misfortune at the Palais Garnier's would be enough to send you scurrying to Paris."

"Paris is my favorite city," said the Prince of Lies. "Though I do miss the regular performances of *commedia della ghigliottina* in the public square.

"I may not always be seen, madame, but do remember—I lurk backstage, waiting for my cue." He tapped idly back and forth between two high notes, the sound light but needling. "And so I know about the letters you've written: a disgraced legal scholar; that philosopher jailed for his little pamphlets; even a deacon, inquiring when the Feast of Saint Cecilia falls this year—I once attended a Black Mass in Trastevere... very posh."

She sat down on a tufted pouf. A retort climbed to her lips—sharp, practiced—but the sheer ridiculousness of his countenance made it escape as a laugh, short and bright, quickly hidden behind the back of her hand.

"After all these years," she said, "I still don't know how to address you."

"Does it matter? I shed names so readily." He stopped playing and conjured a burning cigar. It looked precarious in the curve of his beak. "The contract you signed in blood is binding."

The pungent and sickly sweet tobacco irritated her throat. "Binding," she echoed. "And yet, am I the most famous singer in France? Not now."

"You were."

She stood, strode to the piano, and slammed shut the fallboard. "Unless you plan on dragging me to Hell at this very moment, I stand here deposed. That was not the spirit of our agreement."

The Devil cannot blink. "Ahh, you remember the days when the curtain did not rise for you, when composers did not create arias, entire operas for your voice. The handkerchiefs of patrons have grown dry—no tears for Carlina Biabcarolli."

Her mouth went tight. "You use my name like it's yours to give back."

"I had planned on taking you in September. Not this year. I adore opera with all its tragedies, I thought, Let her sing until she's lost a few teeth. The local patisseries will ensure that would happen.

"But then I heard the pleas of Mlle Daaé—"

"You promised her the very same role!"

"Not at all. That would be farcical. No, Christine offered her soul to be the most captivating girl in all of Paris. She wanted the stage, the suitors, the allure."

"Semantics. And now she had not only the attention of the vicomte but also a madman," Carlotta mused. "The Opera ghost."

"It is difficult for me not to complicate lives while I await deaths."

"And why have I not suffered your whims?" Despite the Devil's promises, her struggles to reach the lofty heights of lead soprano had never been as easy as she thought they would be. Cold days. Hungry days. Those early days that required she gnash teeth at the incivility of men while singing and dancing in tired brothels and seedy music halls.

He shrugged. "Perhaps I never needed to. What matters is what you will do next. I offer you the chance to break our agreement."

"A chance for freedom?"

The cock's head dipped in an exaggerated nod. "Perform one task, a simple thing, like blowing out the candle before sleep."

Out of her singed throat came another bitter laugh. "Cease being coy, Monseigneur. What would you have me do?"

"Murder Mlle Christine Daaé."

Carlotta walked over to where the Devil sat and slammed shut the fallboard. "Do you think me some anile cow? Murdering her would be a mortal sin, one that forfeits my soul to you as much as signing your accursed contract."

"You are the clever one, Carlotta. And yet, not so clever...."

"Why do you want her dead?"

He dropped the ash from his cigar onto the piano. "The means to an end. The Vicomte de Chagny is a wealthy man. He ascribes his good fortune to hold Daaé in his arms as something ordained by Heaven. To honor her, he has already begun the renovation of a dilapidated church in the North. And with that will come a renewal of faith in the community, in the countryside, where I rarely walk these days.

Carlotta knew the rest; a life of opera prepared one for a terrible ending. "And if she dies, then he will be heartbroken."

"And in grief, there will be no church, no prayers offered to the Lord." The last words caused him to spit as if the taste of even that pained him.

"I refuse to be a pawn in this." She began to gesture, imagining a backdrop of flames as the music swelled. "If I must be damned because of ambition, then I hope the congregation's pious hymns are so loud they inspire me in Tartarus to accompany them—"

"Oh, cease the prattle. Such theatrics are wasted on an audience of one. Think more on this: if your hand will not be bloodied, then Christine returns to the Palais Garnier. And to the Opera ghost, whose desires will claim the girl. If she refuses him, he will kill her. If she succumbs out of pity, the vicomte's stomach will turn, and his heart will harden.

"In either case, I prevail."

He lifted the fallboard. "And you?" He ground the sputtering end of the cigar against a white key, scorching the ivory. "You need not conspire, nor lift a hand. Unless you want to reclaim what I have taken from you."

Carlotta blinked, seeming stupefied as she considered the cruel paths awaiting Christine upon the girl's return.

"So reconsider my generous offer. Earn back your soul, if only for a short while." He chuckled. "You may even find a traveling pardoner who will sell you an indulgence."

Offended by the first bold insult in years, she stiffened. Her exit involved a flourish of contempt with an undercurrent of despair.

She breathed in the salon, a garden of floral perfumes, a menagerie of animalic musks. The complains over the warm night and warmer wool, and the babblement that wanted to spread like fleas on fur.

She found Christine and her royal beau talking with M. Luigini about his work.

"Forgive me, messieurs, but I must speak with Mme Daaé." Carlotta gently laid a hand on her arm. "Let us confer," she said." And when she leaned closer to whisper, "You and I have been terribly wronged by the same brimstone bête noire," she noticed an unsightly mole below the young woman's ear. Two dark hairs bristled from its midst.

"I-I…"

"Go on, my ortolan," said de Chagny. "Talk of the stage with one who has stolen the hearts of audiences for years." He kissed Christine's cheek, then told Carlotta, "But tell her no secrets, Mme Biabcarolli, on how to charm men; I would not have any more rivals for her hand."

Christine did not follow Carlotta easily. She tried to shake off Carlotta's grip on her arm.

"Do not profess anything before listening to me," Carlotta snapped. "Behind a closed door, proof of discretion."

Christine stopped, and however she found weight to Carlotta's demand, she assented, allowing herself to be led through the tastefully furnished apartment and to a pair of glass-paned doors leading to a quiet balcony.

Christine hesitated. "Carlotta, please… I think—"

"Yes think, think on what I am about to tell you. Do not let yourself be distracted by the view." Carlotta turned the key in the lock and gestured to the balcony.

IN THE ABSENCE OF CLERGY, the Vicomte de Chagny conversed with the only other pious man at the soiree: the professor. Carlotta discovered them in a gentle dispute over whether any of Pharaoh's men might have held their breath and escaped the Red Sea.

"Forgive the odd argument, Madame Biabcarolli," said de Chagny. "Seeing M. Luigini reminded me of his *Ballet égyptien*, which, when mentioned to the professor—who truly ought to have been a theologian—turned his thoughts to Exodus."

Professor de Fontenelle inclined his head. "I hope I don't bore you. Madame Biabcarolli is young enough to indulge fancies... yes, fancies rather than suffer the digressions... of an old man."

"Where is Christine?" the vicomte asked suddenly.

Carlotta smiled. "We spoke briefly. The night air didn't agree with her, so I believe she's gone."

de Chagny's expression shifted to open surprise. "But why wouldn't she come to me first?"

"The sensibilities of a girl her age..." the professor began with a voice turned to treacle by wine.

"You underestimate her. A disservice to her ambitions," Carlotta interrupted. "You'd best prepare yourself. There's more anguish on the horizon for you than any ghost could contrive."

de Chagny paled. "What are you saying?"

But Carlotta was already moving past him. "I've done all I can."

Throughout the rest of the evening, she nearly returned to the music room. She denied the Devil satisfaction. In the morning, her servants would send for a carpenter to board shut the door to that space.

As the guests slowly departed—often with one last statement of loyalty to her talents and predictions that soon the stage would be hers again—to which she agreed, though the late hour made her suspect herself to be lying.

She found the professor leaning against a wall, his bandage askew, his gaze fixed with the intensity that only an empty bottle brings, on a painting of two hares rearing high before they do battle.

"I shall have a carriage called for you," she told the old man.

"My dear. Do not think of yourself as cursed." He gathered his feet under him with effort. "You are no Job. Not at all. And the Devil could not have brought the chandelier down. I think… I think it was one of the early Church Fathers. The Devil knows no crafts… no craftsmanship. He cannot create with his hands. Certainly, he is no saboteur."

"If I meet him again, I will remind him of his failings."

de Fontenelle smiled. His collar was stained burgundy. "What he ruins…. He trades in illusions, you see. The Devil cannot create. That is reserved for us… and God, of course. Six days, but I cannot believe…"

A servant gently took him to the stairs and walked him down the street.

She strolled around the empty salon. And her thoughts could not stray from the professor's words. What if only a charlatan with savoir-faire called upon her this night. Yes, an ancient one, but so ancient that even he has grown careless. What was it he told her?

You are the clever one, Carlotta. And yet, not so clever… Perhaps that had been a deeper taunt than she heard.

When Christine stole the attention of the entire salon… that had been unnatural in its efficacy. But where had the Devil's hand been in Carlotta's ascent? Where was the sorcery?

Hadn't she trained? Practiced until she was robbed of her voice for days? Wept as she abandoned rest--or the many joys a girl should know at such a young age. A pursuit of perfection, but a pursuit of her own endeavors.

What if the Devil's only trick on her behalf had been to tell a lie— one so seductive, so artfully timed, that *everyone* believed it? Whatever you desire, all for the same price. Could he truly claim her soul with a contract signed in blood, all flourish and threat, yet lacking any clear obligation? Had it ever specified what he must do to make her "the most famous singer in all of France"? Or had the Prince of Lies simply recognized her potential—and seen how her ambition made her gullible?

Her spirits lifted. Perhaps she was not damned after all. Her decision to warn Christine of the Devil's plan had not been necessary to save *herself*— but still, she was glad she had done something noble.

In that small moment of pride, she picked up one of the last pink biscuits from a tray the waitstaff had not yet cleared.

"And what if I'm wrong," she muttered and took a small bite.

It was too late when she noticed how much sugar dusted the biscuit. One of her molars began to ache. Aghast, she dropped the sweet onto the polished floorboards—so like a stage, waiting for the next act.

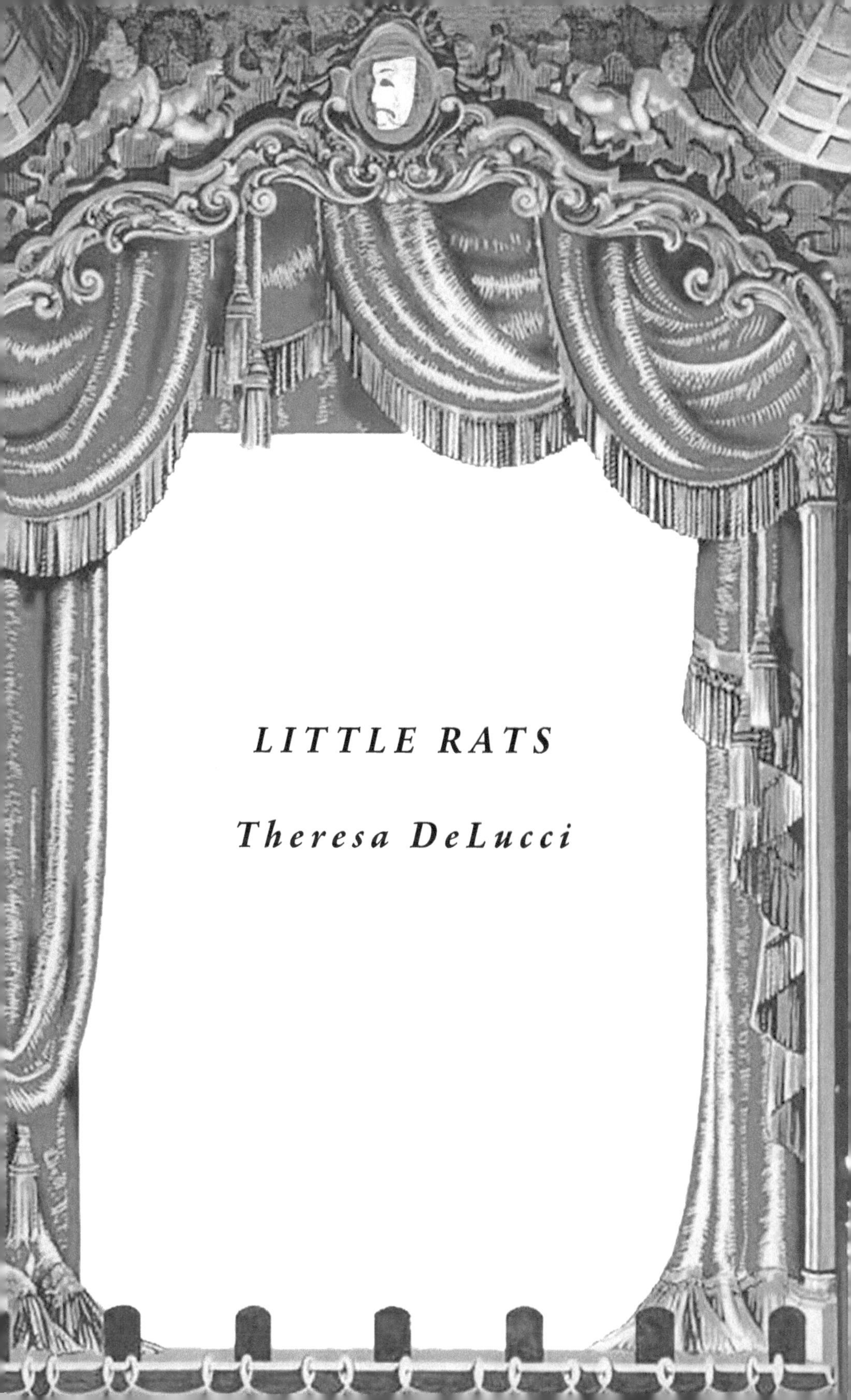

LITTLE RATS

Theresa DeLucci

OW LONG DID IT TAKE your eyes to adjust to the dark of the Foyer de la danse before you could see us? Did you miss us in our little shrine of cool, dead marble and gold friezes in the heart of the opera house? Gather your peers around you like a mantle. Just another frock coat and top hat smudged against the wall. A featureless, pale face hung on swirls of cigar smoke.

Sitting with the other sponsors, so at ease, all of you with legs wide open to infinite possibilities, but only ever pointed towards the same, most predictable one.

How wonderful it is to believe oneself beyond limitations.

We are the background against which the star dancers and singers can shine all the brighter. We are small and common. Easy to overlook.

But we can see you. We can see in your dark.

This time, we saw you first, and now we can lead the dance.

The penny papers will say our mischief began at the Palais, where all the striving, soiled ballerinas of the *corps de ballet* perfected their trade, but the truth is that we had each come out of our mothers with the same affliction. Once, we were thirteen hairless girls, all bred in the same warrens of Paris, where the gas lamps had yet to reach, and laundry lines sagged overhead between tenements stacked so tightly together only shadows touched the ground. Our eyes were accustomed to the dark long before we arrived at the Palais Garnier.

While we trained, there was no world outside of the Palais. Sunlight existed only by a stage manager's design. We stole food from the kitchen and huddled together on our straw mattresses. If the opera house was a galleon ship, then we were the little rats scampering within the labyrinth of hallways and hidden passages in its belly. Squeezing between discarded sets. Climbing over pulleys and rigging in all the unlit places forbidden to patrons, even the most important audience to us, the sponsors.

That was never the real reason we were called little rats, but it was the kindest one.

You must remember that even little rats have feelings to hurt.

PAIN NEVER LIES. YOU MUST remember this, too.

We were trained to learn all the boundaries of our bodies and then ignore them. It was impossible to spend so much time together without learning your sisters' limits even better than your own. We could decipher the popping sounds in our joints, whether wet dirge or dry staccato. Meals were rare events, and our bones could catch the most flattering glow from the gas lamps. We felt the heat of blisters yet to bloom. If a toenail had grown a millimeter too long, we knew when it would slough off.

The floorboards were rich with the blood that leaked from our shoes. We have bled in every room of the opera house, from its toilets in the basement to the private bedrooms upstairs. Where there are girls, there is blood.

What body is born without pain? The corps was just that—the singular body we must become onstage.

(Josephine had the longest, most elegant clavicles. Marguerite's turnout was straighter than a hairpin. Lisette could lengthen her body with ease, like saltwater taffy pulling apart. Suzanne's eyes were only the deep purple of blackcurrant liquor when she spoke the truth.)

One theme played within the chambers of all our warren-bred hearts. The first notes were the anxious timbre of uncertainty about our next meal or what happens when our fathers vanish, sent to prison or gone by their own choice. Always sooner, and never later, begins the relentless allegro of keeping pace with our mothers as they outsmarted debt collectors or vagrancy charges, as we lost our only favorite toys being shooed between windowless rented rooms, watching our mothers get their pink tails caught by one new stepfather after another.

What else were they to do with daughters who were pretty, if not beautiful; talented dancers, but only just? When we were packed away to the Palais, we were sold the dream of the security a suitable patron of our arts could provide with a contract, who could make any one of us stars in such a marvel of a city, such an age of astonishment.

But we are quick studies.

Thirteen little variations in crises, building upon each other in time towards a fixed end. That must be why it felt so natural to dance as one corps onstage. We could always recognize the choreography of each other's lives.

Natural does not mean without pain.

PEOPLE FORGET THAT LITTLE RATS are clever escape artists. We were well-practiced in the ways to burrow deep inside our own minds, where the grabbing hands of sponsors could never touch. Our minds can leave our singular bodies behind whenever we wish, so what did they think would happen when they taught all of us how to dance as one corps?

A hundred superstitions keep a theater from collapse; even the most famous divas know this. There is a god for every candle in the opera house, each witness to even the most private performances demanded of us. Over the slab of a sponsor's shoulder, we look to the gods and goddesses laughing and fighting and raping between the golden vaults of the Foyer's ceiling and cast ourselves among them. We might not be able to read—what use were letters to us? Then or now?—but we learned their histories from music.

Mother Hera. Father Zeus, who was a swan himself, sometimes.

Sister Sibyl.

No statue in the Palais captivated us like the *Pythia* at the bottom of the Grand Staircase. She was not cold stone but living bronze. She swooned atop her tripod, her heavy breasts bared in a disheveled dress. Her snakes and wild curls roiled under the candelabras' flames, but she was no Medusa. She was mad with holy smoke and looked down her outstretched arm as if she was pushing a terrible vision back onto the men who came begging a young girl for Apollo's grace.

Whoever sculpted her understood that Pythia would look more powerful if she looked frightening.

Every evening, we pass Pythia's alcove when we are swept out of the dormitories downstairs, through the administration offices, and into the dancers' private entrance to the Foyer. As sure as the left slipper must go on before the right, we have to touch Pythia's foot and ask for her blessing each performance.

We speak to her directly. What do little rats have to fear from her, or the god of a sun we will never see again? She is trapped in her shrine, too. She swells with the prayers we have fed her, all our midnight secrets and dreams; she sees even the prayers we dare not speak in the light.

Our touch has rubbed the bronze of her skin oily and smooth. The sprays of baby's breath we tucked behind the *Pythia's* base have dried and crumbled to dust weeks ago, but tonight, we kiss her feet and burn our lips.

We tell you these things because we need you to understand what was lost.

There are holy grounds even *you* may not walk without punishment.

IT WAS TOO PERFECT A harmony that the most praised dance of our final season at the Palais happens during the finale of *Il ritorno d'Ulisse in patria*, when Penelope's twelve maids are sentenced to death.

No less than a dozen little rats of the corps would do for cleaning up the vanquished suitors' blood—silky red scarves piled on the stage; no male dancer goes en pointe. We always had a thirteenth ready to take an absent sister's place if needed. It often was.

(Lisette has to sit for that old man and his pastels. Josephine got evicted for the second time this year. Marguerite's mother is in the hospital. Suzanne's headache is just too much tonight.)

Life pulsates through the grand chandelier, and it is what we have for a sun. It never sets. It is a light made for illusions. Under it, our white plumes and bleach-stiffened skirts transform us into precious cygnets. Our gray skin won't show through the greasepaint. We know exactly how to dance as girls with virtue left to bargain. The audience will hate us for it, but they will remember our end more than any of the principal dancers'.

Contrition wracks every angle of our disloyal bodies as we dance adagio to the gallows. The scene-changers below have their own choreography with the set pieces. They hide the ladders we use to reach a platform high out of view and wheel a grand white screen across upstage, between our mark and the proscenium. When Ulysses and his son throw their ropes up to the rafters and exit the stage, we hook ourselves into our waiting harnesses like the rigging coordinator taught us in rehearsals.

Behind all of this an immense spotlight points at our backs, whiter and more focused than the grand chandelier, casting our black silhouettes onto the screen.

And then we jump off the scaffold, six by six.

Twelve sullied maids hanged for the crime of surviving the wrong way.

We never believed Penelope would have taught her girls to jump willingly like that. They would have had to push us. What else could the maids have done but say yes to a suitor, or a sponsor, when there is no other way out of the corner at their backs?

The audience has paid to see us die either way, but we know only swans can die with honor.

BEFORE WE WALKED INTO THE Foyer the night we met, the evening prayers went differently.

"Sister Sibyl, what will become of me," someone whispered, though we could never agree who whispered first. Just that we all had the same thought to shout out Pythia's answers. It was as if one week no one played this new game, the next, it was every girl's favorite.

"Madame Noé will lash your thighs for coming into your last jeté so late."

"You'll never grow tits like mine, Marguerite!"

"Dance for the god who loves you and make no resistance."

Suzanne's bruise-colored eyes were dark, and her reedy voice filled the alcove.

She pulled her hands away from the foot of the statue fast, as though she had scalded them on a hot kettle. Suzanne, whose talent for imagination was even better than her dancing, who could make us believe in any dream. It was natural that she was the sister gifted with Pythia's vision. Gods love those who pray to them the most.

"Yes, yes," we agreed, "The bronze feels warmer today, does it not?"

WHERE IS THE HARM IN revealing the stagecraft, now that it will never be repeated?

Look at the dangling legs of the hanged girls in front of the spotlight until your eyes get so used to seeing us, your gaze softens. You can almost look through us, seeing but not seeing. We are still in silence. Beads of sweat roll down our back and drip on the stage, wetting dried flakes of old blood.

When all the amphitheater's lights blink out at once, our silhouettes instantly become white afterimages on your eyes. For seconds, we are ghosts. It will work with any light, but you must not try the trick using the sun, or we will be the last thing you ever see.

We need only a little time to climb our ropes out of view and unhook our harnesses. Then we hurry down the catwalk's stairs to get backstage. We are ushered to the mouth of an abandoned service passageway that leads upstairs and into the loge.

"Your turn, Suzanne," Marguerite whispers, nudging her.

We move, quick and deft, in single file along the narrow hallway, one of the many paths in the Palais never intended for patrons. The corps becomes pulsing blood in the veins of the opera house. The lanterns along the walls create rare, oily puddles of light. We walk with our hands outstretched to edge between the rough plaster. The air is wet and still from our panting on the backs of each other's necks.

We pass behind the back of a large window, seeing our deserted classroom from behind the barre, where the large mirror is hung. We are walking backstage on our lives.

Lisette yelps in the dark. "Suzanne, what's wrong?"

"The wall," Suzanne gasps. "Did anyone else feel that?"

We will snarl together in an unlucky pile of bruised limbs if we stop there. We cannot stop.

"Do we always take so long?"

Did Josephine say that, or did we all think it at the same time?

We hear the faint trill of a flute and surge towards the sliver of light at the far end of the passageway.

We emerge in the loge and our male counterparts, the vanquished suitors, corral us into the second orchestra box just before the grand chandelier is relit. We hit our mark in time. We sneak sidelong glances at each other, exhaling soft, relieved sighs. We overlook the audience as a silent chorus of the newly dead.

You are a man of discerning tastes. If you had a choice, we are quite sure you would never miss a single performance.

WITHOUT THE LIES WE TELL ourselves, life would be too much to endure.

(Marguerite thinks it's not so bad. Josephine tells herself that anyone in her family would do the same for her. Lisette has to believe that things will get better. Our time will come, Suzanne says.)

Would a god *not* have hair a shade of gold to rival the gilt friezes of the Palais, to make the stage manager's sun seem pale? Would he *not* be tall and slim as a woman, with elegant cheekbones of his own to catch all the candlelight? A god *would* sail around heavier, cruder men as if he floated on air, surveying the perimeter of the Foyer for a spot to perch and let the little rats come to him.

Thirteen sisters orbiting closer and closer around your sun. Press another glass of wine into our hands. Ask us to tell you how we got to the orchestra box so fast. Spin us around the salon in your arms, nevermind the sharp pains in our feet. Pretend you do not dangle the promise of rent money and beef by the pound. Ask us again, just less sweet.

"Can't we keep a little secret or two?"

(The correct answer to this is always no.)

Our will dissolved like sugar cubes beneath the measured drips of your flattery.

At least, that's the excuse we gave for forgetting ourselves and feeling those pinpricks of jealousy when you finally led Suzanne away from the Foyer in the late hours of the night. But the spell of you broke a bit when we accepted that Suzanne deserved her claim to the god she created.

"I really shouldn't show you backstage, but...."

(No one of us confess to saying that. It was not our fault.)

Did the creaking of our ropes play in your ears long after the curtain fell? Perhaps you alone could see them still tightened around our long necks, the way you played with us like marionettes in a market square.

We see the lies that you tell yourself: Because you are a wealthy man, you are wise. You are deserving, righteous, sane.

"HE LIKES COLD ONES," SUZANNE said. We sat on the scuffed floor of our classroom in a semicircle, leaning in to hear her under the recitalists' piano playing.

"Cold what," Lisette asked.

"*Girls*, stupid," Josephine answers, shaking her head.

We looked at each other. We all knew sponsors who would hound us to the grave if they could. It was not such a leap to imagine sponsors who would go a little further.

"I had to lay on top of the comforter, freezing, in front of the open window for twenty minutes. By myself," she added pointedly. Time alone was time wasted. "And when he finally did enter the room, I still wasn't allowed to move or make a sound.

"The hardest part was trying to keep my eyes open without looking at him," Suzanne continued, picking at the frayed seam along her doll's cheek. "I tried to imagine anything. A gull, the Seine. But all I could think about was what if I died with my eyes open and he was the last thing I saw forever?"

Suzanne hugged herself, fanning her thumbs over her spindly arms.

"Madame says he asked about my contract with the school," Suzanne said.

<u>That</u> got a few gasps. Little rats don't get those kinds of long-term sponsors, especially not ones as old as Suzanne.

"What if he gets one?" Josephine asked. "I couldn't do that for months."

We nodded, pretending any of us would be given a chance to decline, pretending like we weren't being chased by the same sorrows, all the next moves mapped out ahead of us.

"Some god," Lisette sneered, breaking our quiet.

"Well," Marguerite shrugged. "Orpheus prefers dead girls, too."

Laughter can take a little power from a terrible thing, so long as it's done from a safe distance.

MEMORIES DRIFT DOWN UPON OUR eyes like plaster shaken loose from the walls:

Madame Noé has caught a smaller mischief of us downstairs, huddling around the *Pythia's* base in her alcove. She taps her walking stick on the marble, then gestures its silver tip towards the office, to the Foyer. We disperse before we can catch Madame Noé's stick and before Suzanne can relay what Sister Sibyl says will become of us. If she has indeed said anything that was meant for all of us, and not just her favored adept. Some remember that Suzanne's eyes were light, though, and others remember them being dark. We all agree the bronze skin of the *Pythia's* foot was warm, yes, yes, very warm indeed.

All the painted gods of Time and Heaven's muses pirouette around the base of the grand chandelier, counting down the hours. Ulysses returns to his homeland and hangs Penelope's maids, six by six, for the third time that week.

Josephine is the spare little rat for that evening's performance, so she is already in the Foyer before the second act. She stands next to the black mantle of the fireplace with a mind pointed towards her next meal. She startles from her reverie when the tall, slim man with golden hair sidles up beside her. She is still talking to him by the fireplace when the performers begin filtering into the salon.

Marguerite and Lisette stroll past them, hooked together at their pinkies.

"Stay warm," Marguerite whispers.

The man with the golden hair was not meant to hear that, but he did. Lisette should not have looked right at him after Marguerite spoke, but she did. Josephine should not have lost control of her face and let her mouth twitch up just so at the corner. But she did.

This memory is sharpened by regret for all the times we thought about what we could have done differently but did not.

The Foyer is most beautiful seen from the second floor, standing under the tiled arches along the veranda. The alcoves are almost like whispering galleries, the way the voices below are borne up on smoke, made soft and muted like light through haze. Suzanne leans against a column, smoking.

"Oh, dear, Sister Sibyl," Josephine asks, with her tired end-of-evening smile. "What will become of us?" She holds two fingers out for Suzanne's cigarette.

Suzanne looks into the loge at the man with the golden hair approaching the veranda. He side-steps through the crowd in a solitary waltz, clutching two glasses of Cabernet to his heart. Would a god *not* shrink from the slightest brush against a lesser creature? He stops short of joining them and gestures for Suzanne to come to him. Quickly.

She gives Josephine her cigarette, whispers in her ear.

"She said I need to leave here now."

"Don't we all." Josephine takes a long drag and closes her eyes. She exhales slowly, trying to picture it. "Promise you'll send for me when you do?"

When Josephine opens her eyes, Suzanne is already turning away.

"I know I will," she says and, her hand is reaching out to the man with the golden hair, or maybe she is really pushing the terrible vision of him away.

WHAT COLOR WERE HER EYES?

No one had answers everyone could agree on, but everyone did have their opinions. Did she not drink a lot that night? She always seemed far away in daydreams, perhaps she was hiding a secret habit or a lover. Everyone knew who she was last seen with and how much you give to support the opera. You are a wealthy man, so of course you are faultless.

We cannot claim to know the exact moment she died. That was beyond even our corps. We only recall an unspoken, nameless tension following us around the Foyer after that evening's performance, like we were waiting for permission to scream.

Perhaps you did not mean for us to find her body, but we did. Though you did not see the three girls huddled together on a straw mattress in the far, shadowy corner of a dormitory room downstairs, far from the bedroom upstairs where you were supposed to be, we were there. We were sleeping. Until we were not.

Without a squeak, we squeezed together tighter and watched, frozen. None of it made sense, to wake up and see a sponsor in a private room only for dancers, looming over the white bundle on the bed. We might have stayed asleep if you had not reached for the doll on the nightstand, if you had not knocked that hairbrush to the floor.

Why had you taken the time to tuck it into bed with her? Was it a last kindness or the most private joke? There was never a hope of understanding the tune that fueled your heart, that last little obscene act proved it for certain.

We saw, too, how you had gotten into the room when we watched you leave it, through a paneled door that no sponsor should have ever known about. You can go where we cannot, so why would we expect to find you in one of the only areas of the opera house where even our mothers were forbidden? You had a way of getting your way. Men like *you* cannot trespass when the world entire is already yours. But the opera house keeps its own order.

Did you know that you left behind a of piece of your shadow? It sank into the grain of the floorboards, and we never saw it follow you out of the room.

Our screaming would not stop for a long time.

The lamplighters found her shoes in the passageway to the loge. Her shoes were returned to the dressing room; even now they still hang from a hook on the wall, waiting to be filled with more blood. Her body was quietly carted away through a back door at sunrise, bound for a mortuary on the Left Bank.

If a group of rats is a mischief, what is a little rat that has died alone?

There is no name because nobody important thinks she needs one.

Her name was Suzanne, and she was not the first girl to ever be erased.

A group of ballerinas is a lamentation; that we do know.

How did you decide what respectable amount of time had to pass before you could return to the Palais? Nothing had happened, after all. Nothing of importance. The Foyer remained lively with patrons and performers holding court in your absence, but each night we recognized a piece of you in other sponsors that we had never noticed before, even in men that had seemed to treat us with kindness.

We are quick studies.

Without needing to be told, we knew you would return before season's end. Would a god *not* want to survey the damage left in his wake? What would be the point of going to so much trouble otherwise?

Besides, there are always more little rats to play with if one gets broken.

Were her eyes open or closed when she died?

We made the rehearsed dirge to our nightly execution, yet our real sentence was having to traipse through the passageway that we started calling Suzanne's. If ever we had moments of forgetting Suzanne was gone, she was there with us as we felt our way along the walls behind the scenery of our choreographed lives. She was a shorn-off limb that our corps could still feel.

Nightly, we dreamt of her in the passageway. She slumps against the wall with her legs out in front of her, wearing her leotard. The toes of her white slippers almost touch the opposite wall. Sometimes she is flush with too much laudanum and looks as if she is only a sleeping porcelain doll, and we shake her until we are the ones who wake up. But there are nights a bruise starts to purple her neck, and she is a broken toy. Her eyes bulge and stare down the long, uneasy dark.

We knew that you would return that night, and we knew that the missing part of our corps was never as lost as we thought. We kissed the feet of the *Pythia* and scalded our lips.

We heard Suzanne's soft, thin voice once again and we listened.

Follow me, she said.

MADAME NOÉ'S WALKING STICK PROVIDES the drum of our heartbeat as we dance into the Foyer.

Boom. Boom. Boom.

This is the moment we start our real dancing, not the kind we came out of our mothers doing, as our mothers did before us, dancing on the edge of a hundred knives pointing to the same cold, empty ruin.

The corps dances with something new and just as unstoppable.

Twelve little rats making their own unbothered, private preparations, putting their left shoes on before their right, feeling the tug of invisible tethers lacing up around their ankles alongside the satin ribbons. A man stands by the open jaws of the fireplace with hair so gold it looks on fire, or perhaps it is because they do not avert their eyes or look downcast. We see him just as he *is* and it will always ignite a rage in him.

This way, Suzanne repeats.

Twelve shining girls in their white plumes, skirts puffed out like sailing clouds, take the stage, and the music we dance to is not what the audience hears. With every turnout under the light of the grand chandelier, shards of futures reflect back at us, carried on that old, familiar tune:

Without the Foyer, there are neither sponsors nor suitors to keep us hidden away from their wives in a little furnished apartment on rue de St. Denis. A few more fat, green-hazed years of absinthe at the No. 7 or The Dead Rat, all the places sacked little rats stuff their deformed feet into heeled shoes instead of slippers and sell dances, sell their pink tails.

Time limps ahead. A dancer's body ages not just in years, but in injuries. Pain never lies, but opium does. Some dancers will grow old. No longer will they be little rats, but aging women with cramping stomachs, swiping bread from café tables, losing hours and inches bent over laundry piles, bent over cribs. When we bury our arms in trash bins and piss ourselves with drink behind a bar, will they look right through us like ghosts?

Then the workhouse, the madhouse, the poor house.

Who will relay what our bodies speak when we lie atop our mortuary tables? Will they even close our eyes before they pull the white sheets over our heads?

No, Suzanne says, *Come here.*

Onstage, the heat of the spotlight bakes their skin, and the fighting suitors are pink-faced little boys next to the way we move. We are one pair of legs slicing through the air without any care for contrition, we leap so sure we might be using dust motes as stepping stones, our head is raised and our arms beat into the air in single formation, we are transforming, taking flight into the only sun we have ever known.

THERE'S NOWHERE ELSE FOR YOU to look but at the girls dancing into the shadowbox and up the ladder of the hero's scaffold.

Six by six, the maids leap off the platform and into white-hot oblivion. Against the useless screen, twelve pairs of black silhouettes shaped like bony girls dangle above the stage. They hold the audience rapt in that moment; they need to be sure that the obscene girls got what they deserved, that the libretto is just a bit safer with the little rats exterminated.

The audience stares into a light that is far too brilliant for even the most exalted stage manager's design, the kind of light to make their eyes start to ache.

When the grand chandelier overhead goes dark, it feels like mercy. We twelve little rats will still be hanged on the back of their eyelids when they blink, only now we glow as white and pure as they wanted us to, if just for a few heartbeats too many.

How long will it take for their eyes to adjust to the dark and let us fade away?

Enough time for us to clamber up our ropes and race each other backstage. Time enough for us to scurry inside the waiting passageway, certainly. Before the audience can realize we will never be coming out of that tunnel again. We have already wandered off course, following Suzanne's music around an uncharted turn.

(Lisette hears the music as the sound of a blue door in a childhood home creaking open; Josephine is pulled along in the gentle undertow of a wave crashing ashore; Marguerite listens to the sound of a ball bouncing down the hallway and a little boy's giggle. Suzanne, when she went, heard the beating of wings.)

We come forth dancing towards the tune's source and away from the opera house, to where no mortal eyes will ever see us again.

Except for you.

Time pirouettes in the space between the walls, and we watch as you claw at your own eyes even as your screams grow faint behind us.

For you, our image will never fade away. We will burn on the back of your eyes every time you shut them. We will burn a black so true, you will see us even brighter in the dark. Around every corner remaining to you, we will be waiting there.

For you, there will be thirteen of us.

And we will be laughing forever and forever out of reach.

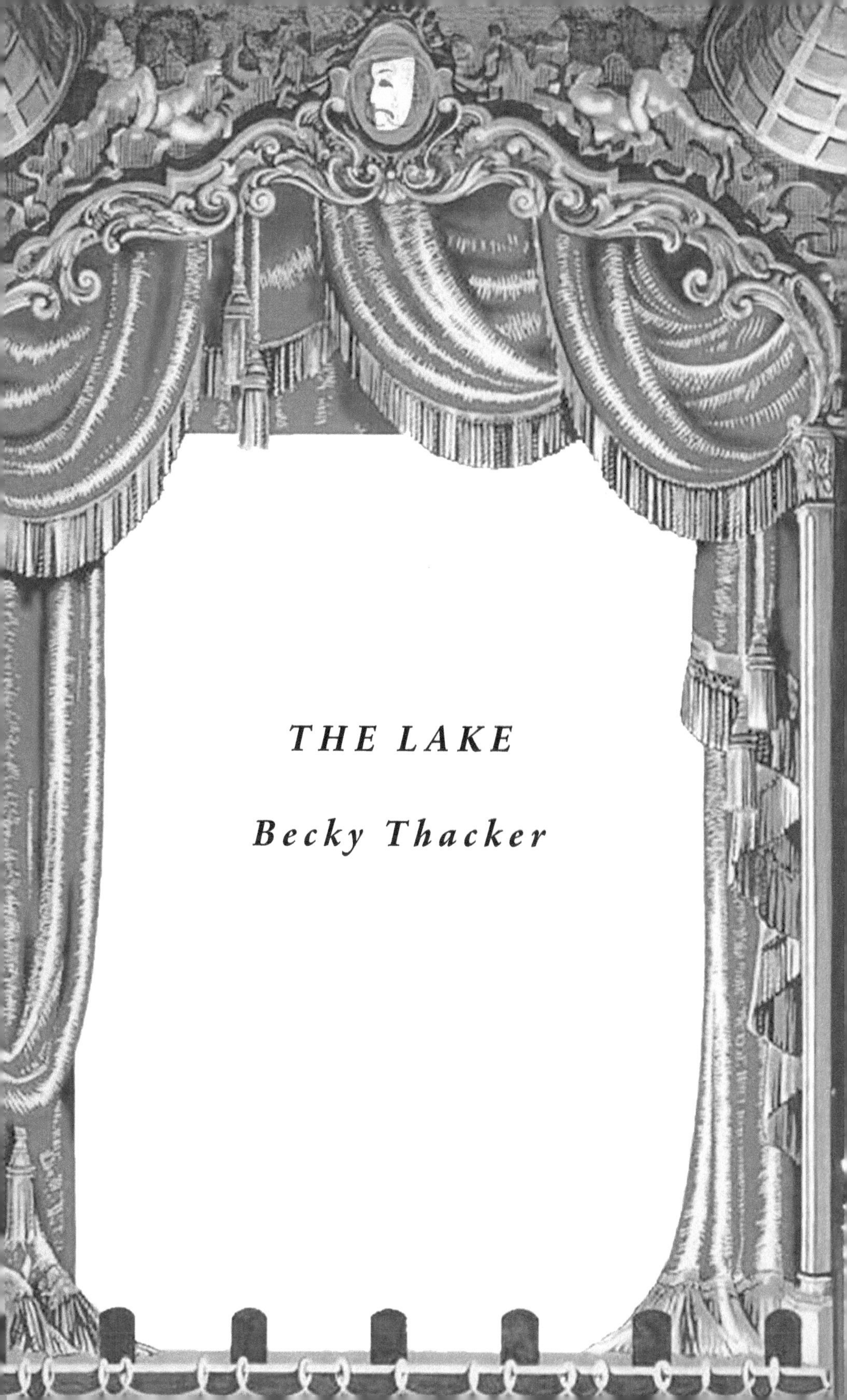

THE LAKE

Becky Thacker

The Rat

IT BEGAN WITH THE RAT—a great, scaly-tailed fellow missing part of an ear. As it swaggered away, I noticed he was endowed with testicles the size of grapes. I stamped my foot and hissed at it to speed its departure. He turned and hissed back.

Rats are, as everyone knows, nothing to exclaim at in Paris. In Palais Garnier, however, patrons do not expect these creatures to distract from their pleasures. Thus, we employ ratcatchers to control the population above the cellars and cats for below. Some escapees frequent my vaulted lakeside sanctuary, where hardly anybody comes except me.

I do not like rats. I particularly did not like this arrogant, overly masculine individual. Again, I stomped. He looked at me, then turned and sauntered away. Enraged, I grabbed a piece of brick and hurled it at the beast. A lucky throw, that. Injuries from the Salle Le Peletier fire had rendered my right eye nearly useless, and the impact of the missile against the flank of the rat astonished us both. He staggered sideways and—*splash!*—into the black waters of the lake. I smiled. A smile felt strange upon my ruined mouth.

A word about this "lake." It has been beneath the Palais Garnier since the opera house first rose above the foundations. It is not large, but nobody admits to knowing its depth nor what, besides rain from the roof, continues to feed it. To me, its vaulted silence has been a refuge from my many pains and sorrows. Its very presence has long quenched some of my rages.

When I first happened upon this subterranean pool, I could not tell how extensive it was. It wasn't until I came back with a dark lantern and walked about its edges that I realized its vastness. A dory was pushed against the wall near the staircase; probably, it was there for the use of workmen. In time, I dared try the oars and clumsily paddled around the perimeter. Through the low archways, I wended my way, finding landings in stygian, cavernous rooms where, it was apparent, nobody had been expected to return since their construction. I returned to them and furnished the most secluded of them for extended encampments.

To most, the understory where the lake resides is not an inviting locale. Since it is below ground, no natural light invades. One must bring a light, which will provide feeble illumination at best. Shadows flicker around the pillars on which the vaults rest; the light fleers along the damp stones arching above the lake. Silence is only broken by the susurrus of one's own clothing, punctuated by unsteady drips of condensation into the water's surface.

I have followed a few rare visitors down here. In my slippers with soft leather soles, I can walk silently or, for my amusement, step loudly once, twice, from behind my pillar in the darkness. The steps echo.

"What's that?" quavers a guest.

"…that…that…that…," the darkness answers.

Another boldly questions, "Who's there?"

"…there…there…there…," responds the croft. Or perhaps the echo is me.

I might toss a pebble into the water, which deliberately gulp it down. I allow silence to settle once again and the visitors to complete their business and leave. Or, once or twice, as they tiptoed toward the exit, I whispered a breathy, "Heh…heh…heh…." Which, when pitched over the surface of the water, echoes quite splendidly. It is guaranteed to provoke an exclamation and, once, from a burly workman, a falsetto shriek as he hurried out. I was hard put not to laugh aloud.

The rat fell into the water, somewhat dazed from the blow, but swam vigorously toward the steep, slippery shore. As it neared the brim, I booted it on the end of its wrinkled snout, and it fell back into the deeper water, sinking precipitously out of sight. I stared; rats are excellent swimmers, as a rule. It popped back to the surface and swam more strongly for shore until, suddenly, it was drawn backward by something that, I surmised, had grabbed its tail. Its eyes stared into mine as it was drawn slowly back from the shore. It gave a squeal; almost human, it seemed.

And it sank below the surface. Ripples wrinkled the water's surface where it had been. Then, it resurfaced three meters from where it had sunk, front paws vigorously beating the waters but to no avail. The creature gave a final cry, a wail, really. Its final look at me seemed reproachful, as though I had stabbed a guest at my dinner table.

Circular ripples spread from where the animal's snout disappeared. A flash of something white moved beneath the surface and vanished. The ripples broke upon the pool's edge, rebounded, and crossed with their fellows to form a delicate pattern of lace before they waned, and the lake was still once again. I backed away from the edge.

Pity

I DO NOT FEEL PITY AND have not since the fire. I feel disgust for the fool who designed Salle Le Peletier, a "temporary" edifice, all wood and plaster, with a network of leaky pipes to carry the gas intended for lighting stage performances. The only surprise is that the building stood for 50 years before an open flame from a poorly welded fixture began to gyre and dance wildly across the underside of a stage set. Like a spark to gunpowder, the result was explosive. It burned for 27 hours before the entire blackened ruin into the cellar.

In the first hour, it burned my beloved Giselle to death. Her burning costume rose about her like petals of a scarlet chrysanthemum, and then—*foom!* I will never forget that sound or the subsequent shrieks of my darling. Her hair burned. Her eyelids burned. I burned as I endeavored to beat the flames away from her face. We were surrounded by a circular wall of flame, and finally, I lifted her in my arms and carried her through a living, roaring wall of heat and horror. We plunged through, and I made for a side door. We fell onto the stones of Rue Pinon.

"You're safe, my darling," I panted as I rolled her on the ground, extinguishing the last of the flames. Her eyes! Oh, her eyes! No longer the harebell blue I cherished but black, sunken like dried cherries in their sockets. I reached for her hand, raised it to my lips, and it fell back to the cobbles without the skin, which remained on my palm like an empty glove. A toad's croak came from her throat, the last sound I was to hear from my Giselle, for she stopped breathing immediately after.

These details remain seared in my memory, but I do not clearly remember much of the hours after that. There were strangers, trying to be kind, sending my darling's remains away from me and sending my living remains to Hotel-Dieu Hospital. The months to follow, I know, were a living hell. I recall the wet bandages, soothing at first, wrapped around my head and face. Blind and nearly deaf, I was unaware of the putrefaction that set in. The raging fever rendered me senseless for a time.

When I returned to myself, my grief for Giselle returned also. I had nobody to share this grief with. Save for the doctor, all turned away in horror at what I had become. It is a kindness that, as I healed, I was not allowed a mirror. My face no longer had feeling on the right side. My eye functioned, but the scars covered it, so I only saw lights and shadows through the gnarled eyelid.

I mention these details only to emphasize why I could no longer feel pity for others. I received no sympathy from others for the loss of my Giselle, for my own ruined face, or for the ruins of my career in the ashes of the accursed Salle Le Peletier.

In place of sympathy, I received a mask.

"Monsieur Erik," said the young nurse in a flirtatious manner, "We have a surprise for you."

I was not fooled.

"What is it?" I growled.

The young nurse tittered anxiously. "Our artisans have created you a face."

"I have a face."

"But Monsieur, your face is…gravely injured."

"Better than anybody, I know that."

"I don't think you do," I started. The voice behind me was firm and male. This doctor had visited me a few times, and I felt that honesty lay behind his dour expression.

"We have not allowed you a mirror all this time because we had hoped we could do more for you. We cannot. For your own protection, we have made you a mask."

"Protection? I don't understand."

"Your face, Monsieur. It is ruined. You no longer have the face of a person. It is the face of a ghoul. A mask will render your appearance unusual. People will stare. Without it, people will shrink back in horror. Women will shriek. Children will cry. I am sorry."

The mask, made of hammered tin and padded inside with wool, looked like the mannequins in shop windows displaying hats. It had bland contours, eyes with no lashes or brows, and a nose and mouth that looked like anybody's or like nobody's.

"These straps will hold it firmly in place. Is it comfortable? Now? Good. Would you like to see it in a mirror?"

"Yes."

The mask moved stiffly against my face as I spoke. A mirror was brought, and I beheld my masquerade-ball countenance. Enough. Abruptly, I pulled the mask up and away and looked at my image. The young nurse gasped. So did I.

When the hospital released me, I hastened to the site of the new opera house, only to find it in use as a store for the military. A war! What use then did anybody have for a musician, particularly one whom nobody could bear to look at?

Palais Garnier

WHAT WOULD ANYBODY DO IN my position? Indeed, I moved into the military storage cum prison surreptitiously. The understory was labyrinthine; over time, I shared its dens and cubbyholes with soldiers, thieves, young lovers, and many sorts of denizens high and low. This populace unknowingly provided me with food, clothing, bedding, and coins of smaller denominations. Water for bathing, I drew in a bucket from the lake below the cellars. I never bathed directly in the lake; its dark waters were not inviting.

I had found a secure niche beyond the lake's vaults, which I furnished as a sanctum. Over time, it became quite a luxurious hideaway, reachable only by the small rowboat that the workmen had left in the vault.

From one of the young swains, whose attention was focused on his lover, I helped myself to the fine black silk cloak with red satin lining, which I wear daily. It is light yet warm and swirls deliciously around me as I flit down corridors and into niches. From glimpses in dark recesses, this garment has earned me the sobriquet "the Phantom" or "the Ghost."

The dull, lifeless days passed into weeks, then months, weary life with no friendship or love and no hope of anything better. More than once, I had considered throwing myself from the heights above the stage or falling into the lake's depths with a stone tied around my neck. What has prevented me? The music! I needed no love or companionship to enjoy each performance, and I was content listening to the singers as they practiced for each program.

One day, as I groped my way through a passage between two walls of the tiny warren of rooms of the lesser dancers and choristers, I stopped in my tracks. That voice! Was it Giselle? Has she returned to me? True, my dearest had been a dancer rather than a singer, but she often sang to herself as she practiced. She was possessed of a lovely, clear soprano, always on pitch, a delight to my ear. Through the wall in the Palais came a voice nearly identical to Giselle's, practicing a snatch of the current program.

Make no mistake—I well knew that Christine was not Giselle. Still, as my lovely little dancer lacked wealthy patrons who might ease her way into the first ranks of the ballet, Christine similarly had to bury her exquisite voice in the lesser ranks of the chorus. However, as the Phantom, over time, I have been remedying Christine's lacks, and, as all Paris knows, she has taken her place in the front ranks.

Marceau

ALAS, IT APPEARED THAT I was hoist by my own petard. I couldn't blame Vicomte de Chagny for falling in love with Christine. Had she remained safely in the background of the chorus, he would never have recognized her as his childhood sweetheart. I could not blame Christine, either. He is a handsome devil, this Raoul. How could I remind her of her admiration for me as her unseen "Angel of Music" when she thrilled to the stirrings of new-found love?

Visiting my lakeside retreat would clear my mind and allow me to solve this heartbreaking problem. And so, I made my circuitous way to the lower vaults, down the stone steps, slippery with moss and condensed moisture. The silence pounded in my ears, and I felt my shoulders relax and my hands unclench. Peace reigned.

Swinging my gold-tipped cane in one hand and my lantern in the other, I sauntered along the shore, but what! What was this white bundle of sticks floating against the shore? I set down my light and reached with my cane to pull the bundle closer; as I disturbed the surface of the water, an answering disturbance appeared toward the center of the lake. A flick of some flat, white object broke the surface, then disappeared again. Closer, then, a ripple in the water. I pulled back hastily. The ripple veered and then subsided as though the object had dived back to its depths.

Cautiously, I pulled the bundle to the side and hoisted it on the end of my cane and onto the land. Bits fell into the water again as I did this, as meat will drop off the bone as you ladle it from the soup pot. Precisely the same, in fact. This bundle was the bones of an animal, held together with bits of tendon and scraps of woolly fur. Closer inspection proved it to be the remains of a small dog.

I knew immediately. It was Marceau!

I should explain. Dogs are not welcome in the opera house, of course. So naturally, there are always persons of privilege who insist on smuggling in their horrid little beasts on performance days, thus assuring that they will disturb the most exquisite moments with their yips and growls.

Only recently, one of these little shit engines had broken loose from its mistress, who set up noisy lamentations all during the intermission. The woman's several swains shouted and whistled up and down the corridors, as did she.

"Marceau! Oh, my little darling, where have you gone?"

The wretched little beast managed to slip into one of the backstage passages, whereupon it accosted me as I hid behind a drapery. It barked and growled, which attracted some of the ballerinas, who then gave chase.

I managed to duck into one of my nooks, and apparently, Marceau had also managed to disappear. How he made his way to the lake remains a mystery, though he may have been chasing a rat. I surmised that he fell into the lake while seeking a drink and either drowned or met the fate of Monsieur Rat.

The exact cause of the rat's and the dog's fate remained a mystery I was curious to solve.

Philipe de Chagny

How I despise that odious man! While I feel a rivalry with his brother, young Raoul, I do not hate Raoul. I have a fellow feeling toward him. Do we not share a deep-seated love for the talented Christine? His older brother, however, has nothing to recommend him. Cold and condescending, he sniffs around the backstage of the Opera house like a mangy truffle hound. What is he looking for? Why, to discredit Christine in the eyes of her lover! He also discounts her talk of a hidden teacher who comes to her at night, her revered "Angel of Music," myself! I have heard him with my own ears; he jeers at her. He says I do not exist, but then he says he will hunt me down as one would a mouse inside the walls and expose me to the world as a charlatan with no musical talent.

To this end, he has begun to snoop where he has no business being. His attempts to find my covert recesses are laughable, yet I resent his harassment. I cannot concentrate on my courtship of Christine while being pestered by this annoying man. It is a distraction.

The Solution

A solution presented itself as I rowed across the lake to one of my landings. The lack of rainwater meant the lake level was slightly lower, allowing me to row beneath a low arch well away from the main cavern. There is a ledge, too narrow to be of much use but wide enough for my purposes. I store various emergency supplies there, including several lanterns filled with paraffin. I had brought some choice tinned biscuits and a bottle of cordial to add to my store.

As I rowed back to my launch area, I felt a distinct bump against the bottom of my craft. I paused, oars lifted from the water and dripping on the dark surface below. Raising my light from the bottom of the boat, I tried to peer over the side. This shifted the gunwale dangerously low to the surface. It really is a tiny boat. As I straightened, holding the light aloft, I glimpsed something large and white that flashed quickly past the boat's prow. I gasped. My heart beat in my ears, and I saw pinpricks of light. I shook my head to clear my sight. Setting the lantern down, I grasped the oars again and rowed speedily to shore. As the boat scratched its chin on the tiny spit of gravel, I hopped forward and scrambled as far from the water's edge as possible.

Ripples lapped the shore from a source I could not identify in the stygian murk over the lake.

"Who are you?" I called sotto voca to the presence. "…you…you…you…" came back mockingly. After a moment's silence, I whispered across the surface, "Are you hungry?" "…ungry…ungry…ungry…" it sighed back. I retired to think.

And I did think and came up with what seemed a simple plan. It would require careful timing, but I could count on that man's arrogant, headlong rush to capture the Phantom to aid me.

I sent the man a note, an invitation of sorts:

Philipe de Chagny:
(I omitted his title, knowing that would irk him in his arrogance.)
Meet me in the scenery room at 3:00 tomorrow morning if you are unafraid. When I have vanquished you, I will kill your brother and wed Christine. Come alone, or I will know you for the coward that you are.

I signed it with the name that most annoys him: *The Angel of Music.*

The scenery room is lined with many cupboards. Some of these have false backs that open into hidden passages. I planned to hide in one of these slightly before the appointed time.

Alas, for the best-laid plans. As my pocket watch told 1:30, I loaded the boat with a large jug of paraffin to fill the largest of my lights. My hands shook slightly from nervousness, not because of the laughable Comte de Chagny but because my mysterious underwater friend had grown bold. Each time I had rowed to one of my lakeside hideaways, this creature had bumped against the bottom of my frail craft as if to topple it. I had begun to think it would ram a hole through the boat's flimsy hull.

I lit my small light that night and set out across the water. I turned my bow toward the farthest niche and rowed with all my might straight there. Holding the bow rope, I scrabbled clumsily onto the ledge. I pulled the boat tightly against the side of the ledge and reached down for the paraffin jug.

"Aaiee!" I shrilled like a mezzo-soprano. The great fish, for fish it seemed to be, lunged at the boat and nearly jerked the rope from my hand! In the dim light, I could see its eye, dull and gray-black. It seemed to study me before turning away. The creature appeared two metres long! Impossible, I thought. Trembling like I had the ague, I pulled the boat close in again and snatched the jug to me. In my fright, I nearly overbalanced the side. I saw the water ruffle as the creature shuttled back and forth along the far side of the boat.

I filled the largest lantern and lit it. I turned the flame to its lowest setting, which would show far across the water but last for many hours.

"My friend, if you allow me to pass once more this morning, I promise I will bring you a gift the next time my boat embarks on your waters."

It circled lazily closer. I could see a bit of the head; pale whiskers, as long and thick as driving whips bracketed that wide, frowning mouth.

I seemed to hear it say, "I am no friend, no companion. I will see you sleep in the dark waters, and sooner than you think."

My launch of the tiny craft would have been admired by the ballet master. With the lightest, most delicate steps, I lowered myself to the floor of the boat, sank lightly to the seat, and took up the oars. I dipped the outside oar into the water, only to have the creature smash into the blade.

"Shhhh…" I whispered soothingly, either to myself or to the animal.

"ssshhh…." floated across the water back to us.

I gripped the oars more firmly while relaxing my arms, the better to pull smoothly and evenly across the water. My underwater accomplice—or was he my adversary?—bumped into the hull of the boat the entire way across the water. Never had the short journey seemed so endless!

However, I arrived safely to the shore and scrambled to dry land. I pulled the boat higher ashore and rolled it over. There was what I took to be a drainage hole in its bottom, sealed with a deeply-set cork. I loosened this cork to the point where it sealed the bung, but a merest nudge would dislodge it. Oh, so carefully, I turned the craft back over, holding the bow above the ground with its rope. I moved it to the shore and let it glide into the shallows, out of the creature's reach. I anchored the rope underneath a stray chunk of building block.

I hurried up the stairs, pausing at the top to look back across the lake. The light I had left on the far ledge shone dimly across the midnight darkness of the undercroft. From here, one could imagine a poorly hidden lair tucked among the lower arches.

I hurried to my recess behind the scenery room. My quarry soon arrived, alone but for his sword. He entered and looked about impatiently. He paused, muttering to himself.

"Ah, you dared to keep our rendezvous! Congratulations on your… bravery." I spoke mockingly, pitching my voice to the corner of the room.

"Where are you? Show yourself!" demanded Philipe.

"Ah, can't you tell? Over here. No, here, you stupid man. Can you not hear?"

As I moved about in my passageway, I taunted him to lure him deeper into the labyrinth. "Behind the closet, you buffoon. No, not that closet. Are you an imbecile? Yes, this one. Strike a light to the lantern on that table and follow me down this corridor…coward."

"You are the coward! Hiding and running away!"

"Then run after, if you dare."

He lit the small lantern and ducked through the tiny door at the back of the cupboard. He was too unsure of his bearings to do without the light; I could see him clearly, but he could only see me when I chose to reveal myself. He knew nothing of how sounds carried within the various hallways and cubbies, where my voice would echo, amplify, or fade.

I sidled down the narrow passages, now and again providing tantalizing glimpses of my cape, now closer, now farther away and farther away, allowing my voice to fade to greater distance. At last, I left him in the corridor, which would allow him to stumble onto one of the doors to the stairway of the lake.

I slipped through a small hidden trap door leading to my darkest recess. At long last, the Compte blundered through the door to one of the stairways and came down to the shore.

The Lake

"I see you…" I whispered into the echoing vault. He looked vainly for the source of the sound.

"Put down your light, moronic man," the whisper came back across the water to him. He set it down and looked around again. Finally, his eye fell on the dim light reflected off the distant archways.

"How did you get there?" his voice thundered resoundingly.

"You will never find the passageway," I taunted, "I merely wanted you to understand that I exist forever beyond your reach."

He stomped back and forth along the shore, cursing extravagantly, but finally, the fool descried the boat through the archway to his right.

He did not pause to consider why a boat would be conveniently floating near the shore but splashed into the shallow water and stepped into the boat. He pushed off with one of the oars, and I was pleased to hear the bottom of the boat scrape slightly against the gravelly shore under it.

He began rowing with energetic strokes toward his destination. A few meters short of the ledge, he realized that his craft was filling with water. He did not know that a pale shadow beneath the lake's surface was eagerly circling.

He failed to see this, so intent was he on finding the Phantom behind the still-glowing lantern on the narrow ledge. He pulled the boat beneath the low arch and then close to the ledge. Standing shakily in the bottom of the boat, he poked about the ledge with his sword.

"Wrong again," I called to him and stepped into view on the opposite shore. He bent over to peer under the arch. I believe, at this point, he saw me. The boat rode lower in the water, and he turned it about to head back across the water.

"You will never make it back to me, foolish man."

"Do you think I don't know how to swim?"

"Your sword will weigh you down."

"I am no weakling," he retorted, and to prove this, he dove over the side of the nearly sunken craft. He came to the surface, swam a stroke, and then ducked beneath the surface. A moment later, his head broke above the water.

"My God! What is that?" he cried. I raised my light beside my face; I am sure he saw me as I removed my mask with the other hand. He gasped, and before he could take another breath, he disappeared again.

The next time he appeared, swimming vigorously, he spat out a mouthful of water and was able to gasp, "Help me!"

I called to him. "Farewell, Sir Comte!" This time, I am sure he saw me before going down again.

The last time he broke the lake's surface, his wild eyes stared at me. "Mercy, Monsieur," he gurgled.

I called to him as he struggled to stay afloat. "I will convey your good wishes to your brother, the young Vicomte, the next time I see him. I may even let him live."

Even at that distance, the despair was evident in his eyes. He disappeared for the final time.

I turned my back to him contemptuously, mask in one hand and lantern in the other, and began to saunter to the stairs. I paused and looked back. The ripples glided to the shore, bounced back, and met more ripples, wrinkling the lake's surface like a crepe. The lake became smooth once again.

I considered the situation. I could now continue my courtship of Christine unhindered by Philipe de Chagny, but more problems now presented themselves.

Would the creature remain in the lake or escape through whatever hole had allowed him to enter the lake? My boat was gone. However, was I to convey Christine to my sumptuous den beyond the water?

I dismissed the concern. Boats? The Opera contained many boats in the scenery room. I would find a craft suitable for my beloved.

I addressed the creature. "We have helped each other, Monsieur Predator. I have brought you a meal, and you have rid me of a problem. We are even. Perhaps you will allow me passage in the future."

I watched the lake for some sign the creature heard me, even so much as a ripple, but the surface remained an eerie black mirror. With a bow of my head, I began the climb back to the Opera house.

THERE IS INDEED A "LAKE" in the underground passages of the Paris Opera House. It's a cistern fed by roof water, and while it is nothing near the size of the Phantom's underground lake, it is extensive enough for the Paris fire department to train there. It is rumored that a large white catfish is living in the lake as well. But how it got there, nobody dares tell.

EXEUNT.
FLOURISH.

Peter Dubé

IE AND LEARN. I BEGIN this way not because the more common "live and learn" is untrue, but because it is woefully incomplete. Death—after all—reveals so much: the dark and then the awakening, the simultaneous liberation and constraint, timelessness and insistent instantaneity alike. The marriage of opposites and a fatal lack of intimacy.

To us, death has revealed a paradox. Once the search for a phantom enlivened this place. The searchers found only a man—the man I then was: angry, filled with a passionate rage at the injustices I had suffered. A man willing to live in a kind of permanent exile from the world provided I could seek an awful vengeance. Willing to terrorize , to kill, to destroy mindlessly. Now, however, these halls are stalked by veritable phantoms that go unsought. Phantoms like the man, or thing, I now am. All but motionless in the end, dwelling in a half-life of shadows. What became of the old rage and the strength that fed on it? Both simply gone, vanished ... There are phantoms and then there are phantoms; that much we have learned. The darkness has been a great instructor here in the magnificent classroom in which we now find ourselves contained.

This place, the aptly name *Palais Garnier*, is a case study in ways that far exceed simply my companion and me. It holds undying images of Orpheus and Hermes, unchanged by their passage through the underworld. Its sweeping staircase, surfaces of marble and artificial zodiac overhead never alter. They too are changeless. All of this wonder: the passages and salons, these proliferating layers of shadow and glittering golden counterpoint *endure*. That is true as well of all those false worlds wrought on magical flats and packed away backstage: foreshortened pyramids, impenetrable forests, shorelines battered by an unvarying tempest.... And my favourite among the sets—a great church in flames.

Despite having been host to the horrors of my rage once upon a time, this place is, and always has been, a sort of jewel box. A decorative container made to enclose precious things, objects rich and beautiful. And we—in some ways its most precious trinkets now, despite ourselves—are trapped in it and can never leave. But these artifices edify as they dazzle, just as they were meant to. More contradictions, more mystery.

The music, the great performances can walk out of this place in the memories of the men and women who come to be enchanted and who leave transformed. But after so many years I can only think that we.... We have been forgotten. And we can never leave.

I know for a certainty, from the gossip in the halls and anterooms, that the tale told by the Persian, as he was then called, though he's had other names, was never truly believed. He was too insistent that he *should* be believed, and too flamboyant in his presentation. He was often too flamboyant. The extravagance of that astrakhan hat still summons a smile with each recall. Seeing it was a small pleasure, and I had so few in the days of my anger. The written accounts that followed, moreover, and I have seen my share over the years to pile up since the crucial moment made its brief-lived stir—provoked speculation and credence in equal measure; they amused and frightened, entertained and provoked, but could never be confirmed. Tall tales bestrode the days for a time, but became a sort of legend, and the events themselves have now vanished into time. The truth passed into the dark with the protagonists and my old vigour alike.

The truth is that Christine and the *Vicomte* never did go North; they died. But no one sought them out; they went unfound and unsaved because *le tout Paris* believed they had escaped, and hence never really looked for them. I of course was known to have shuffled off the mortal coil and was left in peace. Of a sort. Having heard and seen so much and for so long, it is curious that the one thing that remains misty to me is how I then came to this place, or rather, how *we* did.

I awoke, I know not where. I remember no details of that indefinite place. However, I have the sense that we were called here to the *palais* from some nothingness. That we came in response, appropriately enough, to the call of music, the very magic that was the heart of our mortal lives. Or partial music, perhaps. Something that felt like melody but for which I have no fitting word. I know music well enough and know that this summons was *similar*… but not identical with it. I was in a space without forms when it came; I saw nothing, heard nothing and was surrounded with only the possibility of shape and sound—not its actuality. Still, I could move in my way and followed this possible, this rapturous, fabulous something through veils of grey and off-white, shrouds of rippling shadow. I perceived gaslight, fire, glitter and kept going, through what might have been streets, or could have been caverns. I moved without feet, without hands for climbing, but no obstacle prevented progress. I moved with certainty but without knowledge. I had no sense of what was happening. Only the might-be-music signified.

I remember knowing who I was, and I remembered my suffering and my crimes alike since, in a sense, they were who I was, who I had been. A horror, a killer, a living fear. But I saw and felt nothing of the place and present. I had no sensory apparatus to do so; was I nothing but remembrance then? A nothing who could think? Because I did.

The moon was overhead, I thought. Directly overhead; it did not move. Not an inch, not a spot, not a smidgen. Nor did morning come. Where was the sun? Where was time? The wind came, a breeze. It passed right through me.

Below: the streets. Unpeopled streets. Where were the crowds? I saw no bodies, but could pick out their shadows, nonetheless. What was going on? I anticipated crowds and saw none. Yet heard something. And in the distance saw the dome of the *Pavilion de l'empereur.*

In what might have been a breath or could have been a season, even a year, I arrived here. I remember slipping through the strings of a lyre: Apollo's. I recall passing through a window, or was it a mirror? Entering a glistening marble hall and being swallowed. Then I fell. I plunged through blank space, through marble, through porphyry, and through gold. I slid past candles and painted surfaces and then through what might have been caves. I reached and stopped at water, but did not sink. I walked, or did what passed for walking. Then I met her; the first perception I was certain of, and she was wrapped in music. The very glory of sound that had been our transport. Stunned, I thought, I asked—how deep was her kindness, her pity? I knew from past gestures, a gentleness, a kiss, it was deeper even than the waters on which we stood. It gave me peace; it brought on calm.

Then the question became who are we? Who travels on sound? Who might these waters reject? We rested on its surface, our footsteps causing not a ripple, no proof of movement whatsoever. No evidence of our being. Or being there. Imperceptible. Or so it seemed to me. Though I knew *she* knew my presence. And so, I moved towards her calling out her name.

"Christine!" For a moment even the memory of the old pain faded.

And the answer came but it was not her voice, nor my own echoing through the cavernous space. From some deep well of sound I heard a garbled response, not quite comprehensible… but that I would still swear sounded like "angel of music" to me. Though it could not be. And I say as much after having seen years of the impossible parade through these august halls and vaults. So laden with legend. So heavy with account. And have heard of even greater oddities taking place beyond these busy walls.

All that aside, she knew I was before her. And in time we "spoke" though the word is imprecise. We recognized each other, and we knew the space we inhabited. And would.

I moved towards her, closer and closer. She spread her arms, extended them to me. I wanted to rush, but only glided. I reached her and passed through. No touch. No contact. Whatever I was passed through the shell of whatever she was and left her behind.

I turned back to be sure. It was confirmed. The glittering shade from which voice flowed was there. We would spend weeks trying to make sense of this extraordinary moment. We would attempt the embrace time and again, day after day. Every attempt producing the same result. Frustrated one day, I attempted to lift a candle, my hand passed through the gilded candelabrum and yet the thing rattled as it did. I tried again, this time to tilt a chair: a not dissimilar result. I couldn't grip the thing; my hand traversed the substance and yet the inanimate thing *did notice* it seemed to me. But touch each other? Never. She and I could never come to grips. And yet we could make sound. Of a sort.

Sound we could make: song, whisper, echo, if rarely totally clear speech. That was my salvation; I could in my way talk to her at least.

For some time, we tested what was possible to us. I learned in running through the ranked flats that one might tip over as I did so. Landscape. Architecture. Mythic adventure. That tumbling opened the door for us; some amusement might still be had. When the battlements of Elsinore fell, I threw back my head and let the words of my *Don Juan Triumphant* ring out in the empty hall. It lacked body but could echo off the roof still. Resounding if hollow. Rich in timbre if paradoxically—at the same time—thin. A vibrato lurking, as ghostly as we, in the background. For a moment I felt my old vigour, transformed, fill me once again. A memory, but one embodied, or given new and ghostly form. We learned in this testing of our limits that the folk in the seats could hear something of the noise we made, even if faintly or unsteadily. And more than once as we reached out towards them, we heard them speak—of a coldness in the air, a chill and unusual current of air or a breeze rushing by. I found that very interesting. Very interesting indeed. And though real touch was impossible we could unsteady hair or hatpins, collars and scarves and brooches in small ways. Make them fall from necks and ears, send them tumbling some slight distance. That too pleased us. Of course.

In time, with such tests done and validated, our learning created possibilities. We could, we realized at almost exactly the same time, have fun. We had much time to fill after all. Who would have thought that hauntings arise from boredom rather than bitterness?

At first, we did small things. We would pass down a row or aisle watching the patrons turn in their seats seeking a cause for the chill — some suddenly open door or window. Some wayward wind. Finding nothing. Soon enough we would jostle their jewels, send an earring falling to the floor, or a necklace tumbling. This amused us greatly; the concern shown by the *grand dames* was near panic beneath a genteel front. For a while this was enough. Over time, however, we discovered there were some that could "see us," though the characterization is inexact. They could make out some cloudy thing in their presence, but "sense us" is a better word than 'see". That possibility would prove to be great fun indeed. We were glad of it.

WHEN WE STUMBLED UPON SUCH a case, Christine and I would turn around him or her, pulling hideous faces, grimacing and gesturing menacingly as we moaned with long, slow breaths. The chosen individual, whether it was by actual sight, or some other means of perception invariably responded. Pulling back, turning away, or — in the most memorable cases—running from us headlong. We delighted in this; such moments were the only times in long years when we found it in us to laugh out loud. To our delight, our laughter appeared to be even more frightening. The targets' fear grew wilder. Only once did we question this game of ours. Wonder if we were guilty of cruelty. On that occasion, a man in middle age ran from us in utter terror. Headlong he tore towards the exit. He tripped; he fell to the glossy marble stairs with a violent noise. There was a terrible moment of stillness. In the dim light we beheld the most extraordinary thing. A mist, thick and ovoid rose from his body. It split into parts; what seemed like a pair of legs, a left arm, then a right. We saw, turning to each other for confirmation; we saw what had to be his soul leave his body. I remembered the rage that led to a man hanging in the opera. This was different though—an accident. Still, if I could have, I would have taken Christine's hand in mine.

Were we to have new company? Despite our best efforts we were often lonely. We knew each other too well, perhaps. A change might have been welcome.

But no; the misty shape rose towards the distant ceiling and vanished at length. There was nothing to hold him here, unlike us. We must stay; he was free, his spirit was not tied to the Opera. Only the motionless flesh remained on the ground. A small crowd of people gathered around it. We withdrew. After that we returned for a long while to our smaller pranks. Vanishing jewels. Cold breezes. And sound. Indeed, our love of sound grew vaster as it reached back to what we loved in it in life.

It was then we started to sing again. As we had before. Sometimes we would sing after the curtain came down and as the audience departed. Those nights we could see their steps visibly quicken as they made their way back to the world. Sometimes we would sing even as the performance unfolded, our voices blending with those of the living; then some heads would turn, scanning the room as if in search for something. A handful of Paris' eminent ladies would lift hands to their brows. Some slight, decorative young man might straighten suddenly in his seat—suddenly overwrought it seemed to their companions, who leaned in to whisper in their ears. Others in the house brought their hands down on their armrests with uncommon force. Even we could hear it; in some indefinable way the quality of the sound in the massive hall had changed. Had been transformed; it was wonderful.

At length we even began to sing when the Opera was closed, the auditorium and boxes empty. We would sing only for our own pleasure. In the sound we could find something, at least, that resembled life. The rush, the climb and the descent. The long, sustained notes the evidence of both strength and struggle. We were our true selves for a moment again.

Days and weeks, months and years ticked by filled with tricks and music. We were changeless, but we knew that the world, outside our palatial home, and prison, had moved on. The patrons spoke of it. New tools and new people. Proliferating railways crossing all of France, all of Europe. Great fortunes were being built and falling. Hideous crimes took place. Great artists saw their fame grow and their works take on vast weight. And war. Rumours of war came too: in murmured conversations, carried on in voices thick with tension. The world kept turning. Kept changing. Only we stayed the same. Each endless day and every dimly-lit night free of variation. Or mostly free of it. This drained us.

I can recall one completely unexpected night, however. It came during the time when the talk of war was almost constant and affected even us. Often, I would long to hold my companion in my arms and comfort her; this was not possible. We would sing together instead. Despite all efforts, the talk of war went on, grew louder. Soon great whistling roars filled the air and something terrible shook the ground. The crowds at the Opera grew smaller. We were more and more alone. Though never entirely alone, never completely at peace. There were nights we moved though hall, the corridors, the hidden chambers in perfect silence looking for something for which we had no name. We would have cried but were unable.

Then another strange thing came. An unhappy thing. One night a small stream of richly-dressed aficionados filed into the auditorium. One after another, or two by two, they came and found their seats The minutes ticked by. In short order a pair of strangely-dressed men came in. Both wore pitch black tunics and highly polished knee-high boots. On both heads was an equally black peaked cap adorned with a grim, grinning skull. It was like nothing I'd seen before, as were the expressions on the faces beneath the brims. Usually people enter the hall smiling, eagerly anticipating the music they know is to come. Not these men; they were ferociously serious. Faces set, almost grim. There was no evidence of anticipatory joy in them. They walked in stiffly and were greeted by an usher, who began to guide them to their seats which, it seemed, were expensive ones, very near the front of the hall.

Their voyage was not to be long. The small group were a little more than half-way down the aisle when I saw first one, then another, then several more men rise from their places and slip into the aisle behind them. It must have been six in all and they walked swiftly, but with care to make no sound, until they were right behind the grim pair.

Two lights flashed, reflections of the dim house lights off steel, two knives. The blades vanished in a flash, the twin weapons buried into the lower back of two of the sinister invaders. One hit the ground in an instant then some strap or garrote wrapped around the one who wouldn't fall. He fell.

We waited. Where was the mist?? Where the spirits fleeing the finish of the flesh. There were none. Just crumpled corpses sprawled across the luxury of marble. Nothing else. But where were these men's souls? Who is without such? Could one come into being without one? Can one destroy it even while living? I cannot know. I suspect no one can. Still, I can say, I saw no evidence of spiritual existence in these men. Nor did Christine; she said as much—crying out in the very instant.

The curtain did not rise. But the news to reach us through the much diminished crowds in the weeks and months that followed the violent night grew stranger and more sinister. The world had taken a truly dark turn it seemed, though we would never see it.

So, we sighed, and we sang, alone in the dark. We rose and sang. And would do so for years.

Standing in the dark, facing each other, we would offer up music! Our voices would rise, strong with passion, trembling with the sense of something just out of reach. Some knowledge, some understanding. We would choose, increasingly the most tragic moments from the canons of opera. The tone of our voices echoing and sobbing as we did. Longing, fear, and desolation became our repertoire. And our pranks and japes became less frequent. They had lost much of their sparkle for us. It took but little time before the tragic arias became the dominant strain of not just our "public" haunting, but of our private communion as well: the music we would make when the hall was largely empty, and no one strode the stage—when no crowds made their way to seats or lingered at the bar finishing slim flutes of champagne. Still Mimi would die in our voices; Cavaradossi ever faces his end.

Time and again I would attempt to take my companion in my arms as our last plangent notes faded; time and again I would fail. Over and over touch, even the merest contact was impossible. As it always had been. And yet the feeling of failure was radically transformed for us as the world changed. Even second-hand, as the news of the transformations came to us, it had an unusual weight.

It troubled me. It troubled me at my heart, as it were, in the deep places of my aging soul.

So, I asked Christine how things were for her. In not quite words, in not ordinary music, but I asked, and she heard.

Her answer unnerved me. "It all feels rote, now." At the end of the phrase, she fell silent My malaise deepened because I knew too intimately what she meant. Nothing meant anything anymore.

I told her more of my thoughts. Was it possible that we had fallen out of the world… that there was nothing left for us here but to get out of this mad halfway place? And is not the true depth of our tragedy not only that nothing happens to us, nothing matters to us, but that we are acting out roles, merely playing the imaginary personae that we ourselves created ages ago, but that we no longer have the power to realize. We can never change, grow, deepen. We are forever as we are. We are timeless and might last forever. Just like these myths painted on the walls of our palace-prison. But, terrible truth, eternity is not for the likes of us. It is for objects, not subjects.

And, worse by far, though we are both trapped, we are in essence alone. We can never again touch each other. We can only share the idle games with which we try to fill the great hole of forever. And they are failing us.

What can be done. I heard her in my way.

We can create new roles, like we used to. I have no idea where the thought came from.

We can sing ourselves out of this trap. It is the only meaningful contact we've had in decades; perhaps we are permitted it for this very reason. Whoever it is that permits now.

But we have been singing for all of those decades her answer came back.

Yes, I said, but we have sung, in all this time, only for an end. To frighten, to fill time. We must sing now only for the music. As we did when we lived. We must sing not to kill pain, or time, or ennui; we must sing for the rapture of the sound. We must lose ourselves in it utterly, abandon instrumentality, leave behind purpose. We must dissolve in the act of creation; this is an ecstasy every artist knows. A place every one of us has been. But we must turn ourselves over to it; having only half a form anyway, we may achieve a more perfect dissolution in creating. Fade from these shades we have become and perhaps be united in a new thing. A sound. A sound that might at last be remembered and carried on. That might in a way we both know, live. I felt Christine nodding at me, and at the angel of music she loved and dreamed still of knowing.

So, I sang. I opened myself up, all voice, and the sound came rushing. This was not the song we'd served up to the *palais* whether empty or overfull; this was my sound, calling out to join hers. To become one glory of music.

And she joined me.

The music rose. Our voices ascending, tremulous at first, but in the swelling the sound becomes a mass of glittering particles. As if our breath and call filled with invocation and praise were enough to strip the gilding from the balustrades and frames, cornices and cupolas and send it forth, a tempest of light. I hear the glitter, then I see it. Then as the legion of tiny lights rush for some central point, the vision is transfigured. The motes of luminescence are swarming through a denser space, a black one—both thick and heavy. Soil, or loam perhaps.… They move with lesser speed but greater determination as if tunnelling towards some impossible-to-know destination. Some source. Rushing with an effort that is clear yet incomprehensible.

I see, at last, the goal. A knot, translucent, the thing shimmering too. A nucleus. Or egg. A seed. The glittering torrent, our voices, rush to it and circle; orbiting the thing and yet still very much our swelling song. It seems, somehow, the seed itself is us, condensed and transformed by a great weight of earth and resting at the deepest point of some enormous chain of caverns. We are returning gold to the deepest part of the world, from whence it came. Coming home.

And then another change. The dark seed thuds like a beating heart, the rhythm of our singing as its guide. Or are we pulled into the pace set by the thing? Rise. Fall. Rise. Fall. Rise. Until.…

The seed cracks open and extends these nimble tendrils. The light of our singing is swallowed up by them. Absorbed. But we sing on. The tendrils, spreading roots whose substance is all voice. Entwining and extending. Seeking out hidden worlds and entangling. My voice, Christine's, given form and substance beyond simple song. The roots dig, tunnel and discover. They pass teeming insects; ignore the dark earth and simply spread. Splitting the seed, breaking its walls and making new space. Then a thick new shape and volume suddenly erupts. Erect. Heading straight overhead. Where the vault might be, were we still in the familiar trap of the Opera. We are not; our rising voices given body rear upwards. Meet the pressure and push on. Strike sunlight. One deep breath and the expansion. The body-voice stretches, vibrato, falsetto and the note. That one! The voice spreads its arms. And there are more arms yet to spread. They extend as did the roots. Two more boughs break free of the rising trunk. The song yields growth—a tree; the golden sap of life, all sound, made to quiver, shaken by the wonder caught in our throats. Its last exultation as it joins the sunlight once again. Among the roots we watch it find its home, our shades shivering as others enter the horizon. More shadows for companions. Still the sound spreads out a branch that reaches into a miraculous city I almost recognize but don't. Another bough embraces shining wind and shakes as a flotilla filled with tales reaches a new world. The tree of our singing, fed by our song, our breath, our unnatural life, spreads out through universes past counting while we cannot move; our voices joined in the rapture grow and we can only fade in this achievement. The tree extends and all at once, I see it bloom ever so briefly—erupt in flower. Every bough and twig afire with colour and perfume.

My voice catches in my throat. Christine's stumbles by my side. Her hand reaches towards me. Will it touch; it passes through. The song falls, its timbre dripping from the fading blossoms. Suddenly, breathless and anticipating, the song is gone, as if a great curtain had fallen, vast as a horizon, impenetrable and final. Darkness takes the world and a wondrous black light, glowing without revelation—illuminating nothing—beckons from a far horizon. Further yet.

And then, at last: silence takes the stage, and we are done. We exit.

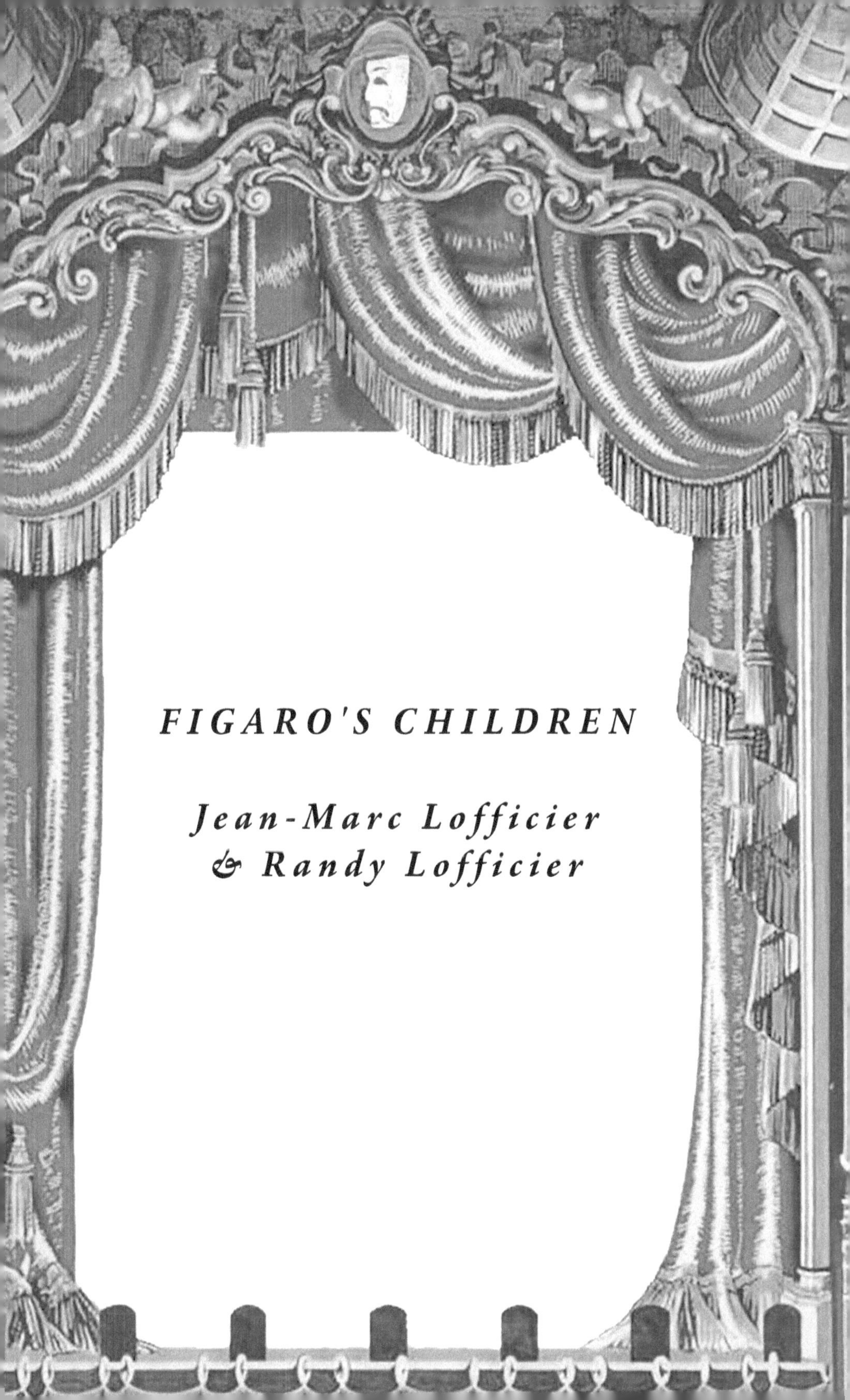

FIGARO'S CHILDREN

Jean-Marc Lofficier
& Randy Lofficier

F IGARO WAS THE ONLY ONE in the Opéra not afraid of Erik.

Figaro was a cat.

Pardon, Figaro was a *chatte*, a lady cat (in every sense of the word), but it had always been a tradition to name the Opéra's cat Figaro, and gender had not been deemed enough to upset that tradition.

Every rat the rat-catcher did not get, Figaro made a meal of it. She was welcome everywhere, above and under the Opéra.

And, as we said, she was the only resident of that prodigious building who was not afraid of Erik. She purred when he caressed her, came occasionally to visit him, begging for treats (she loved dates) and generally behaved like a proper little lady around him.

There was one man, however, who did not like Figaro: Antoine Manoukian, a *machiniste* who, unbeknownst to Management, raised rabbits in a hutch in the third level. Manoukian thought that Figaro ate his baby rabbits, and truth be told, not all baby rabbits' disappearances could be blamed on rats.

When the season came, Figaro had kittens. In those days, the Rue Scribe was a notorious Heaven for cat dalliances.

Manoukian was prepared to put up with one Figaro, if only because he knew that to do otherwise would mean to be ostracized by the rest of the staff, but not a chowder of Figaros.

So, very stealthily, he managed to grab all the helpless little kittens and stuffed them into a bag, weighing it with a stone, intending to drown them into the Lake.

Mewling bag in hand, he approached the dark water's edge.

Antoine Manoukian's body was found floating in the Seine the next day. Cause of death: drowning, presumably accidental.

Figaro's children still roam free today under the Opéra.

Ask anyone.

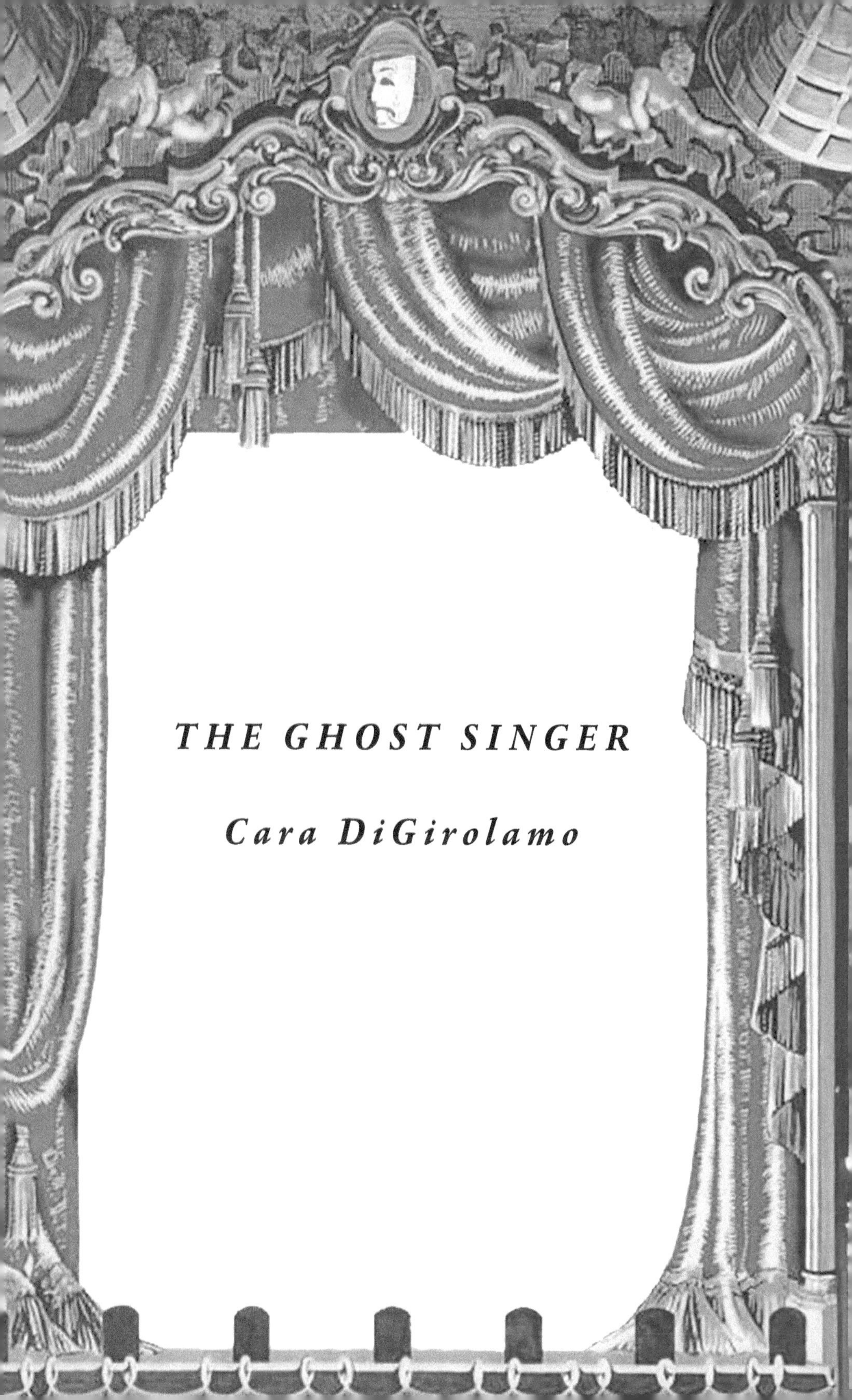

THE GHOST SINGER

Cara DiGirolamo

MY INTEREST IN THE OCCULT began at age fourteen when my parents took me to Paris. The trip was excitingly impromptu, and I was mesmerized by the electrical exhibition, the modern buildings, and most of all, the opera.

The news was thick with curious rise of Mlle. Christine Daae and her patron, the Opera ghost. I begged to attend the one-night performance of *Don Juan Triumphant*. My parents did not find the subject of Don Juan suitable for a girl my age, so instead we attended a matinee of Gounod's *Romeo and Juliet*. The following day, we heard of the chaos at the evening performance: the kidnapping, the torch-lit hunt through the basements for a monster, the falling chandelier. An old friend of my father's, Count Luis Diego, died that night, in his box at the opera. He was ninety-six and had a bad heart, but the nearness of death shocked me. When I looked again at Paris, I saw the world transformed, made of two connected parts—both spirit and science, with a permeable veil between the living and the dead.

I did not then understand how right I was. Much later I discovered we had gone on holiday because a young woman had been found dead in a flat only a few doors down from our Oxford house—her face slashed to ribbons and a rope around her neck. "Apparently, after being attacked in her own home," the *Oxford Gazette* reported, "Miss ——— hanged herself, for what life could a disfigured woman hope for?"

If my parents' intent was to protect me from the horror of death, they did not succeed. The disaster at the Palais Garnier led me to attend my first séance, and that to everything that happened after.

A few years later, in London, I attended a séance conducted by the famed Madame Giry—once a dancer at the Palais Garnier. I had not been able to settle in at school and my parents worried I was not mature enough for courtship either, but I distracted myself from these troubles with spiritualism. At the séance, I met the most handsome young couple I'd ever seen. The young lady—tall and fair, with sharp blue eyes and a boyish figure—was *Australian*. She had a confidence to her step and a pertness to her words— talking of growing up "mustering" sheep on horseback and shooting tiger-snakes in the "bush"—that impressed me deeply. She'd been to finishing school in Switzerland, she said, "but the finish didn't take." Her husband was the younger brother of Anthony Flyte, M.P., one of the young lights of the Liberal Unionist party. Anthony was known to be the concerned, sober, and serious sort. His brother was the opposite—charming, handsome, and prone to tease, with a long narrow chin, skeptical eyebrows, and flowing sand-colored hair bound by a ribbon into a romantic queue. His name was Leo and hers Catherine and he called her "Kate" and kissed her in public. I fell in love with love the day I met them.

We introduced ourselves in the crowded parlor of Madame Giry's rented salon, over insipid tea and cheap biscuits, as everyone recovered from the thrill of conversing with spirits. Such beautiful people overawed me, and to make conversation I started rambling about my favorite topic—my spirit guide, a little Apache girl called Lilhe'e. We'd met during my first séance in a shabby

English tearoom in Paris, and I'd asked to speak to her at every séance since. My despairing father tried to remind me that the Apache were the most violent and dangerous of Indian tribes in the Western Territories of America—they would set upon even their brothers in their berserk blood-lust!—but I would not believe a word of it. Lilhe'e seemed the sweetest girl, even if each spiritualist spoke in a wildly different version of her native patois (one had even made her sound like a French gangster) and, after that first night, invariably called her Lily. In my last session, Lilhe'e had told me of her journey to a holy mountain, where she walked through dreams seeking her sister who had been stolen by Death. It was very exciting. I'd hoped Madame Giry would continue the tale—a talking bear had just appeared—but unfortunately, I had not received a message from the Other Side at this particular event.

After relating all of this, I noticed, to my horror, the crinkled eyes and quirked smiles of the young couple and realized from the strain in my chest that I spoke for full minutes without stopping for breath. I gasped air in, and as a distraction from my silliness, quickly asked them who *they* had hoped to speak to. Madame Giry had not addressed a message to them either.

"Her mother," said Leo. Kate batted him on the arm. "Or perhaps *not* her mother."

"Oh no," I said. As if talking too much wasn't bad enough, now my excitement seemed tactless; other people were here to assuage their grief! "She has passed?"

"No," said Kate. "She said she would send me messages by the spirits, since she can't be bothered to write letters, and telegrams from Australia are too expensive."

I took a moment to understand, then I choked out an awkward laugh. Leo and Kate joined in, and my awkwardness faded into delight at being in such friendly company.

They were both like that, always joking, calling each other "darling," and being the most charming and sociable people I'd ever met. I was a silly child who talked too much about the spirits, but they didn't mind. That very day they invited me to lunch, and in no time at all, I had become their particular friend. They took me to the opera and parties in London, and in the summer, they picked me up in Oxford on their way to Flyte house in the Welsh Marches for what Kate called "tremendous larks." There Leo tossed me up to ride pillion with Kate, and we'd charge up into the hills for a picnic. In the afternoon, Leo and I lounged in the shade—him finishing the wine and me the cheese—and cheered as Kate cantered across the field, showing off her new tricks. The most terrifying one was where Kate, astride a broad-backed stallion wearing only a blanket and bellyband, drew her feet up, tucked them under the band, and rose to ride while standing. She threatened to learn to stand on her hands on horseback next. Leo taught me to choose good wine and be rude in French, Kate taught me to spin her silver pocket-knife on my finger and tie twenty different knots (though the only one I remembered was the Australian quick knot—uncomfortably similar to a noose), and the three of us argued for hours over croquet. That time was, for me at least, an idyll.

I met Leo's brother on those visits—Anthony—an earnest, heavy-browed young man, very serious about politics and deeply uninterested in spiritualism. He kept offering me improving philosophical books and disquisitions on natural history, which I found dull. He did like cards though, and I often partnered him at Russian Whist.

Though my parents were puzzled as to why this nice couple had taken such an interest in their silly daughter, the Flyte's friendship was, I am sure, what finally convinced my father I was mature enough for my debut (—that, and because after my mortifying ramble in Madame Giry's salon, I no longer asked to speak to Lilhe'e at séances). But on the summer night my parents hosted a small supper in my honor—we were not rich, nor noble enough to need to pretend to be—I wished my coming out party had never come. For instead of Leo and Kate arriving with good humor, charm, and laughter, dreadful news buzzed from guest to guest. A terrible accident had happened at Flyte manor, and young, beautiful Catherine Flyte was dead.

I FLED THE SUPPER AND didn't leave my bed for days. I sobbed heaving, wretched sobs, thinking of Kate's fearlessness and the wonderful tricks she did on her beautiful horses, how she'd wrapped a firm arm around my shoulders, and told tall tales about Australia (bouncing rats as big as a man, really? I didn't believe a word). I thought of how devastated Leo must be, and wept until my nose was chapped and my eyes were so swollen I could hardly see.

One memory made me feral with grief. Up in Kate's dressing room at Flyte house, while getting ready for a dance, Kate had spun me around to admire my dress. "Lovely, Rosalie," she said. "Leo will think so too. But if you're looking for a fellow, be careful. Leo's the jealous sort. He'll go into a tremendous rage if anyone dares be inappropriate." She tapped my nose teasingly. "Luckily I can be as inappropriate as I like." Then she kissed me, which was very exciting, though not particularly inappropriate.

I ached for her sisterly affection and Leo's brotherly defense of my honor. But my status as their cherished friend had died with Kate.

In the fall I met Leo again. I came upon him in an Oxford park quite near my family's home, sitting on a bench, as deflated as a pneumatic bicycle tire with a puncture. He'd cut his hair short; his long thin cheeks were now hollows. To me he looked like Jean ValJean, just out of prison, out of temper with this cruel world but too broken-down to rage at it. I told him just how sorry I was, and just how horrible it felt. Then—impetuous as always—I hugged him. He seemed startled at first, then overcome. He held me back, and I could feel his body tremble as he started to sob.

I DIDN'T THINK OF IT as a courtship. How could I? This was Kate's husband! My fierce belief in the existence of the spirit world made remarriage after death as shocking as remarriage after divorce was to a Catholic. They were still in love, still wedded. How could he adore anyone else? I was simply comforting him in his grief. Once he'd wept in my arms, I knew this was my divinely appointed duty. So even though my parents protested, when Leo returned to Flyte house, I went too.

Flyte house—once a bright and welcoming country estate—had become dour and dim with Kate gone. Most of the rooms were shut up, and only a few stone-faced servants remained. Leo ate little, drank excessively, and hosted no parties. Anthony stayed in town at his club, only coming down on the train for a few hours each month to meet with his steward.

On days when Leo shut himself up in his room and would not deign to be comforted, I found myself at loose ends. I roamed the old haunts where we three had spent the summer, but they were places of mourning now, and in each one I wondered if this was where Kate had died.

I finally decided that I needed to know. But when I asked a stableboy to direct me to the place, to my surprise, he shrugged. "It was in the house," he said. "I can't say where."

I realized then that, like most everyone in town, I had *assumed* that Kate had died in a riding accident. This was logical, with her half-trained stallions and tricks you'd see in traveling circuses. Darker ends had been suggested by those who thought Kate brazen and Leo dissipated. Some said she must have been pretending to be the young Annie Oakley and shot herself in the head. Others said she had smiled at a visiting vicar, and Leo—mad with love—had scalded her with boiling oil. Still others diagnosed the pox. Her honorable friends ignored such dastardly comments. Yet, the suggestions all had one element in common. They were disfiguring—a logical inference, as her funeral had been held with a closed casket.

The servants at Flyte house found my curiosity about Kate's place of death distasteful, but the more my questions were deflected and dismissed, the more desperate I became.

Eventually a young maid succumbed to pestering. She hadn't been in the house at the time, she said, but she'd heard the kitchen rumors. After supper the evening of her death, Mrs. Flyte—Kate—had gone into the gunroom, possibly to prepare for a hunt that weekend.

"If there were another reason I wouldn't know it, Miss," the maid said, in a difficult to follow Welsh lilt. "And I would not say it. Some in the kitchen whisper that homesickness got the better of her. But Mrs Kate was not at all prone to the melancholy. Bold and brash, perhaps, but so good humored—when Mr Leo is peevish, and Mr Flyte chiding, she can make them both laugh." *Could* make them both laugh. But neither the maid nor I corrected the phrase; we simply regarded each other in mutual anguish.

There had been a storm that night—an early summer roil—and what with the thunder crashing, the wind making shutters slam, and the limbs of trees cracking off like pistol shots, no one could say for sure whether anything they'd heard came from inside or outside the house.

"Mr Flyte pedaled over from the station on his new safety bicycle that night," the maid said. "The butler met him, wet as a water-rat, took his coat, and ordered a bath, but Mr Flyte seemed agitated for other reasons. He asked after his brother and sister-in-law. The butler told him that after supper Mr Leo had gone to his study and Mrs Kate to the gunroom.

"Then, hardly a spell later, Mr Flyte bellowed for a doctor. He burst out of the gunroom with Mrs Kate in his arms, all blood everywhere. Then he cried out 'Get my horse!' and rushed out of the house. Myrtle found Mr Leo curled up in the corner of the gunroom, white as a sheet, hands all over blood, shaking like a ghost had visited him. When I came back from my half-day, there were still rust-brown patches of dry blood on the table and floor. It stained, so we had to burn the furnishings."

Hearing the story did not soothe me. I was now desperate to know what dreadful accident had caused Kate's death! Had a pistol accidentally gone off when she was cleaning it? Had it been an accident at all? Someone had stolen the contents of the poor box at the church that same week-end. Perhaps a roaming vagrant had slipped in during the chaos of the storm, and, caught thieving, had stabbed Kate and fled.

The only person who surely knew was Anthony Flyte. But he had not returned to the mansion since I arrived and seemed unlikely to do so. Of course, I could not ask Leo. I would not dare remind him of such horrors.

I also could not countenance the idea mentioned by the young Welsh maid that "homesickness had gotten the better of her." Laughing, good-humored Kate would *never* have taken her own life.

But *had* she been laughing and good-humored in the months before she'd died? We'd taken a trip to Brighton in the early spring. Kate and I walked the chilly beaches while Leo, deeply unimpressed with February, drank brandy and coffee and read papers in the hotel. Kate had gazed silently across the mist-strewn grey sea with eyes just as grey and opaque.

"I'd like to go to America," she said, her voice quiet, as if she'd forgotten I was there. Then, in an abrupt change of attitude, she turned to me with a wicked smile. "You should come. Just us. We could go all the way West—seek out your little Apache dream-walker friend."

I had been too embarrassed by the mention of Lilhe'e—and astonished by the idea that she might be a dream-walker and not a ghost—to think much on Kate's tired face and longing gaze at that time.

Leo preferred quieter entertainments now that Kate was gone. We walked around the pond and sat quietly on the marble bench beneath the statue of Orpheus grieving and playing his harp. Even though we did not often speak of Kate, her presence was like the invisible Eurydice, gone before us, and we too weak, too human, to bid her return.

One evening, when the shadow of Orpheus stretched far enough to touch us, Leo turned to me and asked, "You loved Kate, didn't you?"

"Of course," I said, because . . . of course.

His face went a little pale, and his long narrow chin seemed sculpted from glass. "You never thought that she could . . . could *choose* to leave me. Did you?"

I shook my head, surprised by the question. They'd often argued—but they fought like siblings, fierce and merciless, yet always ending in jokes and laughter. No one was as loyal as Kate, or as unwilling to hold a grudge. "I couldn't care less about what they think," she'd always say, when people thought her Australian manners brazen or rude. "So why get upset? Living well is the best revenge."

"What would you say if you knew that—" Leo hesitated. "--that someone you cared for had done something dreadful? Something God considers . . . unforgivable?"

I felt like I'd swallowed a cannonball. Someone who did not know them might wonder if he were implying that Kate had been unfaithful. But that was not the 'leaving' I feared he meant. If Kate had left him—and the world—by the dreadful, unforgivable means of her own hand, I did not want confirmation that it was so.

But if she had done such a thing, would it change my feelings for her? "I don't think what someone does has much to do with whether you love them," I said, because it was true. If I could see Kate again, of course I would still love her. Leo's hand pressed over mine, and his grateful, sad eyes, made me wish I could be angry at Kate for abandoning him. But I only wished that she had trusted me enough to let me try to soothe her pain.

About a year after Kate's death, Leo showed signs of recovery. He started riding again, and he laughed at the silly things I too often said. He decided I needed to be more cultured and showed me the art prints and curios he'd collected during his time in Hong Kong. A year to the day after Kate passed, he came out of mourning and began wearing his dandy ties and waistcoats once again, taking me to lunch, and escorting me around the city.

Six weeks later, he asked me to marry him.

Perhaps it was foolish of me—all my friends told me so—but I had never imagined that our relationship was romantic. Of course I'd said "Yes!" to his sweet and earnest face—his slender, sculpted chin quavering with hope. But afterwards my own eager response shamed me. I had said yes without even *thinking* of consulting Kate.

Leo seemed surprised when I brought it up, but after I explained everything (and wept significantly) about how I could not bear to do anything that would make her unhappy or interfere with their reunion in the next life, he nodded, a firm set to his jaw. "Of course we must ask her," he agreed. "We will consult a medium."

There was a complication to this plan, however: a year before, in 1888, Margaretta Fox had confessed that the Fox sisters' communication with the spirits had been a hoax. Suddenly there was a new vogue in debunking spiritualists, and mediums were becoming far more cautious about what they promised to deliver.

We met with three, each of whom said that Kate enthusiastically supported our marriage; I wasn't convinced. When the first relayed her message, I knew Kate wouldn't have said it in such a formal way. At the second, I scoffed at the idea that Kate would think herself unworthy for not giving Leo children. The third gave Kate an absurd Russian accent; Leo and I made fun of her the whole way home.

Although we laughed, Kate not appearing left me worried and disheartened. I knew those mediums had never met her, in this world or the next. Perhaps it *was* true that we were only atoms, imbued with a little life and no immortal soul. Did that mean I would truly never see or speak to her again?

As I was already staying there, Leo and I began to reopen the Flyte country house and invite our social circle to visit. Even Anthony ventured down again. He called me in for an interview and asked if I was very happy, and if I had ever been interested in another man besides Leo. This question surprised me, until I saw him glance down at my hands in a pitiful sort of way, and I realized—to my utter shock—that Anthony Flyte *admired* me.

I immediately told Leo about the conversation, and he clasped my hand warmly—though, admittedly, a bit more fiercely than usual—and laughed. "Why wouldn't he admire you, Rosalie? You are the perfect, sweet, helpful, innocent girl. His favorite sort."

As I did not like being called innocent or sweet, this annoyed me. We cheerfully argued, and I complained about his bruising grip on my hand, which he brought to his lips to kiss better.

Then, as tenderly as he'd always kissed Kate, he kissed me.

A few months into our engagement, Leo asked me if I had heard of Madame Sara Mirza, the Persian Singer.

Madame Mirza was not a medium, he told me. She did not speak for the spirits, nor did she claim to summon them. She was an opera singer— though not a particularly well regarded one. Her face did not appear on the posters for Berlin's Staatsoper, or La Scala in Milan. Her haunting, distant mezzo-soprano was not the currently popular voice of the verismo era. But she had no shortage of invitations from a different sort of theater. Her performance was known to create an experience for those in her audience, one that put each listener in touch with the spirit they most longed to see. This left them shaken and moved, knowing for certain—by voice and look and word—that they had been, for the length of a song, reunited with their lost loved ones.

"I'd like to receive more than another of those unconvincing messages," Leo murmured into my hair as I examined the program he'd brought from town. "Perhaps she could let us talk to Kate herself. There are a few words I still wish I could say."

Most curiously, in her early career, Madame Mirza had been in the chorus at many ill-starred performances—with fires and on-stage deaths. She had even been on stage at the Palais Garnier the night the chandelier came down.

Like Leo, I did not want to hear Kate's words ventriloquized through some stranger's voice. I wanted to meet her face to face, hear that charming accent, and see those laughing blue eyes. I wanted to ask her the dozens of questions I had thought of while missing her, and to swear to her that I was no husband-stealing Jezebel, that I would only take care of Leo while she could not. But it was the singer's connection to that night at the Palais Garnier that made me certain she was exactly the right person.

So, Leo and I invited Madame Sara Mirza to Flyte house.

MADAME MIRZA WAS YOUNGER THAN I'd expected, but she had the lustrous dark eyes and glowing skin of someone who would look young for many years. She spoke English with a French accent, and French with a Russian accent, and though I do not speak Russian myself, Anthony, who did, said her Russian had an Armenian accent, though how he could tell, I will never know. Her frame was diminutive, but solid around the hips and stomach, and if she had been less poised and intent, I might have been disappointed. The combination of her unusual features and the reserved and icy intelligence behind her eyes made her terrifyingly beautiful—and also, unexpectedly, familiar. I wondered if I had seen her somewhere before.

She came a few days before the house party Leo had arranged—her performance was to be an evening's entertainment for the group—and as the lady of the house, I was required to entertain her. Unfortunately, this was a challenge as she did not ride, nor chat, nor enjoy fashion magazines, nor want to talk about spiritualism. She did, however, enjoy long solitary walks. So, I sent her out on one each morning, then quickly read the entire news-paper, collecting any topic of conversation I could find. It was deeply awkward, and for the first few days, I suspected that Madame Mirza was enjoying my discomfort.

But then we talked about Kate.

I didn't bring her up. Leo and I were cautious about how much information we gave mediums ahead of time, but it wasn't surprising that Sara Mirza knew about her. Her death and my and Leo's engagement had been the talk of the town for some time. My news-paper forays had also resulted in the discovery that Madame Mirza knew *everything*—the plans of anarchists and communists, the duplicity of the nationalists and the imperialists, the struggles of the temperance reformers and suffragists, and she had arch, dry opinions about them all. Why wouldn't she know about Kate?

Still, I was surprised when out of the blue she asked me if I had liked her.

"Of course!" I said, "She was boisterous and brave, never afraid to tell someone exactly what she thought of them. I do not think I have ever been so fond of *anyone*."

Unexpectedly, she too looked fond, in a way that made me trust her.

"So, you did not plot against her to steal her husband?" she asked me. I was so offended that she laughed. She was astonishingly pretty when she laughed, utterly unlike her usual stern glamor.

After that I told her everything about Kate, about our adventures, her worst jokes, and how she'd made me feel pretty and smart and grown-up when no one else did. I only kept to myself those moments when—I now realized—she had been sad.

Madame Mirza warmed to me and invited me on her morning rambles, which were unexpectedly energetic. We traversed the wood on animal paths instead of the bridle ones, dodged brambles and climbed over fallen logs that she would often walk atop, carelessly juggling a set of unusual objects she had brought along with her.

"I'm not a dancer anymore," she said, when I gawped at her leap from one unsteady fallen tree trunk to another. "But I do like to keep my foot in."

She also told stories. She claimed they were tales of Persian kings—all very romantic—but some were obvious retellings of potboilers I'd read in mystery magazines.

I asked her about the events at the Palais Garnier, but she said it was too tragic to be the subject of gossip. "All I can say," she advised, "is that it is a great evil when a person is driven out of the world, and just as much of an evil when people call obsession 'love'."

I begged for more, but she said it was so long ago she hardly recalled, then let it slip that it had been her first job after running away from an arranged marriage. This distracted me with wildly romantic impressions of her fleeing Persia in a camel caravan or by pirate ship. These inopportunely verbalized fancies she terminated abruptly with a raised eyebrow. "I was at school in Zürich," she said. "I took the train."

I cannot say what about her was true and what was invention. Anthony is sure she was some scruffy nobody who'd made up her history out of whole cloth, but he didn't hear how matter-of-factly she'd said, "I took the train." That story, at least, I believe.

THAT NIGHT, A MEMORY THAT I had forgotten returned. Kate and I had been poring over magazines in a tea room while a young man played jaunty popular tunes on the piano. Kate opened a spiritualist periodical to an article about a "Ghost Singer," who'd made a stir at a theater in Monaco. It included an etching of the unnamed woman's face. Kate paused to stare at it, then let out a low whistle. "She's spectacular, don't you think? If I were a ghost, I'd hang around her just for something to look at." Then a frown. "You know—she looks like a girl I went to boarding school with." She laughed and tossed the magazine at me, her cheeks flushing pink. "If it is her, she was the first girl I kissed. I would have kept in touch, but she got expelled for cheating the other girls out of their money at cards."

Kate had been to school in Zürich too.

WHEN THE HOUSE PARTY GUESTS began to arrive, I ended up with a thousand tasks and a score of servants to supervise as they prepared the food and rooms. So, Madame Mirza returned to her solitary walks. The morning of her performance, I had to hurry down to the gatekeeper's cottage to make certain he knew who was coming and to keep the lanterns lit; Anthony had an appointment in town but was hoping to catch the late train back in time for the show.

Near the gate, I caught a glimpse of Madame Mirza in the wood, speaking with a figure I didn't recognize. They did not seem to have noticed me, so I stepped behind a tree and stayed as silent as possible, endeavoring to hear what they were saying.

They spoke in soft voices, in a language I did not know, and I wondered if it was Persian. (Of course, it could have been Italian or Swiss-German or nearly anything, as my languages were limited to English and French).

The person appeared to be some kind of vagrant, dressed in a heavy wool coat with no buttons, the front tied together with twine. They wore a hat with a wide brim and a scarf wrapped up past their nose, but that was not enough to hide the horror of their face. Two parallel scars ran down one side, ugly and fleshy, like long poker burns, or like someone had sawn rough cuts with a breadknife and infection had lifted the skin between them like a rising cake.

I did not want to know what had become of their eye. Luckily it was patched.

I liked Sara Mirza, but so many spiritualists *were* con-artists. Was this her confederate? Did they plan to rob us?

I remembered the rumor that a thieving vagrant had murdered Kate and shivered. The thought was foolish and unlikely, but I couldn't help but wonder if he had returned for a second act.

When I returned to the manor, I spoke to Leo about my concerns.

"You agreed to invite her," he said, sounding a little snappish, as he sometimes got when he found my childishness annoying instead of amusing. (He'd gotten short with Kate too—for different reasons—but she wouldn't put up with it, and they'd descend into a blazing row.) "We have guests coming. We can't just turn her out and not have any entertainment for them."

"I wasn't saying we should do that," I protested. "I just want to be cautious. Make sure there aren't any tempting diamond necklaces lying about, that sort of thing."

Leo sighed grouchily, then agreed it was a good idea, and called for the butler.

I forgave him his short temper because of the worry I read so clearly on his face. We had been to so many mediums, and I was never convinced. If even Madame Sara Mirza could not assure me that Kate approved of our marriage, he might wonder if I would marry him at all.

I would have. How silly of him to worry. I would have.

A HOUSEFUL OF FRIENDS GATHERED in the salon that evening. They were Leo's friends mostly, but all of them had welcomed me.

I'd found that unsettling at first. When our engagement was announced, Leo's friends all said that I was better for him than Kate. She'd been too wild, too loud, too forward. She'd driven him mad with worry with her daredevil stunts and her colonial rudeness. Leo's brother should never have sent him off to Australia to meet rough girls like that, they said. *I* was preferable, because I was cautious and calm and gentle. I made him more like me, they said. But I thought the opposite. Kate had made us both vibrant and lively and chaotic, and, without her, we were shadows of who we could have been.

When Leo touched my hand that evening, I felt like he knew that too. "Is this it?" he asked. "If this time, Kate says it's all right, will it be all right?"

I was struck by his look of gentle and hopeful sorrow. If Kate had been there, she'd tell me to stop letting him wallow, to "buck him up"—or some silly Australian expression. At that moment, I decided that whatever 'experience' Madame Mirza gave me, I would take it as a positive sign.

I squeezed his hand, and like Kate, I kissed him, right there in the salon. "Yes," I said. "It will be all right."

Surprised, he pressed both my hands between his and smiled. The earnest expression made him look a fool, as if I had stolen every thought from his brain. He'd often looked at Kate like that. Truly, he loved us both.

THE PERFORMANCE WAS TO TAKE place in the downstairs salon. It was a long room with continuous french windows along one side that looked out on a veranda. As it was late enough in the year that the sun would set before we started, the curtains were left undrawn. At the front of the room, the footmen had built a small stage from which Madame Mirza would sing. They'd hung black lace drapes across the back half to make a little backdrop for the stage and set up two dim globe lamps along the front of it for footlights. Otherwise, the room was dark.

Leo and I sat near the front. I heard whispering and giggling around us—skeptics saying the darkness was a perfect cover for trickery, believers telling them to enjoy the experience, opera lovers guessing at what she would sing. Then a soft chime called forth silence, and Madame Mirza stepped through the backstage drapes and onto her stage.

The shadows made her intense eyes startling as she focused on each of us in turn, like she was reading the sin and goodness on our souls. She stood like that, just looking, for an uncomfortably long time, the only sounds the breaths and foot-shuffles of the audience. Then, without any prelude, or any accompaniment, she began to sing.

The song was a haunting version of Mozart's "Queen of the Night," that mad howl of a mother exhorting her daughter to kill, and I knew then that the rumors were true. Her voice was not the most pure and sharp, and the piece had been pitched down to fit her lower range. But the feeling and the darkness in her voice and in the song made every syllable tug at the veil between life and death.

As her song ended, the echoes of her voice fading among uncertain applause, the gramophone clicked on, and a recorded orchestration began. Trombones blared, violins squeaked anxious staccato rhythms, and Madame Mirza began to sing an intense modernist piece I hadn't heard before. Yet, in the subtle movements of her body and the way her shadow shifted and flickered on the lace curtains, I knew that in this piece she *was* the ghost, bringing a warning and a devil's bargain.

When this aria ended, my body felt numb and strange. It reminded me of how I'd felt during my first séance, enervated by hope and fear. But this performance was even more overawing. The veil between this world and the Other Side seemed to have grown translucent, and though it was only a reflection of our little audience in the glass, for a moment I thought I saw, through the french windows, a gathered army of the dead.

"Here is a song you will not know," Madame Mirza said, as the music behind her shifted into a softly haunting clarinet. "The opera is based on an ancient Persian tale. In it, a young woman, beautiful and with many graces, weds a handsome foreign stranger. She loves him ardently, and goes with him to his castle in a far off land. They expect children, but do not have them, and slowly her husband's love and kindness transform into possessiveness and jealousy. She does not know what to do. She dreams of the ghost of a beloved friend who whispers warnings of a secret darkness inside her husband. The young lady refuses to believe foolish dreams. Still, her love is altered by her fear and loneliness. She begins to wish to leave the castle."

A few women giggled. "Is this Bluebeard?" one whispered. "Is that an ancient Persian tale?"

"I don't like this," Leo muttered, a frustrated edge to his voice, as if he had been expecting something that hadn't come. "She's a singer, not a storyteller. She should stick to what she's paid to do."

"It's just context," I reassured him. "Usually, the master of ceremonies would give it, but it's only her tonight."

Leo's shoulders relaxed and he squeezed my hand. "Of course."

"Finally," Madame Mirza continued, "she goes to her husband and says that she desires to travel across the sea, but not with him. She loves him, but she cannot live with her own fear and uncertainty any longer. He does not understand and grows frantic and furious." She stepped toward the footlights, and the shadow of her body twisted and grew, becoming that of the dark husband, gaining power as his anger rose. Her voice too, took on the tones of his bewildered rage. "She may not go. She is *his*. But she is determined, so he catches up a blade and cuts off her face."

A shriek came from one of our guests—a few gasps too. Beside me, Leo's face went white as marble in the dimness. He looked ill, on the verge of retching. I felt sick too.

"She fights him, but he holds her by the throat and slices the knife down her cheek, then again, and then, with clawed hands, tears at the broken flesh to peel up the skin between the slashes."

"Ho there!" exclaimed a young man. "Isn't that quite enough--"

Madame Mirza did not let him interrupt. "Her body might leave him," she continued fiercely, "but she is his, so he intends to keep all her value. He will mount her face in his trophy room and know that he has not lost anything of worth. For a woman's value is in her face and her womb. The rest of her is so much refuse." Leo hissed in a sharp breath and seemed about to leap to his feet. The whole room shuddered in distress. Then, abruptly, Madame Mirza ended the tale. "Here is the lament of the young wife's ghost."

The piercing, glass-rattling cries of the wild verismo aria shattered my already attenuated nerves. It was in French, and to my surprise, I did know it. It was one of the few songs from the Ghost's *Don Juan Triumphant* that had been copied and unlicensed song sheets sold. I knew then she had lied about the source of the song. Why? As an excuse to tell that story? One repeated line transfixed me. It did indeed match the tale she'd told: *Not only me, not only me. He has done it before, and he will marry again.*

Suddenly, a thundering crash came from outside; then, inside the room, the sound of hurrying footsteps. Madame Mirza's voice cut off in the middle of the song; the gramophone screeched to a stop. She looked up. Two strange green lights began to glow behind her.

"She's here."

The atmosphere, the music, had done its work, and half the ladies in the audience let out a delighted shriek of fear. Some of the men tittered nervously. Beside me, Leo gave out a rough laugh that held a note of panic. He liked everything to go just as he'd planned, but Madame Mirza was already far off script.

The singer closed her eyes, and then, quietly, intensely, she spoke. "I have a message."

The room went as still as the silence after lightning.

"It is from a girl—a young woman—called Lilhe'e."

She did not pronounce the name as Lily. Its mention stopped my heart in its tracks. How could she know that name?

"I--" I began, not sure how to respond. "She's my friend."

I glanced at Leo's sweaty face, his long jaw tight with corded muscle, and I wondered, suddenly, if *he* could have told Madame Mirza about Lilhe'e. What if he'd thought I'd never believe Kate had been contacted unless the message came through Lilhe'e?

Madame Mirza's eyes flashed open, but they were not her usual deep, thoughtful, skeptical eyes. They looked empty, like her mind had stepped aside to channel the Other Side.

"Run." It wasn't Madame Mirza's voice anymore. It was Lilhe'e's—only not the silly voices the spiritualists had given her throughout the years—the one I'd always heard in my head. "It isn't safe here. Run. I will tell you what you must know, what you already fear, if you find me."

I was too panicked to do anything. The whole room exploded with whispers, curiosity, questions. I could feel everyone's eyes fixed on me and Leo in the front row.

"*Why? Where*—" I started. Did she want me to run all the way to the New Mexico Territory? But before I could form my question, Leo leapt up.

"What sort of message is that?" he demanded. "What about the— Don't you have another one?"

Sara Mirza fixed him with a cool glare. "I don't take money for false messages."

Leo's cheeks went a vibrant red. "How dare you say that! Get out of my house!" He grasped my shoulder tightly. "You're another charlatan! Here to make trouble!"

Behind us, in the back of the salon the door opened, and Anthony came in, tiptoeing with comical caution. "Sorry I'm late," he whispered. "What's going on? Is there a free seat?"

The wind blew the door shut with a bang, and a flash of light—lightning?—illuminated the veranda outside. Beyond the french windows stood a tall figure in a wedding veil, facing away from the house.

Kate.

The whole room knew it, breathed it, believed it.

I could feel the wonder in the way Leo's fingers loosened on my shoulder. *"Kate,"* he whispered. Then I saw him look at the audience and realize that he wasn't the only one who could see her. The wind blew her veil, and, like a telepathic idea had been sent, we knew she was about to turn. A strange pallor crossed Leo's face. "No," he stammered, his voice shaking. "They won't understand. Don't—" The figure seemed to shift. "Don't turn around!"

Abruptly, he charged forward and burst through the windows, glass shattering. People leapt up and screamed. Anthony shouted, "Leo!"

Leo didn't let the flying shards of glass stop him. He grasped the woman on the other side—was it an angry or romantic embrace?—but she came up in his arms too easily, like a hollow toy.

A dummy. A doll.

She hadn't been going to turn at all.

Leo froze, bewildered, and looked back into the room. His eyes fixed on me, and mine on him. Around me, the room was like a half-broken wave of chaos. People were shouting "It's Kate! It's really Kate!" but also "A fraud! A con!" No one could see anything for sure, until Anthony bellowed, "Enough," and switched on the electric lights.

Madame Mirza was gone.

"She can't have gone far!"

"The safe! Check the safe!"

"The jewelry boxes in the bedrooms! The silver!"

Everyone charged about, trying to be helpful. Anthony did his best to organize servants and rein in the guests, but he kept glancing to me and Leo. Leo was white as a sheet and quavering. He still held the dummy dressed as Kate, eyes fixed on its smooth, featureless face. I stared at him, at the dummy—a clear ruse, a fraud—and yet . . .

He will marry again.

I ran.

. . . find me.

There was only one exit Madame Mirza could have taken out of the room, so I went that way. When the corridor split—right to the center of the house, left to the west wing—I turned left, away from the cries and carrying on and sounds of running feet. In the silent depths of the west hallway, I heard a quiet footfall in the corridor above. *There.* Up the stairs I went.

At the end of that hall, I thought I saw movement; so I chased it. Another stairway, another corridor, another turn. Then a brief glimpse of a closing door.

I burst through that door and found myself in Kate's old rooms. They were cleaned and stripped of her personal things, but they hadn't been refitted for a new use. This was the room where Kate had kissed me and told me that Leo would go into a rage over me. It was empty. I heard another quiet movement—behind the closet door? I lunged, jerked it open, and rushed in.

No one was there.

Then, behind me, the door clicked shut, and the latch, which had always been loose and had trapped many an unwary housemaid—even Kate a few times, though she could easily knock it back up with her pocket-knife— rattled down into place.

"I *don't* give my blessing, you know," hissed a far too familiar voice from the darkness. "You get away from him. As far away as you can get."

I knew for certain then what I'd known deep down since Sara Mirza had spoken Lilhe'e's name, or perhaps since I'd seen the vagrant in the wood.

Kate wasn't dead at all.

IF YOU KNOW A HOUSE well, you can move through it unseen. A flick of a silver knife, and you are free. Then, unnoticed, you traverse the corridors, even as agitated people run here and there and the servants hurry to assist. You know where to stand to not be seen when the door opens and Anthony ushers Leo to his bed, giving him a shot of brandy and some opium pills he has on hand. "It's the shock. Some nasty joke. Don't say anything more. I'll tell everyone it was just the shock."

You can wait there, right in his room with him, until the drugs take effect, and then, when everyone is searching the grounds for thieves, you can slip back out, still unnoticed, and go back to the place you'd been all along. Right?

IN THE MORNING, A HOUSEMAID found me trapped in Kate's closet. She called for Anthony, who woke me gently, with a soft touch on my arm.

"Are you all right?" he asked.

I nodded, keeping my hands wrapped in my skirts, unwilling to summon words to speak.

"The butler mentioned that you'd warned him to prepare for a possible robbery. Clever of you. Though getting yourself trapped in a closet..." He lifted an amused eyebrow.

That was moderately humiliating, but I'd accept it.

"Unfortunately, Madame Mirza—or whatever her name actually is— knew where the key to the safe was, somehow. We've been cleaned out." He frowned. "Jewels mostly—none of Mother's, or yours actually, only Kate's."

He seemed bemused by that. But I wasn't.

He gave me a brandy and then promised to wait faithfully in the hall outside when I said I needed to see Leo. In case I had a swoon, he said, after the distress of being locked up all night.

I stepped into my fiancé's dressing room and saw his body dangling from a cord suspended from a hook in the fireplace. I screamed myself hoarse. Anthony rushed in and went white with shock. His knees gave out, and yet the look on his face appeared to be relief.

NO ONE KNOWS WHAT HAPPENED to Madame Sara Mirza, though I assume she has an abundance of assumed names to be getting on with, and, of course, she now has all of Kate's jewels as well. No one else saw the drifter she was with, her half-ruined face, or the way she had moved, with a light, athletic step I'd recognize anywhere.

I hope they're happy together. Perhaps they went to America, like she'd wanted to. Trick riding and spirit singing would do well in a traveling show.

I am quite happy myself. I married Anthony last year. I seem to have a talent for soothing other people's grief, because I hardly had to be sympathetic at all before he was crying in my lap about Leo and confessing what he'd done.

It had all started with an awful incident while Leo was up at Oxford. He'd met a young woman of no background and made her his mistress, and then he'd been horrified and betrayed when he discovered that his money did not guarantee her loyalty. Anthony had helped him cover his tracks, and then sent him to Hong Kong and Australia, in the hope that a harder life would set him straight. When he returned with Kate, they had seemed so in love that Anthony hadn't worried. But then rumors came to his ear that Kate had been asking questions about Leo's time at Oxford and been seen spending time privately with a strange woman—a spiritualist. Everyone whispered about how those grifters knew too much.

He'd rushed home to confront her, to find out if she knew about the girl at Oxford, to make certain she would not say something foolish. But he had walked in on a horrifying tableau in the gunroom. Leo had Kate pinned to the table, a hand pressed tight over her mouth. Her silver pocketknife was beside them, all over blood. Leo had carved up her face, and now he was clawing it to bits, his fingernails deep in the ugly wounds.

Anthony had struck Leo down in one blow and carried Kate off to the doctor. She had fainted and stayed unconscious from blood loss for nearly a whole day, which gave Anthony too much time to think. When she woke, her face a mess of stitches, an infusion of blood and fluids still seeping into her veins, he'd brought her the valise he'd found in the gunroom, and money that he'd stolen from the church's poor box—he would not risk Leo discovering she was alive because he'd written her a cheque. Then he asked her to disappear.

"I told her that she must never return to society or speak of what happened," he said, staring down at his own hands as if imagining his brother's bloodstained ones. He, an MP, would contradict her if she tried. "Then I threatened her. She was ugly now. The world would recoil from her face. What sort of public life could a disfigured woman hope for?"

He hated that he had said that—and the way she'd quailed at his words. But he had to protect his brother.

Anthony loved his brother, knew his good temper and his charm. He did not understand why a woman's disloyalty could drive him to violence. Still, the mistress had been low-born, and if what Leo told him was true, Kate was wild—perverse also, liking to wear men's clothes and flirt with women. The fault must have lain with them.

But then Leo proposed to me. Anthony told himself that I was different. I was a good girl. I would never dally with other men or grow suspicious and talk to low-class people to ferret out his secrets. Still, he was afraid. He would never be sure I was safe, and he loved me, so how could he bear that?

"I'm glad he made the right decision in the end," Anthony said. "That's what— That's what justice would have done. Hanging."

"Yes," I said.

I'm all right, Kate had said to me, as I touched her poor face in the darkness. *I might not be too pretty, but I won't live as a ghost. I'm free.*

I stood beside Anthony at Leo's memorial, and while he shook hands manfully with every mourner, I kept my hands in my muff and greeted everyone with a brief incline of my head, just occasionally making eye-contact through my black lace veil.

Everyone thought I was exceptionally pathetic and ladylike—not like that wild Kate who must have driven Leo mad. They didn't know it was because shaking hands would have been far too painful, what with the rope burn on my palms.

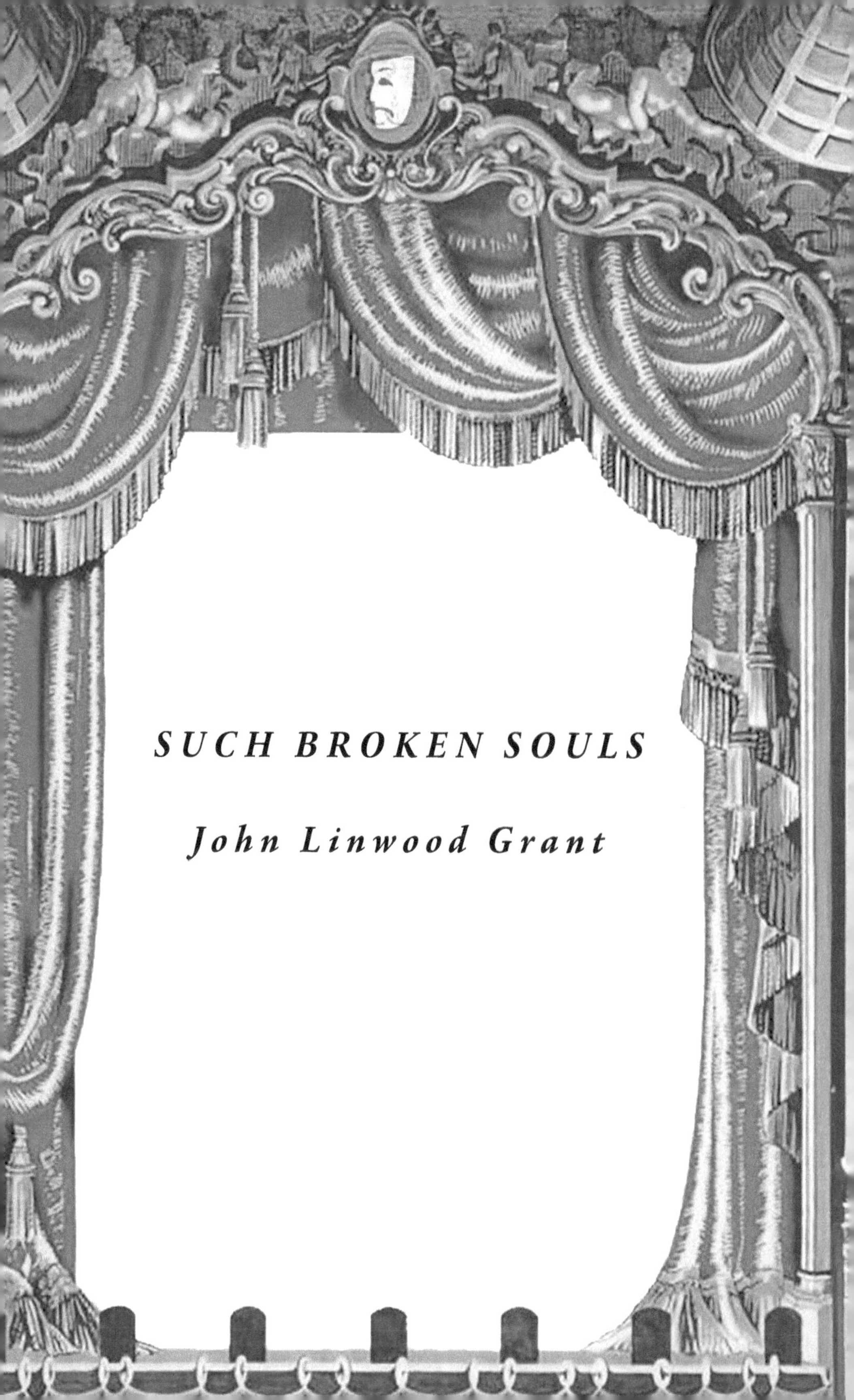

SUCH BROKEN SOULS

John Linwood Grant

THEY WILL TAKE HIM FROM his mother's house, and it will be on some quiet, perfumed night when no one is prepared for such an intrusion – though the nature of the act itself will not be unexpected. His mother, his sisters, will weep and cry out; the others of that place will stand back, their eyes averted. Beneath the Yildiz kiosks there are many rooms where people are reminded daily of the sultan's deep and unassuagable paranoia.

They will take him, slipperless and terrified, and he will not be seen again. Not by that decent woman who raised him, nor by little Aliye, who giggles at her brother's fond humour, nor by sullen Fatima, who wishes to study the sciences, who holds in her heart the same disdain for the demands of Abdul Hamid II, master of the Ottoman Empire.

And so I, who love him, have no choice but to go to Paris – to return to that edifice of sewers, sedition and stale wine which I swore was dead to me. For the sake of one who will otherwise be taken from his mother's house, I must go there to allay the sultan's fears, and gain a reprieve for my soul-mate.

I must hunt and find Ceset.

The Corpse.

Paris, March 1882

THERE IS NO JOY HERE, despite the raucous cries of drunks and street-hawkers. All is a facade. The more obvious ruin of a decade ago has gone, though there are walls, buildings, even whole streets, still scarred by Prussian artillery and then the Commune's self-inflicted struggles. I do not wish to think about the Commune, but as for the Prussians' role, I believe Bismark would have seen all Paris made rubble to achieve his goals. Perhaps it would have been for the best, for there is that ruin also which remains within the people, a furtive mutual distrust and meanness. Not enough years have passed, despite their pretences.

I have rented lodgings in Montmartre. The concierge of my building is a brutal old woman. I can imagine her as a *petroleuse* during the Commune, cackling as she sets fire to her own city, and informs on her neighbours to the Committee of Public Safety. I paid a month in advance to secure the apartment from her. It is a small, mean apartment, but it it is situated not so far from the Palais Garnier in the next arrondisement. The Paris Opera.

"You hear me, *hein?*" She smears the front step with dirty water. "You Turks, so proud and clever, but only your gold lets you sit and drink with decent citizens."

"I am a Frenchman." I hardly care what she thinks. "I was born in Rouen, tutored in Paris."

"So you say." She squints and then goes inside.

Her remark is useful, I suppose. I need to be tailored to fit the landscape, to blend in. My clothes are broadly Western, but cut for the East, and I have become used to wearing the Turkish cap.

A tailor off Boulevard Haussman tuts, measures, tuts again, and promises me a suit within two days. He provides me with a nondescript felt hat and an overcoat which almost fits. In the mirror, I am Thierry Leduc, an idle man of letters. In the mirror, I never fled Paris under the Commune, never enlisted again in the service of the Ottoman sultan – my tan comes from some time spent in Marseilles, and now, more than ten years later, I am home.

I like this fellow no more than I like the true one.

RESIT BALIK IS A PERFECT agent, born for the secret police. He is furtive, callous, and his intelligence is that of a malicious hound—his appearance is much the same, sullen and red-eyed. We meet in a nondescript cafe off Place Pigalle, where he chain-smokes and complains. He knows me only as Maréchal, a trusted agent. I never used my true name in the East.

"The Persian would not speak to me—his servant sent me away." He toys with a small cup of thick, bitter coffee. Five spoonfuls of sugar. "I could, of course, return one night with a heavier stick…"

"You've done your part." I try to sound unconcerned. The Yildiz Intelligence Agency is known for its love of 'corrective' beatings, the removal of an ear, a finger, a toe… whatever will remind people that they are always watched. I had hoped that in the West, the sultan's agents would be of a higher calibre. Perhaps they are, in the places where it matters.

He sniffs. "This Opera ghost—he could be no more than a fever in the child-minds of those who work the stage. A superstitious lot at the best of times. Or a beggar, living off scraps left by the wealthier patrons, hiding in the cellars by day."

"They say here that he is dead."

"There you go, then. A ghost cannot die; a beggar's death is no matter for us."

"But if he was—is—Ceset, the architect of our master's secret places and devices, then the matter must be settled. There must be proof either of his end, or his further plans."

He gives a grudging nod, and passes me a handwritten list, along with copious notes, all in Turkish.

"You have everything for now," he says. "Do what you must do. I have other tasks upon my shoulders."

When he leaves, I read the papers which outline his work thus far. They are competent, concise. *Someone* had lurked within the Palais Garnier, and there had been fatal events. A stage-hand hanged or garotted; a Comte de Chagny found drowned in the cistern below the building. Witnesses were unreliable, contradictory. And the main characters involved with the Opera ghost, a young man and woman, lovers, had reportedly left the country, destination unknown.

The nature of my quarry? Here they talk of his true name being Erik, a disfigured, disgruntled singer. There was even a notice in one of the papers not so long after the Comte's murder: "Erik is dead." At times he was said to obscure his features with a black felt mask; at other times he wore a deaths-head, the face of a corpse.

Many suspected the latter to be yet another mask—but was it? For although I do not say so to Resit Balik. I am convinced that I was once acquainted with the Opera ghost, long ago and in another, distant place. And if so, I worry at the talk of his demise. Such a man does not die easily.

I will have to visit the Persian.

Constantinople, September 1868

I HAD ALMOST COMPLETED MY examination of a thick sheaf of Russian papers—land treaties, dull stuff—when I was interrupted by a runner from one of the kiosks. Twenty minutes later, I stood before a harassed *agha*, an administrator, in his office at the Dolmabahçe Palace.

"You must meet with a man," he said, "And must not have met with him. He is French, and there can be no misunderstandings. You are French and, I am told, to be reliable. You will know if you see deception. This is the word of *my* master." And I had no doubt he meant the sultan himself.

I went where I was bid, and in a room which I did not know existed, hidden deep within the palace complex, I waited. The light was poor, the single large desk strewn with architectural drawings; there were no seats. Curiously, a violin and bow lay in one corner, as if dropped there a few moments ago. I tried to make sense of one of the drawings – some sort of trapdoor and pulley system? – but failed. They said that the sultan's masons and artificers were guided by an outsider, a man who chose not to be seen, and from those drawings, I suspected I was about to meet him.

I heard a faint grating sound, and the next I knew I was sure that another person was in the room. The door by which I had entered was in plain sight, closed – but the palace was well known for its tricks. I turned, trying to show no alarm.

The figure by the wall, seemingly come from nowhere, was tall, extraordinarily lean, with long, dexterous fingers which had the yellowish tinge of jaundice or some disorder of pigmentation. Robes of midnight silk clung like a winding sheet to the body, a voluminous black *keffiyeh* to the head, except for a slit which showed nothing but more darkness where the eyes must surely be.

"I am Maréchal, the translator." I said, less confidently than I would have liked. "I was sent to you."

His gait as he circled the room was that of a night-stalker, a thing which walks through graveyards in those fables told when children misbehave.

Ghul, I believe the Arabic word is. If he had pounced upon me without warning, seeking my throat, I would not have been totally surprised.

I tried again. "I am told there are modifications to be made to the palace. Certain matters of security for the sultan and his immediate staff. I'm sure you have it all in hand, but you know the Turks—they worry so about detail."

A low laugh.

"They worry that I serve only myself, and they are right to do so. But their artisans and artificers are bumbling fools in comparison. The sultan requires genius; I provide that commodity. You must have heard of me?"

I did not wish to seem too awed – or nervous. "An occasional rumour of a veiled foreigner who designs concealed doors and passages, yes, one who has a gift for mechanical marvels. This is not my area of expertise, though – I am a man of official documents and dull reports." And I grew daring. "Some of my colleagues call you…."

"Ceset." This laugh was darker. "The Corpse. My name, however, is Erik, which I will allow you to use when we are alone."

"A Frenchman, by your voice."

"I was once. And perhaps again, but we shall see. So, I assume you are here to discuss the alterations to the Secretariat, and the installation of a passage to the sultan's quarters?"

"I believe so."

He gestured at the table. "You will see the plans. You may even inspect the work as it progresses. There is nothing particularly cunning involved. Doors which cannot be seen by the uninitiated, certain alternative routes, a subtle trigger stone at key points. The priest-architects of the pharaohs would have understood immediately."

As he leaned towards the drawings, his *keffiyeh* slipped, betraying a sharp cheekbone to which the discoloured skin clung like dried parchment, an eye so sunken that no colour could be discerned. I must have drawn in a sharp breath, for he looked up me, not bothering to replace the *keffiyeh*.

"You see? Ceset. I was born thus, beyond help, and so I help myself."

"I… I am sorry, m'sieur."

And I was, though I was also strangely terrified, as if presented with Death Incarnate.

That was my first meeting with him, one of a number in which I sought to serve Abdulaziz without loss of my weak and troubled soul.

If Ceset had a soul, I did not yet know.

Paris, March 1882

THE PERSIAN IS GRACIOUS, AND his servant, Darius, brings us mint tea.

He seems surprised that I know so much of him, but I explain the sultan's people made many enquiries into the history of the masked inventor, magician and musician who came to court. His time with the travelling fairs and shows of Eastern Europe, Russia, even India, and his sojourn in Persia, Naser al-Din Shah, the Persian monarch, may be a cunning man, but he is not sultan of the Ottoman Empire, where mistrust and rebellion clutch the hem of every robe.

"And you, m'sieur, once helped this man escape the Shah, many years ago. You are said to know his skills, his inclinations, and to have seen him here, in the flesh, during last year's dire events at the Palais Garnier."

I am honest, for I will need honesty in return. My host does not argue, but his green eyes gaze upon mine directly.

"How is a Frenchman serving Abdul Hamid?" It is a gentle enquiry, not a challenge.

I tell him, without prevarication. I speak of my youth, and how I travelled to Asia Minor as a scholar and a translator, performing some minor services for the Ottoman court. Under the sultan Abdulaziz, I was a favoured foreign servant, but I grew homesick and returned to Paris at the end of the Franco-Prussian war in 1871, fool that I was. Sickened to see the violence and partisan madness of the Commune, I fled France for a second time, thinking only to resume a quiet life in Constantinople.

"But all is politics to the Ottoman. I survived the fall of Abdulaziz, but was coerced into the service of the new sultan, Abdul Hamid II. At first, I translated reports of French political developments, then it was minor military matters, and so on. Each step seemed so small, but the journey as a whole...."

"You became owned, compromised, an agent bound by the secrets in which he dealt."

"Yes." I see that he understands, but then he was a *daroga*, a chief of police. He would.

The mahogany chair creaks under me as I lean forward. "And now the sultan has seen reports of the Paris Opera, and of one who may be Ceset—Erik as you call him—

the man who designed intricate passages and wild devices for the sultan's predecessor. You were there in Mazenderan under your Shah – you must know what is going through the mind of my sultan, whose constant concern is betrayal, assassination. A man who fears he does not know *all* the hidden ways which Erik might have installed for his predecessor"

The *daroga* sighs. "I do. If Erik were alive, your sultan would want him killed - or dragged back to be locked away until all secrets were known."

I sigh.

"I am given to understand that either would suffice, though, God knows, I am no assassin. Some other would undertake that task. Thus I have pressing business. Last year – the events at the Palais Garnier. I have no interest in fanciful tales, nor in people's personal tragedies – I must hear only the resolution, as you know it, any clue to his final disposition."

"Then you shall."

We talk of the East, and of Erik's past. I have no stomach for recounting the long and often uncomfortable tales he tells me of those times in Persia. Great works were done, and also terrible ones. If they differ from what I know of his deeds in Constantinople, it is only that under the Ottoman sultan, the monster no longer made violent sport of others, nor turned his own hand so directly against his fellow beings. He became more clandestine, more 'behind the scenes'. Was his initial taste for hurt sated in Mazenderan — had he begun to discover some thin thread of humanity within him?

Over more tea, the Persian tells me everything he knows concerning the final days of the Opera ghost, as he is called more commonly here. Of his last meeting with the monster, of how he did receive Christine Daae's papers and belongings, and gave the signal that Erik was dead. He lets me glance through the relevant papers, and I trust him to have shown me all that which I might need to know.

"Thus it is done," he says. "Christine and her true love Raoul de Chagny are lost to France, ensconced in some pretty home in Scandinavia. Not even I know where, exactly. It is for the best."

I ponder on these facts—facts as far as the *daroga* is concerned. I have no doubt that he is being absolutely honest with me. But no body has been found. No deaths-head corpse, at peace at last.

"Do you miss Mazenderan?" I ask.

"Do you miss Istanbul?"

Neither of us speak for some moments.

"It is cold, here," he says eventually. "But electric lights now shine within the Opera House; last year I rode in a carriage powered solely by steam. Erik would have approved."

"He still may." I set my tea down carefully. I point out that The Corpse has lied before, and is a master of deception and misdirection.

"Perhaps he simply wishes to be *known* as dead." I say. "Perhaps, with his twisted concept of human affection, he genuinely hopes Christine and Raoul will find some happiness, and think no more of him. But does such a man simply fade and pass away? *Can he?*"

My host is surprised by my fervour.

"This is important to you—not only to your master."

I think of Fazil. "It is life... or death."

He nods, closing his eyes for a moment, and his expression is troubled. "I will unearth one last doubt I buried, though I should not. If his great score was truly completed – his *Don Juan Triumphant* - then where does it lie? Would he really have succumbed to eternity without it being known of – sent to astound some mastersinger or opera manager, to astound France, the world? He was not a humble man."

"So he would have purpose, a reason to live?"

"I... how can I tell, M'sieur Leduc? I did not say that, and this thought of mine may be yet another fantasy. No more, no more."

The Persian sinks into his chair; I bow and take my leave. At the door which opens onto the Rue de Rivoli, his servant Darius pauses me.

"This must not go on," he says, low, and hands me a heavy silk-swathed bundle, something hard within. "Please, my dear master has borne enough. If you find the monster, put an end to him."

When I am back in my Montmartre lodgings, I peel the silk aside.

Darius's gift is a long pistol, and a curved dagger with an amethyst upon its hilt. The dagger, I have no doubt, of a Persian chief of police.

Constantinople, February 1869

You would think that two fellow countrymen, finding themselves in Ottoman service, might discover - or form - some common bond. Ceset and I did not. I was a mere appendage to the sultan's network of civil servants and agents, a convenience because of my fluent French, Turkish and Russian. I was without influence and offered no threat. Ceset was... another matter. Palace servants feared him or despised him; pandered to him or avoided him.

And my reports to the *agha* – they were required to contain unusual detail, not only on Ceset's plans and progress, but on the minutiae of our encounters. Even though my meetings with this genius were infrequent, I was being used to spy on him, it seemed. I was becoming part of the sultan's intelligence network.

In deciding what I did and did not include, I began to recognise something unexpected, something almost impossible. His age, his deeply unnatural appearance, his accent… despite the fact that he was reputedly widely-travelled, his French held the nasal flair, the gutteral 'r's, of Normandy, of my home region. There were stories, myths, in Rouen….

Might I alone, of all the thousands in the many rooms of Dolmabahçe Palace and the spreading kiosks of Yildiz, know who Ceset truly was?

ONE RAIN-SWEPT AFTERNOON HE SHOWED me a half-constructed automaton, a marvellous thing. Resting on a stone block, at a distance it resembled the upper half of man, and upon the metal head was a mask, its general likeness that of Abdulaziz.

"One arm will lift and fall, as if in salute," said Ceset—or Erik, as I called him to his veiled face. "This will stand on a balcony, slightly shadowed, and so the sultan will be there, even if he has travelled beyond the palace, beyond the city. I have toyed with the idea of giving it a voice – two or three simple phrases – but that is more difficult. I have my thoughts on recording such a sound, however. De Martinville's phonautograph intrigues me. He is a Frenchman, of course."

I had no idea to what he referred but admitted that his creation was a work of a mastermind.

"It is." Ceset had no sense of false modesty. "For some time I have been writing a piece, the score for an opera, one which will sweep all others away. *Don Juan Triumphant*. But paper, paper has its limits, and human performers, they are so flawed and unreliable. Perhaps one day I will have it played by such an automaton, faultless, eternal."

I knew little of music, and could barely read a score, so I nodded, trying to appear enthusiastic.

"Do you sing yourself, m'sieur?" I asked.

"It is my joy, my pain, but I do so rarely in this benighted place. Now, those plans..."

His patience seemed to have fled, for he drove me through the dry details of masonry, support requirements, hidden hinges, and much which I did not need to know. When he came close as we pored over the designs, I was half-curious, half-repelled, by the odour of foxed paper, mouldering leather, which hung about him – not so much offensive, but as if he were constructed of such things, not flesh. His exposed hands appeared like stained, spoiled vellum laid over bone, and I had to stop myself from a flight of fancy that this was not a man at all but an automaton itself, formed from the library and the grave in equal measure.

My report that night was short and said nothing of my own feelings.

TWO DAYS LATER, CESET WAS in a more genial mood – for him – and shared wine with me, at which point I spoke out as I should not normally have done. I tried, ineptly, to test my suspicion about his origins. The more often we talked, the more I heard Normandy in his voice.

"I hear you are widely travelled, m'sieur. I myself come originally from Rouen," I said, putting down the plan of a false floor which opened upon a pit of iron spikes. I did not wish to dwell on its use.

"Indeed?"

"Yes, my entire childhood was spent there."

"A happy time?"

"Oh, I wandered the area far and wide, always listening to folklore and rumour, always too ready to believe. Children love grotesque tales, of course."

"Such as?"

It was now, or not at all. The wine had flowed freely—a Tokay of excellent quality—and it won out over my natural caution, though he seemed unaffected by it.

"Well, I do remember stories of a troubled family near Darnétal whose son was born with a grievous deformity."

"Go on."

"Some said that the father drowned the child in the Seine, so appalled was he by his son's appearance – others that the boy fled, never to be heard of again. Starved or killed by its own condition, was the talk."

"Did these fancies include the family's name?" His response was easy, as if we spoke of nothing more than the shortcomings of the local bread.

"Graille, I believe. The boy's first name was never mentioned. Our local doctor's daughter, a fey, black-eyed girl of seventeen, said that she had seen him when she was small, seen his mockery of a face, before he disappeared. Few believed her."

"Did you?" He bent down to take up the violin, on which he played a few long, deep notes. "Such wild stories are common amongst peasants, after all."

"They are." I gulped the last golden drops from my glass, rose. "I cannot tell you what I thought back then. It was long ago, and I have always suffered from too much imagination."

The lightless slit in the *keffiyeh* regarded me for some seconds.

"We *become* what we imagine," he said, and dismissed me.

Paris, April 1882

I VISIT THE PALAIS GARNIER, but I do not seek gossip or wild rumour. Balik has gathered such common and sordid tales as are likely to emerge; the Persian has supplied more useful material. I bribe a carpenter, who takes me at night to prowl through the cellars and under-cellars, and I can see that it would be easy for any man to appear, to hide, to confuse, and never be tracked down. A warren below a warren. Even with guide and lantern, I am lost numerous times, and must be called back repeatedly from arched, empty vaults, from rooms full of mouldering props, and passages which simply end.

I do note traces of the Communards of 1871: crudely-hacked routes, scratches on the walls. It is foolish to call those people Communists, for although some were, many were anarchists, some were rogues and looters. I was there—the bulk were simply Parisians, with hope for their city but no great interest in the broader politics of the day.

In a remote stretch of the tunnels, below the fifth cellar where the carpenter will not go, I discover the 'Communists' Dungeon', as the Persian's papers name it. There are corpses – not many, but enough. The nature of these depths has preserved them to an extent I would not have expected. There is skin over the bones, though it is drawn tight, and noses, earlobes, eyeballs are gone. They remind me very much of Ceset. Except that they can no longer walk amongst the living. If he—his body—is down here, I cannot imagine where. The *daroga* assures me that the monster closed off or destroyed his most secret ways before his death.

Besides, I know he is not here. I *feel* it, in my own, less-ruined bones. I pay the carpenter well, and remind him that I was never here.

Out on the Rue Scribe, beyond the circle of light from a streetlamp, a shadow watches me. I stare in that direction, making it known that I have seen them.

The shadow passes. For now.

A WEEK PASSES, AND BALIK or one of his men sends me a Rouen newspaper, one small column marked for attention. It announces the murder of a local mason, a widower, aged sixty five. The cause of death... strangulation by cord or thin rope. No suspects, no motive. The Turk knows both of my thoughts concerning Ceset's Rouen origins, and of the Punjab wire, to which the *daroga* had referred more than once.

The dead man's surname is Graille, the name from my childhood memories, and the Persian was sure that Erik's father was a master-mason from near Rouen. What other conclusion can I draw?

Erik has killed his own father.

Is this his final act of revenge, or the latest whim of a malevolent phantom freed from his ties to the Palais Garnier and the opera? He must have many hatreds locked with that narrow, bony chest.

It is the way of the agent to suspect everything, to suspect everyone. I expect that Balik is reporting on me to the court of the sultan – there are too many shadows at my back. Balik is not the only Ottoman agent in Paris, but he is useful, I suppose. If he tells the kiosks of Adbul Hamid that I am being thorough, diligent, then my beloved Fazil remains safe.

The Corpse is on the move.

I may go to Darnétal, where he first faced rejection, though I doubt he will stay there. It must hold only pain for him. If he heads east across the continent, retracing his long journey as a freak, then a performer, my hunt might last for years. I can only pray that this time he remains in France, his natural home—but where in France?

Constantinople, March 1869

Two weeks after the night I shared Tokay with Ceset, I heard that the sultan's secret police had been ordered to apprehend him.

"What is his crime?" I asked my immediate superior, a stout, secretive Turk who prospered, so it was said, not on his palace salary but from the blackmail of certain dignitaries in the Dolmabahçe Palace.

"Knowledge." The man spat. "Our master Abdulaziz suspects the man of ambition, of presuming that the web he builds belongs to him, not to the sultan. Ceset has become too clever. Do you know the consequences of that, Maréchal?"

I did. As for Ceset, he was certainly clever enough to have tasted the wind.

He had already fled Constantinople.

Rouen, Normandy, April 1882

THERE IS LITTLE OF INTEREST for me here, in the town where I was born. My own parents passed away a while ago; and both of Erik's parents are dead – now. Local talk – when I press people – is that Madame Graille took her own life in a fit of madness, a few months after her son Erik fled their home. Monsieur Graille never re-married.

I go to the old man's grave in Darnétal, just outside the town. The small stone bearing only his name and dates of birth and death. More interesting is the adjoining plot, the grave of Amelie Graille. Upon it lie white lilies, strewn there five, six days ago. Around the time of her husband's murder.

The priest looks blank when I ask him if he knows who left them; the gravedigger smiles.

"Ah, a thin, thin man, all in black. He did not stay long. I saw him as I was digging a last soft bed for old Ruillon the Baker."

"You saw his face? Was he masked?"

He frowns. "Masked? Is this a theatre? No, his face was pale, stiff. That is all."

I toss him a franc, and leave. I remember what Erik was supposed to have said to Christine Daae, in his 'last' days: "I have invented a mask that makes me look like anybody. People will not turn around in the streets."

No more the stiff black felt nor the depths, then.

He is alive, if such it can be called. I am certain now.

Paris, April 1882

IF HE HAS LEFT THE Palais Opera, has left Paris, left Rouen, where is he, if he remains in France? There is only one possibility, one connection left. I do not write a report on this, not yet. What do I have to say? What excuses can I give that will preserve Fazil's safety, his life?

When I meet Balik in our usual cafe, he is even less deferential than before. As usual, he smokes thin cigarettes until the stub burns his ugly fingers. Graceless, he has never offered me one, and my own case remains closed – the acrid smoke he exhales is enough to make one wish to quit the habit.

"I have been the dog, and sniffed every corner, every hole," he mutters. "Everything I discovered, I passed to you, and my work will be well-regarded. What have you done, *Frenchman?*"

He uses my nationality as a slur.

I grimace. "Have you been following me?"

A sly smile. "Occasionally *my* people have looked in on you, discretely. You might have needed their help."

Which is clearly not why such surveillance was set in place.

I affect an air of indifference to his remarks. "I will be travelling to Brittany this week."

"A holiday?"

"Of course not, but my next moves are none of your business. The Yildiz kiosks sent *me*, remember. They instructed that I should receive your co-operation."

His thick eyebrows entangle, ease apart.

"Then it is on your head, not mine. As it should be."

He tosses a few centimes on the table, and leaves.

Perros-Guirec, Brittany, May 1882

WHITE LILIES LIE ON THE grave of Christine Daee's father. They must have been placed here only a few days ago. Wilting, but not yet dried or rotted. It is, I am sure, an echo of Amelie Graille's grave at Darnétal. 'You follow me,' say the lilies, 'And yes, I have been here.'

I was not wrong to come.

It is macabre that such a pleasure spot as this coastal Breton resort should be entwined with the life of Ceset. Not that the cemetery itself is a place of any amusement. It is a boneyard. Kennel-sized shelters hold bleached skulls; the long-bones of the dead are packed around the church walls, as if an ancient catacomb had been hauled to the surface and placed on display.

But where exactly will Erik be, and what is his purpose? For that matter, I do not know *why*, after these years, that he killed his elderly father. He has been in France since at least 1870, when he was a contract builder working on the Palais Garnier, according to the *daroga*. Why did he wait so long? It feels like an act of completion, of tying things together - one of the final scenes of an opera.

I must know if some climactic event awaits.

Bypassing Balik, I send a coded report directly to Constantinople myself, by courier. It contains no lies, but it paints a picture of a dogged secret police agent now closing in on his target – clues found along the way, intelligence being gathered. It speaks of a crucial, anticipated event, and the apprehension of Ceset. Balik can argue, but he cannot prove it untrue. Such a ruse should keep Fazil safe a little longer.

I wait in Perros-Guirec, as little seen as possible; by day I read and worry, by night I haunt the graveyard. I do not know if this is whim, or intuition. I do know that Erik came here once, and that Daae's grave has – or once had - great significance to him.

My own state of mind… a certain paranoia has crept into me. I feel I am observed once more, and my nerves suffer. When my hairbrush is not quite where I thought I placed it, I wonder who has been in my hotel room, though the maids say they have not entered. A whistled tune on the streets of Perros-Guirac sounds too close to a signal one agent might give another, yet when I turn, it comes from the lips of a small, grubby child who is idly turning a hoop.

I am not reassured.

ON THE THIRD EVENING I kneel, secreted in the shadow of the sacristy, from where I can see M. Daae's grave. Two hours, three, pass. I am cold, and beginning to think I should shake off this folly, when I hear a violin playing.

Peering from behind a heap of femurs, some of which must be centuries old, I see a lean figure – unnaturally lean – in sombre step towards the grave of M Daae. His face is hidden, fingers dancing on the neck of his instrument.

As the bow scrapes, an urgent discord fills the air, and I must check my anxious breathing—it is bitter, redolent of the darkest sins, the most terrible regrets, to such an extent that I am paralysed. I cannot even unlock my own fingers from the bone-choked wall I clutch.

His back is to me, and his step is slow, measured, as if a mourner at a long-forgotten funeral, yet he continues to play with a fervour that you would think might tear the instrument apart. If the music steals my volition, then the singing which follows is worse – my inner thoughts seem at risk. The voice is sweet beyond measure, but the words, given in almost antique French, are those of Judgement Day:

> *These ruins which you see,*
> *These dark and charnelled bones,*
> *Were fashioned as your final home -*
> *A prison for forgotten flesh;*
> *A rack of pain*
> *On which to lacerate your lost, immortal soul.*

I am hearing *Don Juan Triumphant*. How can I doubt it? It is everything recorded in Christine's notes, and more terrible. If this is the Angel of Music, then he is truly a Fallen one. I close my eyes; my silent lips beg for it to stop, and as if I were heard, it does.

When I dare to peer into the night again, Erik stands over me, violin lowered.

"Did you think I would not know? That I do not understand being hunted?" he asks, his voice sounding amused. What his face might be saying is hidden by a new mask, and yes, it might almost pass as human on idle glance. Wax or ceramic, it has tints of normal flesh, though more white, a nose, patrician, and red lips, slightly parted. Only its lack of motion, and the darker pits of the eyes, betray it.

Crouched by the sacristy, I try to respond. I cannot rise, but I lift my head.

"I… I have no choice."

"So I understand."

"How can you possibly know that?"

Laughter. "A dog told me."

And from under his black cloak he draws out something which he tosses at my knees. It lands with a soft thud which I have heard before, in the torture chambers of Abdul Hamid II, and I recognise it immediately.

Chewed fingernails, dark hair upon the back, the insides of index and middle fingers burned brown-black by the smoking of each cheap cigarette down to the last few strands of tobacco. The severed hand of Resit Balik.

"He came to steal your success from you, and win the sultan's favour. Or to see you fail and prosper by that failure. I did not care for him, and as you and I are old friends, I removed him. The hand you can keep, if you wish, as a memento of this little encounter. The rest of him will not bother you again."

I feel some strength returning to my limbs, but not enough to flee.

"You could kill me, here and now. A knife, your Punjab wire…."

He gives a deeper, more sinister laugh. "And what would that achieve, when you have offered me an unexpected witness to my final and greatest achievement. I began it before Mazenderan, let it grow in Constantinople, and brought it to fruition in my house on the lake. In a few weeks, others will revel in its majesty."

"At the Palais Garnier?"

Scorn greets my suggestion.

"The mewling 'sophisticates' of Paris, who batten on the stale recitation of mediocre operas, each formula worn more thin than a beggar's shoe leather? No, my *Don Juan Triumphant* will be played to people who have the fear of the Almighty in their hearts and a true understanding of Hell."

"Where, then? When?"

"You will be told. And then you, who now know more of my life than even the Persian, may at last understand."

My sense were returning.

"I spoke to the Persian at length. He and the others believe you to be dead."

"Such was my intention, but… I tried to rest there under the Palais Garnier; I could not. My tortured skull resonated to the sounds of my own music; my deformed body would not accept its end. Still, I am a generous man. I used certain tricks upon one of the best-preserved Communard corpses I found in the cellars, and left it where it would be taken for my own remains. I dressed it in the apparel for which I was known. And the Opera ghost was no more. That lie was my gift to the *daroga*, my gift to Christine Daae. It sufficed."

"You never thought people might enquire further?"

"Not the French authorities. No, they are plodding buffoons. Nor the weak, superstitious opera folk. But the Ottoman court, or an agent of the Persian Shah—that was always possible. Or the *daroga* might have regretted his actions, and sought to curry favour, to return to Mazenderan. I do gain some small pleasure, some amusement, from the fact that it is you of all people, my dear friend, who has been at my heels."

I managed to stand. "We were never friends, Erik. I barely knew you, except through my duty."

"You knew me better than the Turks. You did not seek to profit from me, use me, nor flinch in disgust at my presence. For that reason I have chosen mercy."

"You did not show mercy in Darnétal ."

The deaths-head darkens, clears.

"An act long overdue, which I knew would intrigue you. Nothing more. Await my summons, Maréchal."

Then he laughs.

"Or should I call you Thierry."

His black cloak swirls, and I am alone.

Constantinople, December 1877

"The Russians, the Romanians, they are closer every day." An officer I did not know. "That the Bear should prowl at Constantinople's walls...."

I nodded. After living here six years, it did seem inconceivable that life in Constantinople—Istanbul, as many locals call it—bustling but orderly, could suddenly be torn apart by thunderous cannons and Cossack swords. Already I had secreted my original French papers upon my person, and prepared to protest my ignorance of Ottoman affairs. Maréchal must disappear, and those other papers, the ones which proclaimed me in service to the secret police, I would burn if the Russians entered the city. There were neutral merchantmen anchored in the Golden Horn who might spirit me away, if I were swift.

A *binbashi*, a senior army officer who was vaguely familiar, did not agree concerning the city's fate.

"Plovdiv will fall to the enemy, but who cares about the Bulgarians anyway - let them bicker amongst themselves. The British are sending a fleet."

"To aid us?" asked the other man.

"To halt the Bear and ensure a settlement."

I had heard such talk but felt relief at confirmation from a senior army man. A few questions demonstrated that he had certain, genuine knowledge, not just chit-chat from the barracks. Turkish Intelligence was more efficient when it came to foreign affairs than it was with its own people. There would be men in London who sent this news by courier and telegram – men deep in the heart of London's ruling elite.

In the offices of one of the *aghas* I was introduced to a young man named Fazil. He had problems with some of the paperwork which has been sent from Marseilles, urgent matters concerning the French Mediterranean fleet. Naval terminology, ambiguities caused by the use of technical terms. And then there was the situation in Algeria… I was required to advise and assist him, in short. I shrugged and led him to my small office, a sheaf of papers under his arm.

That night we slept in each other's arms.

Do not misunderstand me. Despite a few short dalliances with Rouen and Paris girls in my youth, I had believed myself to be excluded perpetually from the fields of romance or marriage. A man apart, lacking that 'natural' urge to flirt and mate. Not only did I have no aptitude in that regard, but I had no drive for any of it. A pretty girl, a handsome man. These were as sculptures or paintings, easy to identify as tasteful in appearance, but of no personal interest.

Fazil had eyes of amber, a slightly twisted mouth which always seemed to smile, and a panther's grace.

I loved him.

An insanity, you might say. And not only was it an insanity I had never encountered before, it was one which I could not cure. How could a good Catholic embrace such madness? Had I been subverted by too long in Turkish courts? No, I conceded to myself, after much soul-searching. Firstly, I was not an especially good Catholic, being negligent in most of my observations, and secondly, if God had wanted me to be otherwise than I was, then He would have made me so. Was I to be blamed for the choices of the Almighty? The thought was ludicrous.

Over the months, Fazil and I worked together, had clandestine evenings, weekends, in the homes of friends and acquaintances who understood such matters. As an agent I was expected to circulate, fraternise, observe. I did, but some of my reports became fabrications, tales hastily concocted to explain my actions when Fazil and I were ensconced in a bed which smelled of fresh sweat and sandalwood.

Thus we survived, clandestine but bound to each other.

Until the reports of Opera ghost reached Constantinople in late 1881, and some fool of an *agha* brought it to the sultan's attention.

That was the point at which my superiors revealed that they knew far more than they should about my affairs, that they had leverage over me. I was to be the tame Parisian who would scour Paris for Ceset, or his cadaver.

And if I did not...

Perros-Guirec, May 1882

I REMAIN IN THE HOTEL here. Where else shall I go? I fret and turn at night. Have they already taken Fazil, as surety against my actions? I consider informing Yildiz that Balik is dead, murdered by Ceset, and that this is sure proof that I am close to my quarry. I do not do so, in the end, because of any possibility that this will be seen as the monster having control over the game. The sultan is mercurial. Let the Turk stay missing – I will send a telegram which confirms that I continue my work, as if I know nothing of Balik's fate.

THE NOTE COMES AT THE very end of the month, eight days after the encounter in the churchyard. It is handwritten, in an expensive cream envelope delivered to my hotel by a boy who had it from another boy, and so on. There is no point in trying to trace it back further – it clearly comes from Erik.

BE IN LE FAOU ON THE TWELFTH DAY OF MAY

I have no idea where Le Faou is, or why this date is significant. But it is all I have. I need maps, perhaps a guide, and to talk—carefully—to the local people. In French. I also know nothing of the Breton tongue, its strange, soft pronunciation and its ancient words. But I was a scholar, once.

I will surely manage.

Finistère, Brittany, May 1882

FROM PERROS-GUIREC TO BREST, ON a recommendation from a fisherman; from Brest to Landernau, where I hired a carriage, little more than a dog-cart, to take me further. I am in search, apparently, of a place little more than a village, one which lies inland of the Bay of Brest. Le Faou. The only map I have with me is many decades old and torn. Besides that dubious aid, I have a change of clothes, a book of Turkish poetry once dear to Fazil—a present from him before I left Constantinople—and the weapons handed me by the Persian's servant.

The book reminds me constantly of him, and of my own failures. If only he had not been constantly observed. If only I had been more resourceful, we might have both fled that city together and been free now. The weapons, on the other hand, remind me that whilst I can shoot a pistol—just—and know which end of a dagger to grip, I would be no match for a determined foeman. No match at all.

At night, I let down the backboard and make an uncomfortable bed upon it; sleep comes, but not quickly.

I am afraid.

"YOU TRAVEL FOR THE PARDON." A farmer, his wagon piled with fresh hay. He draws up beside my cart on an already narrow lane through the woods.

I let my face show doubt, a touch of stupidity, in hope that he will speak slowly. He is clearly a Breton native, and I have already had too many conversations in Brittany whose true meaning escaped me. I would do better if they spoke Court Russian.

"The pardon." His horse whickers at mine; we trundle along with our vehicles almost touchting. "The pilgrimage to Rumengol."

"No, Le Faou."

"Ah, yes, but from Le Faou, one joins the procession. It is the pardon to honour Our Lady of Rumengol, the Pardon of the Singers." His cracked voice rises:

"Lili, arc'hantet ho dêlliou.
War vord an dour 'ʒo er prajou."

He grins. " 'The lilies, with their silver leaves'. You are what, from Paris, Reims? You sounds so. This is a blessed time, m'sieur, with much music, and a festival after mass. I thought you a pilgrim."

"I suppose I am. So I should head for Le Faou, then after that…"

"Turn east, a touch north of east. You will see them gathered on the roads, in the lanes, preparing for the festivities. If you wish only the Dawn Mass, then that is in three days time, at the church of Our Lady of Rumengol. She cannot be missed, for her bell-tower pierces the sky, and her organ has a mighty blast."

I clutch the reins tighter. Is this it, the moment Erik steers me to?

"I am much obliged to you," I manage to say, my temples tight with thought. The lane branches; we go our separate ways, my thanks upon his rough-clothed back.

The Pardon of the Singers. It can be no coincidence.

Rumengol, May 1882

I REACH LE FAOU ON the day named in Erik's note, early in the afternoon, and head on to Rumengol. This second, smaller village overflows, its one main street awash with humanity - solitary old men, groups of laughing women, neat families, shrieking children. As for their appearance, black predominates, the women with that typical Breton headgear of folded white lace above pitch-coloured dresses, the men in sombre outfits with dark blue sashes around their waists and broad-brimmed hats set upon their heads. This black, though, has no intimations of the graveside – it is respectful, proper. They are proud of their appearance, pleased to be gathered here in preparation for the pardon.

Pulling up the cart a little way from the village, I tether my tired horse to a tree by which fresh grass abounds. The entire place has a festival atmosphere, with rows of canvas stalls set up by the road. The pedlars under the canvas are selling trinkets, amulets, tokens of Our Lady of Rumengol— as well as a range of breads, sausages and small pies. There are cider stalls as well, men with casks of thin wine, for the village inn is small and cannot hold a fraction of those who have gathered – many, many hundreds, perhaps thousands of people.

"They have soup and fresh loaves," says one red-cheeked man, grinning as he sees my confusion, and he points to the inn. "Push in, push in. All are friends here."

"I did not imagine it to be so… popular."

"You are not Breton." His grin widens. "You do not know us, but you are welcome. As for the numbers, we have a new-built chapel on the green yonder, just so all can hear the priests; the singers will gather, in glades, under eaves, and you will hear the beauty of our music. Our tribute to The Lady of Rumengol!"

The farmer on the road spoke truly of the church itself, whose open bell-tower does rise high above this less-wooded stretch of land – nor is it dour, for more tents have been erected nearby, their cloth painted bright reds and yellows, and two banners flutter from the tower. It is a true celebration, not a solemn, thin-lipped observance.

I toss a handful of coins to a one-legged beggar, buy a confection from a smiling girl with a high, ivory-white bonnet. I have no idea what it is for which I wait. To spot a thin, black-clad man with a silent face in such a crowd would not be possible. Either he must plan to come to me, or there will be some signal as to his purpose here.

And yes, my guts are cold with the thought that all this is again deception, that he is not here, and never will be. A twisted ploy, to send a fool such as I to some forgotten corner of Brittany for no purpose whatsoever.

For an hour, three, I doze on the back of the cart; a soft May night has fallen when I awake, and all is the same as before. A fire-eater performs in a clearing, eliciting gasps from the younger folk; fiddlers play ancient Breton airs as they stroll through the crowds, and a number have settled to sleep and prepare themselves for the Dawn Mass tomorrow. Sedate organ music swells from within Notre Dame de Rumengol, which adds to the general feeling of God looking down on the pilgrims with benevolent approval, and the Holy Mother pleased that she should be remembered so.

IT HAPPENS AROUND NINE IN the evening, when the crowds have quietened and the pedlars have curled up in canvas rolls which were earlier their stalls. Braziers and torches light the clearings; the church glows from within as pilgrims holding tapers and candles slip in and out to seek the blessing of Our Lady.

At first there is the sudden stilling of the music from within the church— a moment where one organist replaces another, I assume, or an offering of quiet whilst the details of tomorrow's mass are being prepared—but no. For the organ pipes boom again, but this time with a crashing set of chords utterly unlike the previous gentler tones. I twist around, and see people fleeing Notre Dame de Rumengol, huddling together in apparent shock or standing with their fists raised in outrage.

"The Devil, the Devil is among us!" shrieks an elderly woman before she is trodden to the ground by those who follow her. I rush to lift her up, buffeted by the crowd.

"What has happened?"

"The Devil," she says again, clutching at her chest. "He has ascended from the Pit to play the music of Hell!"

I offer her brandy from my pocket flask.

"Or Death." She shakes her head. "Has Death come to take us, in defiance of Our Lady?"

From her, and from other shocked pilgrims, I hear talk of a huge, black-robed figure which swept into the church and, heading for the balcony, dispossessed the organist on his balcony. This terrible figure was seven or ten foot tall, had flames around its head or eyes which spat sulphur – their accounts are barely rational. All agree, however, that its face was that of a skull, a grinning deaths-head.

"We are judged!" cries out a portly man in simple clothes. He falls to his knees and begins to recite a Psalm.

And all this time the pipe organ bellows out its new score over the fields, over the confused crowds. This is Erik's music, sonorous, penetrating— *Don Juan Triumphant* - but its reception isnot, I think, that which he might have expected. I can see from their expressions that they are not enthralled by his work, but appalled by this sacrilege, this intrusion. I hear urgent talk of this 'demon' who seeks to destroy their church, and how it must be dealt with. Already, blue-clad seamen have started dipping pitch torches into a brazier, jaws set grim as they contemplate their response.

A young priest stands in the entrance of Notre Dame de Rumengol, tears on his cheeks; pushing him out of the way, I press myself through the last of those fleeing the church.

At other times you might pause, astonished by such an interior. To each side of the altar are set huge carved panels which overflow with gilded and painted statuary; angels and saints abound, and an ornate stone canopy encompasses a painted figure of Virgin and Child, her sculpted face serene, and fresh lilies strewn at her feet.

The white lilies of Darnétal and Perros-Guirec.

But the stones around me ache, resonate, with the tortured music from the gallery above the narthex, the organ gallery. He—Erik, Ceset—stands there, his hands playing over the organ keys, his head flung back, unmasked. I had almost thought to find one of his strange automatons placed before the keys, a wicked joke, but no… it is him.

"He is but a man, he is but a man," I tell myself.

As *Don Juan Triumphant* shivers the air, I pause to genuflect—a ludicrous act, I know—to the altar at the far end of the church. Fallen tapers sputter at my feet; a small child cries out from somewhere amongst the pews. I tug the *daroga*'s long pistol from my belt, barely able to make my fingers cock it, but they obey me at last.

And I fire. Not directly at Erik, but to one side, enough that I can be sure that the bullet does not kill. Why? I do not know.

The shot resounds, adding to the vast and terrible bitterness in the music at that point; an organ pipe splinters, but he does not stop playing. Nor, I realise, can he even hear the growing anger of the pilgrims outside.

Running to the door which leads to the gallery, I take the stair two, three steps at a time, heedless of my complaining muscles. Another small door, open, and I am ten feet from Erik, the bulk of the organ hanging above us in all its own gilded splendour. He must know I am there, but he does not turn to look at me; his skeletal fingers are an extension of his will, his madness, as he plays. His noseless face in profile, with those sunken eyes and corpse-cheeks, seems more dreadful than ever.

I dare to move closer, the discharged pistol in my left hand.

"You must stop, Erik, leave this place in peace!"

His hands falter, an added discord to the music.

"Why? Where is the acclaim I deserve, the love I should have received? If it cannot be freely given, then it must be taken through awe and fear."

I feel regret, and… pity.

"You made a choice. You turned that face, that deaths-head, to cruelty and devices of malice; you embraced hatreds and made your spirit more mean, not more bold. You *chose!*"

The music fails.

"Then I am evil?" he asks, as a normal man might ask if you think he has a stain upon his coat.

"You are dead." I let the pistol clatter to the oak planking beneath my feet. With the organ quieted, never have I heard so loud a sound. "Perhaps if you had been loved, truly loved, as a child, you might be alive. How can I know? But now… you are only Ceset. The child Erik died as he fled Darnétal, and you are what replaced him—a tortured, homeless soul. You know only coercion, deception, and the propagation of fear, those properties which my Eastern masters value so much. You should not have returned to France."

He lowers his head and releases a sob which chills me. "I should not have returned to France – for I am dead."

My eyes blur, and I step close to him, take one of his hands in mine. His flesh feels cold, so cold.

The *daroga*'s knife slips easily through his black robes, between his ribs, and up…

When his almost fleshless lips part, and a drop of dark blood appears at the corner of his mouth, I place one gentle kiss upon his parchment cheek.

And at last I see his eyes. Deep sunken, yes, but they are human, if yellow-tinged and strange.

"The score… my *Don Juan*," he gasps. "It is in the crypt below, in a… leather satchel. Do not let them… destroy it. I leave you that, and the plans… the plans of my work in the Yildiz kiosks." More blood, trickling from his mouth and onto my own breast, marking. I have killed a man. "Use… use them as you must."

"Erik, I…"

"Farewell, my friend. Hide me, that Christine never knows I -"

There is no more.

I know that priests and pilgrims will dare to return soon, crosses and torches to hand, seeking to exorcise the monster who has despoiled their sacred place. I must act swiftly.

He is no weight; I carry him with me as I sweep down the stair and seek the entrance to the crypt. I must hide until dark, and convey his remains to a tangled forest glade or an abandoned cemetery—anywhere I can make him truly forgotten. No newspaper announcement; no suspicions as to where his body lies this time. Not even the Persian will be told of what I have done.

Rouen, Normandy, June 1882

THE INNKEEPER'S WIFE REMEMBERS MY family, and tells me that my cousin Albert, a farmer near Caen, is doing well. I have neither spoken to nor corresponded with Albert for almost two decades, not since I first left for Paris. I notice a fishmonger on market day, and remember that we once played together. I do not go to speak with him.

And, by chance, I hear that the doctor's dark-eyed daughter, who once spoke of seeing the deformed, skull-headed boy from Darnétal, passed away some years ago. Cholera.

Everything that Erik claimed was in his slim satchel. The full score for his opera, and many maps, inscribed in astonishing detail on India paper, which charted his major artifices for the Ottomans - those I will keep for any time of darker need. The only other item inside was a single lace handkerchief, such as a young women might carry. I left that buried with his body, in a wild and lonely place I will not name.

'God knows, I am no assassin' I told the Persian in his small, tidy flat.

But now I am.

My report to the Yildiz kiosks has been made. Ceset is no more, and as proof, I remembered the fate of Resit Balik - I sent them The Corpse's right hand, which I sawed off with the *daroga*'s dagger. The task took some time, for the sinews were like steel wires, and the bones harder than they had any right to be.

No bad deed goes unrewarded in the court of Abdul Hamid II. My work will be considered a modest success; Fazil will be safe, at least for a while. But will he welcome back a murderer, a weak soul who has heard *Don Juan Triumphant* and has been changed by it?

On the street outside the *Blue Cock* inn, I find myself facing an old priest. He says he remembers me from many, many years ago, then smiles and recalls how well I sang as a chorister.

"If you are back to stay, Thierry, then you must join the choir." His voice has the rasp of failing lungs. "We are always in need at St Madeleine's."

I plead an urgent errand, and offer the lie that I will certainly look him up later in the week.

My own smile is a mask.

I do not believe I will ever set foot in a church again, not after Our Lady of Rumengol. Let the Lord be merciful to those who deserve it.

If such people exist…

About the
AUTHORS

JAMES BENNETT is a British writer raised in Sussex and South Africa. His travels have furnished him with an abiding love of different cultures, history and mythology. He is a winner of the British Fantasy Society Award for Best Short Story. Bennett's work is known for its rich fusion of myth and modernity, often featuring queer perspectives. His recent collection delves into queer folk horror, Lovecraftian themes, and erotically charged tales rooted in LGBTQ+ experience.

NADIA BULKIN is an Indonesian-American political scientist and author of short stories, largely in the horror genre. She has been nominated for the Shirley Jackson Awards in both short fiction ("Live Through This") and single-author collection (*She Said Destroy*). Describing her work as "socio-political horror," Nadia explores power dynamics, identity, cultural otherness, and mental fragility— often centering emotionally fraught female protagonists . Her writing draws on Indonesian folklore, queer identity, and horror's psychological depth.

JAMESON CURRIER is the author of eight novels, five collections of fiction, and a memoir. His most recent books are his illustrated tales, *Paul's Cat, The Candlelight Ghost,* and *The Man That Got Away.* He is the founder, publisher, and editor of Chelsea Station Editions, an independent press. He currently resides in a farmless farmhouse in the Hudson Valley.

THERESA DELUCCI's short fiction has appeared in *Strange Horizons*, *Lightspeed*, *Tor. com*, *Weird Horror*, and in *Fears: Tales of Psychological Horror*, edited by Ellen Datlow, and received an honorable mention in *The Year's Best Horror Vol. 14*. She has talked pop culture for *Reactor*, *Wired.com's Geek's Guide to the Galaxy* podcast, and *Den of Geek*, where she is a regular contributor. She is also the editor of *Come Join Us by the Fire*, a free horror audio-exclusive anthology from Nightfire Books. She lives in New York City, where she enjoys oysters and cults, but not Blue Öster Cult.

CARA MASTEN DIGIROLAMO writes fantastic fiction--from music that can cause earthquakes, to fairie drag balls, and scholars riding language-dragons. They are a graduate of the 2015 Odyssey Writing Workshop, have an MFA in Creative Writing from the University of British Columbia, and a PhD in Linguistics from Cornell University. Currently they teach English at Capilano University, but they have previously been a fictional language consultant, a toy star window designer, and an instructor in the secret art of Turkish paper marbling. Further fiction can be found in *Beneath Ceaseless Skies*, *Fantasy Magazine*, *Cast of Wonders*, *Daily Science Fiction*, *NewMyths.com*, and *the Deadlands Magazine*.

PETER DUBÉ is a multi-genre writer, translator, and independent scholar. He is the author, co-author or editor of a dozen books of fiction, non-fiction and poetry. His novella, *Subtle Bodies*, an imagined life of French surrealist René Crevel was a finalist for the Shirley Jackson Award, and his novel in prose poems *The Headless Man*, was shortlisted for both the A. M. Klein Prize and the ReLit award. His most recent work is volume of nonfiction exploring the intersections and overlaps of gay men's politics and culture with surrealism entitled *Desire as Praxis: Towards a Queer Surrealism*. He was a member of the editorial committee of the contemporary art magazine *Espace, art actuel* for 18 years and is currently co-editor of *The Philosophical Egg*, an organ of living surrealism. He lives and works in his hometown of Montreal.

L.A. FIELDS has published numerous short stories and essays in anthologies spanning horror, erotica, queer literature, and academic. Her scholarship includes annotated editions such as *The Annotated Joseph and His Friend* and thematic nonfiction like *Gay a Day*, spotlighting LGBTQ+ figures in history.

A writer, an editor and a herder of lurchers, JOHN LINWOOD GRANT's fiction crosses a whole load of genres, although he's particularly fond of dark Victorian and Edwardian themes. He is the co-editor of *Occult Detective Quarterly*, a journal which explores the fictional world of supernatural sleuths, psychic investigators and doomed meddlers.

ORRIN GREY writes disjointed and irresponsible things about monsters, ghosts, and sometimes the ghosts of monsters. His stories have been published in dozens of anthologies, including Ellen Datlow's *Best Horror of the Year* and his nonfiction writing about horror film has been nominated for a Rondo Hatton award. He's the author of several spooky books, including *Glowing in the Dark, How to See Ghosts & Other Figments*, and many more.

JEAN-MARC LOFFICIER is a French-born writer renowned for his prolific work in comics, animation, reference books, and translations. He has authored over a dozen nonfiction guides on film and television and specialty reference volumes on French genre fiction with his wife, including the definitive *French Science Fiction, Fantasy, Horror & Pulp Fiction*. RANDY LOFFICIER is an accomplished U.S.-born writer, editor, and translator primarily known for her collaborations with husband Jean-Marc Lofficier. Randy co-founded Hollywood Comics, advising comic creators in Hollywood. She later co-founded Black Coat Press, specializing in translated French fantastika.

JOSH ROUNTREE is a Texas novelist and short story writer. More than seventy of his short stories have been published in a variety of venues, including *The Deadlands, Beneath Ceaseless Skies, Bourbon Penn, Realms of Fantasy, PseudoPod, Weird Horror*, and *The Year's Best Dark Fantasy & Horror*. His novel, *The Legend of Charlie Fish*, was released to wide acclaim, making the Locus Recommended Reading List, and being named one of Los Angeles Public Library's best books of the year.

ADDISON SMITH has written stories featured in *Fantasy Magazine*, *Fireside Magazine*, *Daily Science Fiction*, and over fifty other venues across science fiction, fantasy, and horror. Addison is known to describe himself as an "amorphous being constructed of suspended cold brew and kombucha."

An amateur naturalist and lifelong reader, BECKY THACKER writes from the Midwest, where she delights in libraries, small presses, and the odd history of the world—and finds inspiration in everyday human strangeness.

About the EDITOR

STEVE BERMAN is an American author, editor, and publisher recognized for his many contributions to queer speculative fiction. He is the founder of Lethe Press, the oldest independent publishing house known for its support of LGBTQ+ voices in fantasy, horror, and science fiction. Berman has edited thirty anthologies. He is a finalist for the Andre Norton Award, the Golden Crown Literary Award, and the Shirley Jackson Award, and he has won the Lambda Literary Award. He resides in Western Massachusetts.